THE ADEARIAN CHRONICLES
BOOK TWO - REVELATIONS

THE ADEARIAN CHRONICLES
BOOK TWO - REVELATIONS

SHANNON M. HARRIS

SAPPHIRE BOOKS

SALINAS, CALIFORNIA

Dedication

My Girl's.
They keep me sane.

Acknowledgments

I want to thank Chris and everyone at Sapphire Books for all of their hard work. A big shout out to Candi for all of her help and insight. And to everyone else who had a hand in making this book a reality. Thank you.

Present day Adearian
Manight
Two weeks before The Festival of the Goddess

Queen Isabel relaxed against the rails of the ship as the rocking of the waves settled her nerves. Being on the open water always brought her comfort and a sense of peace. She made a mental note to do this more often, whether she had the time or not. Since leaving Candor, both her excitement and her fear threatened to overwhelm her, even more so since the Captain had informed her they would reach Manight within the hour. The last time she set foot there, some twenty-eight years ago, she vowed never to return. The invitation from Queen Abigail, concerning the Festival, came as a complete surprise and somewhat of a shock. She debated with herself for months until finally deciding to turn the invitation down, when her daughter, Victoria, expressed her opinion in favor of going. Vic, as she was commonly referred to, wanted to see if all the hype concerning Manight was true. For Vic's benefit, Isabel had accepted and she would keep telling herself that. It didn't have anything to do with the fact that her pulse had quickened at reading Abigail's words written on the invitation.

She didn't dread many things, but she did dread the moment she laid eyes on Abigail again. When she was a teenager, her father had allowed her to study at Shara's University, even though she wasn't an Item

Sorceress. Compared to Candor's teaching style, Manight's was one-sided, but she wouldn't trade her time spent there for anything, especially her time with Abigail. In the past thirty-five years, she often thought about her, but never allowed her memories of their time together to invade her life. Old memories, for everyone's sake, should always remain buried. She smiled and leaned into the rail as a cool breeze swept over. Her life turned out exactly the way it should have and if given the chance to go back and change it, she wouldn't. She loved her husband deeply and Vic was a testament to that love. His unexpected death a few years back almost broke them both.

She pushed off the railing, ran her hand through her long auburn hair, and blew out the breath that she was holding. Her eyes swept the estate and the surrounding shoreline. The sight of the cliffs and the jagged coastline never failed to take her breath away. From where she stood, she could make out the stone wall that enclosed the estate and the top of the Castle. She did a double take and squinted into the distance when movement at the top of the cliffs caught her eye. There was clearly a struggle taking place, but they were too far away for her to make out any specific details. After a few minutes, she gasped and stepped forward when a body fell over the side of the cliff and bounced off the rocks to the sand below. She shivered and rubbed her arms when a second body fell over the side and disappeared into a gray fog.

"Mom." Vic leaned against the railing beside her. "What just happened?"

Isabel couldn't believe what she was seeing. "Magic."

"I know, but I didn't think magic was allowed

within their borders, and shouldn't the guards be on the lookout for bandits this close to the Festival?"

"It's not supposed to be allowed, and yes, they should be on the lookout." She bit her lip and kept her eyes glued to the cliff, cringing when a third, then a fourth body fell over the side. After a few minutes, she could make out two people walking into the forest. The Mages that the royal estate employed shouldn't have allowed whatever had just happened. "It shouldn't have happened and I hope it doesn't take the guards long to discover the bodies." She turned to Vic and squeezed her hand. "We will have to keep all our senses alert during our time here. Even the Royal Mages shouldn't be performing that type of magic inside their borders. Whatever is going on, I'm afraid we will be in the middle of it." Deep in her gut, she knew what had just taken place was one of the reasons Abigail had invited her here.

Vic grinned and bounced on the balls of her feet. "Really?"

Isabel looked at her daughter. Really looked at her. Where had the years gone? Before her stood a twenty-four-year-old, confident woman. From the short, fiery red hair, to the heart melting dimples, she was the spitting image of her father. She couldn't get annoyed at her enthusiasm, because she was the same way when she was her age. "Don't get too excited. We are here for the Festival and the reading. Nothing more. We are guests and as guests we will stay out of and away from Castle business." Maybe the more she said it, the more she would believe it.

Vic planted her hands on her hips and cocked her head. "Mom, really. When have we ever shied away from anything?" She shook her head. "I told you this would be a new adventure for us. Something we could do together. Besides, I brought plenty of notebooks to catalogue our time here. How often do we get to visit another country? Surely," she winked, "I will have something interesting to write about."

Isabel nodded and leaned against Vic, content to stand beside her and watch the port draw closer. One day, Vic would be Queen and she hoped she never lost her playfulness. Even with being blessed with magical abilities, Vic had walked the one path no one expected; she had become a teacher and taught the youngsters the basic elements of magic. She was well liked and loved in Candor, but Manight was not Candor. They would not put up with what they would consider reckless behavior. She would have to keep an eye on her. Whatever was happening in Manight would only lead to trouble. Her eyes closed of their own accord and she took a deep breath when she sensed the shields. "Brace yourself." Crossing through the shields never ceased to amaze her. It was an extraordinary feat how the Mages accomplished it. A moment later, she stiffened and concentrated on the magic swirling around them. The shields were strong, but there was a disturbance within them.

"That's all they have?"

Isabel opened her eyes, wrapped an arm around Vic's waist, and pulled her close to her side. "I told you that our magic was different than in other parts of Adearian, but do not believe for a second that their magic isn't as powerful as ours is. It's just different. You know they have strict regulations in place. It is virtually impossible to break through their shields." She stopped talking when Vic frowned and a dozen different emotions crossed her features in a matter of seconds. "What? Victoria?"

Vic sighed and took a step away from her. "I…I… there's something I haven't told you." Isabel reached for her, but Vic took another step back. "I wasn't completely truthful with you about why I wanted to come here."

Isabel's heart pounded in her ears and she gripped the rail to keep herself steady. They had always shared everything and for Vic to keep something back scared her more than she wanted to admit. "Talk to me."

Vic turned away from her and looked out over the water. "Do you remember about a month, month and a half ago when I excused myself early from dinner? I said I wasn't feeling well."

It was odd at the time, because Vic never excused herself from dinner, but she hadn't thought anything about it. Maybe she should have. "Yes, I remember."

Vic rubbed her hands down her arms. "I felt something." She ran her hands through her hair. "It's hard to explain. I felt." She touched her chest. "I felt someone call me. She needed my help. I felt everything she felt. From the searing heat, to the pain, and the bones breaking." She shook her head. "It was hard to breathe. It was hard to do anything. I didn't know if I would be able to break the hold her emotions had on me. It was like she was projecting onto me." She frowned. "I don't see how that's possible. I thought the only way to project such strong feelings was through a blood link." She sighed. "My questions didn't keep me from helping her, though. I went into the study and pulled Dad's book of spells from the bookshelf. I knew the distance between us was great. It didn't dawn on me until we passed through the shields that I'd already pushed through them once before."

Isabel stiffened. That was the last thing she had expected to hear. "What are you saying?" Why was this happening now?

Vic shook her head. "Mom, you know what I'm saying. I was in your office when you received word that someone attacked Princess Jalen. It was the day after I shielded someone. A woman. It was me. I shielded her." She held her hand up. "I don't know how, but I did it." She shrugged. "It just came naturally. I was pulled to her." She grasped Isabel's hand. "How did I do it and what does it mean?"

Isabel kept her features neutral, but her stomach was churning. Vic was right. Projecting usually only worked on blood relatives or those you deeply cared about. She couldn't explain to Vic what had happened to her, not on this trip. Maybe not ever. Some things were never meant to be brought into the light. She squeezed Vic's hand. "You saved her life. Everything else will fall into place. Some things don't need an explanation or can't be explained. Just be grateful you were there when she called out." Vic didn't look convinced so Isabel decided to change the subject. "You want to meet Jalen? Is that the reason you wanted to come here?"

"Yes."

Isabel nodded. "That shouldn't be a problem, but let's keep everything else between us. No one is to know what you did for her."

"Why?"

"Victoria, you know that if the wrong person found out what you did, you would be putting your life in danger. I won't take that chance with your life." She bit the inside of her cheek. "The magic you defeated must have been powerful?"

"It was. I honestly didn't think I would be able to fight it."

"But you did." Isabel smiled.

Vic grinned back. "I did, but it drained me."

"Performing powerful magic will do that." Vic was one of the most accomplished sorceresses for her age. There were many others more powerful than she was, but she had an incredible ability to focus her attention far better than most. Whoever had tried to kill Jalen would be looking for whoever shielded her and she would make sure Vic had a guard at all times. "We will not disgrace Queen Abigail, Manight, or Candor by practicing our magic within the city."

"Mom, you're the one who gave me a crash course on how to put our own shields in place so we could still use magic in our rooms."

"I am, but at the time I was your teacher, now, I am your mother. Please do not do anything foolish. I cannot stress enough we *are* only guests. While I know I could get us both out safely if need be, I don't want to have to make that choice."

Vic reached both of her arms out, grasped her right wrist with her left hand, and bowed her head as a sign of respect for the crown. "I would never do anything to disgrace you, my Queen, the crown, or Candor. I would do anything for you and our people."

Isabel sucked in a breath. Her little girl wasn't so little anymore. "Lower your arms and raise your head." She ran her finger down Vic's cheek. "I know that. I wouldn't know what to do if anything happened to you."

"Good thing you won't have to find out." She waved her hand in the air. "Enough of that mushy stuff. A girl can only take so much." She laughed.

Isabel squeezed Vic's hand. "We should prepare. The port draws near and according to you, our adventure begins."

Vic pulled her close, squeezed her tight, then pushed her to arm's length. "I can hardly wait." She winked.

Isabel turned back to the shore when Vic disappeared below deck. Vic's confession certainly was unexpected and hopefully wouldn't bring any unwanted attention their way. Secrets long held needed to stay that way, and she prayed they didn't play a part in what was or what would happen in Manight. Some secrets deserved to stay buried.

❧❧❧❧

Lanis leaned back against the door, crossed her arms across her chest, and eyed the Jester, who sat at the table. His brown trousers, white shirt, and black cape were forgettable, but the smirk on his face spoke volumes. If she didn't already know what he was capable of, she would have never believed him to be a Rogue. Did he really know where Anya was, or was he playing games with her? After everything they'd been through, to be blindsided by Anya's kidnapping felt like a punch to the gut. Given the chance to do it all over again, she would have never opened the letter from the Ramden Council. But, in the end, it hadn't been her choice. Anya knew she would never say no to the Council, but she would have said no for Anya. No one's life, not even hers, meant more to her than Anya's. The very thought of someone besides herself touching Anya fueled her hatred ten-fold and she would make sure everyone involved paid with their lives. She pushed away from the door, stepped over the body on the floor, and sat down across from the Jester. "What do you want?"

The Jester leaned his chair back and laughed. "You know, it's funny. Seeing you in front of me now, I don't know what she sees in you." He spat. "You're nothing special."

Elson stiffened beside her and she held her hand up to hold him back. The Jester laughed and cut his eyes to Elson before bringing them back to Lanis. "What do you want?" Lanis repeated.

He cocked his head and stood. "I want what everyone wants. But in this instance, Lanis Welsh, Protector and lover to High Priestess Anya, I don't want anything from you, but I do want something for the both of us." He stared at the body on the floor before retaking his seat.

"She asked you a question, twice," Elson said. "She deserves an answer." He picked up his sword. "If you know where our High Priestess is, you need to tell us."

"Well, my, my," the Jester said. "What a big and strong, dare I say, protector you have." He laughed. "Too bad he wasn't the one put in charge of guarding Anya." He looked at the body and back to Lanis. "Is he the man you put in charge of Anya?"

"He is." Lanis was fast losing her patience, but, for Anya, she would keep her temper in check.

"Good." He nodded then wrung his hands together. "I don't trust many people," he said, looking at them both. "But I do trust one unconditionally and I will stop at nothing, as long as it is within my powers, to see that she is safe. I will not tell you how, when, why, or where Anya and I met. I will only tell you that

I also wish no harm to come to her, but it is not within my power to save her. When she begged me to save her, I told her that that was the difference between you and me. I cannot go against an Oath I have signed, but that you would stop at nothing to save her."

"Wait a minute." Lanis stood and clenched her fists by her sides. "You've seen Anya and she begged you to save her and you said no." Anya never begged for anything. She was always the strong one, the one taking care of everybody else, and the one everybody could count on. What did they do to her?

The Jester stood so fast his chair toppled backward and he pushed the table against the wall. "I did what I could. I live by my Oath; you don't. I did what I could and I could only do that because of loopholes I put in my contracts. I did what I could for you along your journey because of Anya and I am doing all this because of her. If it weren't for her, I would have already killed you. Do not try my patience. You will lose."

"You already tried and failed to kill me once." She waved her hand between them and sat back down. "And we both know you wouldn't try something here." They were wasting time. "If you know where she is, tell me, so I can save her. You're right; I would do anything for her."

"Even give up your own life."

"Yes," she said without hesitation.

He turned away from her and leaned back against the wall. "Because that's what it might take. It will not be easy to get to her. I only had so many options and I chose the one that would keep her alive the longest. I don't know what they did to the cell she's in, or who was in it before her, but she is fading far quicker then she should. Believe me when I say it wasn't easy keeping her alive." He ran his hands through his hair.

She rubbed her neck, looked to Elson, and nodded. He sat down on the bed. "Where is she?"

"First things first. I notice that you're missing someone. Did she get lost along the way?" He smirked.

"She isn't of any concern to you. Answer my question."

"You are no fun at all. Tsk, tsk." He shook his head and frowned. "I really don't know what she sees in you." He shrugged.

Lanis tilted her head back and bit her lip when it dawned on her what his problem was. He was in love with Anya. "Get on with it."

His smirk vanished as quickly as it appeared. "I cannot help you. What I am about to tell you is the only help you'll get from me. There is someone that will help you, but you have to get to her first and it won't be easy."

Great. That's all she needed, another obstacle. Why couldn't anything ever be easy or at least not life threatening? "Who?"

He shook his finger at her then looked at it in disgust. "Pity Manight doesn't allow its citizens to use magic." He shook his hands out. "Where was I?"

"You were about to tell us who we have to see," Elson said.

"No. I was about to tell Lanis who she has to see. You, my friend, will not be going with her."

"We'll see," Elson muttered.

Lanis couldn't believe everyone was being so calm. It was disturbing on a whole new level. "Can we get on with it?"

"Queen Isabel is visiting Manight to partake in

the Festival and she's staying in the Castle at Queen Abigail's request. You need to get in and talk with her. She will be able to help you, but you will have to be honest with her. She doesn't like surprises."

"What can she do?" Elson said. "She can't practice magic in Manight."

"No, but she can practice magic inside the Castle walls. Where do you think the Mages are that protect Hadmore's borders and more especially Manight's? The Royal Estate is the only place in Manight that allows magic." He addressed Lanis. "Be careful; she doesn't take well to strangers. Candor is a lot different from Manight. Do not play games with her."

Lanis frowned. "Let me get this straight. First, you want me to get into the Castle, then you want me to find Queen Isabel and talk her into helping me, but she can be hostile. How do you purpose I do that?"

The Jester shrugged and his eyes strayed to the body on the floor before coming back to Lanis. She couldn't decipher the look in his eyes. "You need her to help you." He ran his hands through his hair. "What I did to Anya will take a very powerful magic to cut through it and that type of magic cannot be found here."

Lanis's stomach dropped. "What did you do to her?" How could this get any worse?

"They have her in a small cell in the center of a Holders outpost set back inside a cave. You do know who the Holders of the Spheres are, don't you?" He looked first at Elson, then Lanis. "He does; do you, Lanis?"

If they had her, this situation was far worse then she could have ever imagined. "I know some. I know they worship Damrek." She shook her head. "I know they are searching for the seven spheres. No one knows much about them or where their hideouts are. I know there is a Book of Damrek, but I've never seen it. Have you?" she asked Elson.

"No."

"I have," the Jester said. "To me, it's just another book, but to them it's their whole life. Lanis, do not underestimate one's love for their God, even if it is a false one."

"Oh, I won't." She leaned forward in her chair. The Jester looked deep in thought, but he also looked nervous. "So you're telling me The Holders of the Spheres have her."

"Yes and you have to understand that what I did, I did for Anya's safety. I enclosed the room she's in in an enchantment. A very powerful spell. Isabel will be able to help with that. No one can enter the room and no one can leave."

What? "Is this a joke? How am I supposed to get her out if no one can enter and leave the room?"

"I did it for her safety. I left a two-week supply of food and water. That's all I could do for her. It is up to you to save her. I told her you would be coming for her. Was I harsh in making that statement? Would you abandon her now, Lanis? After everything."

"Of course not."

"Where is she?" Elson said, standing.

"Follow Laramore's border until you reach the ocean. From there, travel along the water until you come upon a large rock formation littered with several cave openings. The cave you need is the one with a small sword etched into the stone. There aren't any shields guarding the door, but beware, some of the most feared fighters belong to the Holders guards.

They will not think twice before killing a stranger. Stay on top of it."

"Well, isn't that fantastic. Is there any other obstacles I should be aware of?"

The Jester smirked. "Oh, there's plenty, but nothing you'll hear from me." He sobered quickly. "Do take my word. You will need Queen Isabel's help." He sighed and glanced at the body on the floor. "For a favor, I can contact somebody who will get rid of that body for you."

It wasn't her ideal situation, but she would work with what she had. "All right." What was one more favor to owe?

He clapped his hands and laughed. "Perfect." He bowed before her. "Anya awaits you, my Lady. Do not tarry. Time isn't on your side."

Lanis dropped her head in her hands when the door shut behind him, and the quiet inside the room washed over her. Anya needed her and she would stop at nothing to find her.

⁂

Dimitri's footsteps were purposeful and steady as he walked down the long, familiar corridor of the Castle. He tensed, but made direct eye contact with the guard heading his way and nodded as he moved past him. This was not the time to draw suspicion upon himself. Instead of entering the door at the end of the hall, he glanced both ways to make sure no one was coming his way, then opened a door set into the wall, to his left. It took a few seconds for his eyes to become accustomed to the darkness, but he knew the layout of this hallway by heart and his steps were sure.

He had no trouble finding the brick that was raised from the wall. He knocked twice on the wall, pushed the brick backward, and walked through the open door. The two oil lamps that hung from the ceiling cast the room in a warm glow. His steps faltered when he came face to face with the two occupants in the room: High Priest Lantor and his Protector. This was certainly unexpected, considering he was supposed to be meeting the Jester. He kept his face neutral, walked to the cabinet set against the wall, and poured a glass of water. "Can I pour you a glass?"

"No." Lantor shook his head. "My apologies for meeting you so unexpectedly. A mutual friend alerted me that this meeting would be taking place and I took the opportunity to come and meet the man who single-handedly tracked down five of the seven spheres." Lantor clapped softly, then sat in one of the three chairs in the room. He crossed one leg over the other, clasped his hands together, and rested them on his knee. He smiled. "I must say, it is quite the feat what you've accomplished. Five spheres. Remarkable."

Dimitri grabbed a vacant chair, moved it across from Lantor, sat down, and held his glass loosely between his hands. It was a bit of a surprise that the Jester knew about the spheres, but it wasn't unexpected. What was a bit unsettling was the fact that he told Lantor about them. That they even knew each other, and possibly worked together, could aid his cause in the future. High Priest Lantor was a powerful man. He would have to be careful how he played this.

"I have to applaud your efforts," Lantor said. "I've been trying to locate just one sphere without any luck. Tell me, what would I have to do to acquire one?" He ran his hand along the arm of his chair. "What is your price? I am sure you know well enough, in your line of work, everyone has one."

Dimitri stood and swallowed the last of his water. "The spheres are not for sale." Lantor may be High Priest to Novak, but not a lot of people in Manight worshipped Novak. Dimitri would have been more impressed if Tothos, First Priest to Shara, had come to him for a sphere. "Was there something else I could help you with today? I hate to know you came all this way for nothing." He crossed his arms.

Lantor spread his hands out in front of him. "If one wants to know the answer, they must first ask the question." Lantor stood and clasped his hands behind his back. "Tell me something, Dimitri. How are your beautiful wife and daughters?"

Dimitri clenched his jaw and forced himself to stay calm. Lantor was obviously goading him, but he wouldn't let him walk all over him either. "My wife and daughters are fine. You have some nerve to come here and threaten my family."

Lantor chuckled. "No need to get so uptight. A family is a beautiful thing. I only brought them up to remind you that you are not only playing with your life, but also theirs." He ignored Dimitri's glare. "What can you do with only five spheres? You're still missing two."

"Like I said. Is there something else I can do for you?" Dimitri sat back down and rested his hands in his lap.

Lantor nodded, leaned back against the wall, and slipped his hands in his pants pockets. "I propose an alliance. It would be a mutual agreement, and I will use all of my resources to help you find the last two spheres."

Dimitri didn't believe for one moment that's all Lantor was after, but he needed time to figure out his real agenda. He knew others were looking for the spheres, and he'd heard talk over the years, but he'd never heard Lantor's name mentioned. The only way he would get out of this meeting was to agree with his terms and figure the rest out later. "I agree to your terms, but keep in mind we still have to locate Damrek's Cave." His heart sank when Lantor grinned. He knew where the cave was. Now, he had to play along, if only to find the cave. On the flip side, just because Lantor was using him didn't mean he couldn't do the exact same thing to him. He smoothed a crease out of his white shirt. "If I may ask. Why do you want the spheres? You don't worship Damrek."

"No one really knows what will happen when all seven spheres are brought together. I'm curious, that's all." He walked to Dimitri and held his hand out. "I take it we have an agreement."

Dimitri stood, ignoring Lantor's outstretched hand. "We do."

"Excellent." He pointed at Dimitri, then opened the door. "Have a good day."

He knew once he acquired the last two spheres, Lantor would kill him for them and he didn't intend to die anytime soon. He left the room and headed back to his office. Once this was over, he would be glad to be out from under the Castle, and in turn, out from under Queen Abigail. He groaned when he shut his office door and his eyes landed on the man sitting in his chair. What more could go wrong today? The man knew he was never to meet him where someone could see them together. It was amazing to him what some people would betray their Queen and their country for.

"What can I do for you?"

The man stood. "I know who shielded Princess Jalen."

Dimitri grinned and rocked back on his heels. He might have taken a step back talking with Lantor, but this could be the turning point he had been looking for. The grin quickly vanished when the man told him who it was that shielded her. Getting rid of her was a task he wasn't sure he wanted to undertake. To shield someone from that great a distance took the skills of an accomplished sorceress. For now, he would bide his time, and wait for everything to play out.

❧❧❧❧

Isabel regarded the woman standing in front of her with a mixture of disgust and disdain. Upon her and Vic's arrival a short time ago, she had been informed Abigail wouldn't be available until the next day and that Lady Sara wanted an audience with her. Vic, wisely, kept her mouth shut when Isabel had sent her to their rooms to put their shields in place. Sara had been adamant about a private meeting, but Isabel had waved off her request. Barnet, one of her personal guards, along with four of Sara's guards, stood along the back wall of the large sitting room.

Isabel couldn't help the laugh that bubbled up in her when she first entered the room and her eyes latched onto the rust colored couches and chairs that were arranged neatly in the middle of the room. Countless memories of her and Abigail cuddling on the couch bombarded her mind, but she quickly buried them and focused on the present. Her eyes swept the rest of the room; everything was the same except the tiles on the enormous fireplace along the main wall. Abigail had always been a creature of habit and extremely sentimental. It brought her more comfort than she wanted to admit to herself that Abigail had left this room nearly the same as when they were teenagers. She inhaled. Even the lavender that permeated the room was the same.

She kept her expression neutral, but her stomach was churning. If it had been anyone else who had requested the meeting, she wouldn't have given it a second thought, but this was Sara. She didn't trust her when they were younger and she didn't trust her now. Sara's long blond hair hung loose around her shoulders and her sky blue eyes held the same haughtiness Isabel remembered. The white silk dress and blue chiffon over-lay she wore was tailored to perfection and Isabel knew that the ruby that hung around her neck had belonged to Abigail's mother. Isabel didn't believe in wearing your wealth as a way of showing others your value. Her father had taught her to show her integrity through her actions and that's exactly how she raised Victoria.

She slept easier every night, knowing what type of woman Vic had grown into. When the time came, Vic would make an exceptional Queen. Sara, on the other hand, made it no secret that Maya, her second born, should be Queen when Abigail stepped down. But, according to Hadmore doctorate, the heir was always the first-born. In most kingdoms that would be a problem; however, Hadmore had put strict guidelines in place hundreds of years ago that guaranteed the first-born would be acceptable. Jalen, their first-born, was Abigail's heir and for all intents and purposes, she would make a fine Queen.

Isabel picked up her glass, took a tentative sip of the amber colored wine, and looked at Sara over the rim. After a few tense seconds, she lowered it and cupped her hands around the elegantly carved glass. "What can I do for you, *Lady* Sara?"

Sara smirked. "Really, must you stoop to such levels, Isabel? I find it odd that you would come to our Festival of the Goddess." She sneered. "You don't even worship Shara."

Isabel set her glass down on the fireplace mantle and gave Sara her full attention. Something seemed off about her, but she couldn't put her finger on it. The air around her was disturbed. She wasn't one to play it safe, but she would tread lightly. "That is true. I don't worship Shara, but I couldn't pass up opportunity to hear the Prophecy read and by no one other than the High Priestess of Malora herself." Isabel picked up her glass again and saluted Sara. "What is a Queen to do?"

Sara walked to the corner table, poured a glass of wine, and took a sip. "The finest wine my tongue has ever tasted."

"I don't know." Isabel shrugged. "I'm partial to our wine in Candor."

"Then why don't you go back?" Sara spat. "No one wants you here."

Isabel smirked and fingered the rim of her cup. She knew she shouldn't, but Sara always did rub her the wrong way. "I wouldn't say that. I can name at least one person who will be happy to see me."

Sara's knuckles turned white on her wine glass. "You had your chance with her. She is mine," she ground out.

Sara was right; she did have her chance with Abigail, but life had worked out the best for everyone involved. She wouldn't trade the thirty-five years she spent with her husband for anything. A part of her would always belong to Abigail, but fate paved its own road for everyone. She was a magic bound One Sorceress and she wouldn't have given that up for anyone, not even for a life with Abigail. Being a One Sorceress allowed her the opportunity to study from various universities and gave her the ability to learn a wide variety of spells and ways in which to enchant numerous items. To be given the gifts of several areas of magic wasn't rare, but it presented opportunities to her that she couldn't pass up. She would have never been able to stay in Manight, not with their strict policies on magic in place, and Abigail would have never moved to Candor, because she was the only heir to Hadmore's throne.

"Sara." Isabel sighed. "I loved Abagail a lifetime ago. Life worked out the way it was supposed to for everyone. I have an amazing daughter and had a wonderful husband. You have two daughters, a son, and you have Abigail. If I recall, from our youth, you have everything you ever wanted. Abagail will always own a piece of my heart and I won't apologize for that. The past is exactly where it belongs." She lifted her glass. "This is a time of celebration." Isabel managed to hold back a flinch when Sara threw her glass into the fireplace and it shattered. Isabel held her hand up to keep Barnet back.

Sara's eyes locked onto Isabel's brown ones. "The past never goes away. Things always have a way of coming back into the light." She smirked and crossed her arms. "It amazes me how so many people thought they could keep such a secret."

Isabel stiffened, but kept her composure. There

was no possible way Sara could know her secret. Numerous precautions had been put into place to ensure the past stayed where it belonged. If it were up to Isabel, no one would ever know the truth. She placed her glass on the mantle and faced Sara. "Tell me Sara, what have you been doing with your time lately?"

Sara paled for an instant, then moved away from the wall. "Stay away from my family." She turned on her heels and headed toward the door, but before walking out she turned back to Isabel, a smirk plastered on her lips. "I may only be a Lady, but I am *her* Lady."

Isabel frowned. Sara always did have to have the last word. She hadn't intended to strike a nerve with her question, but that's exactly what she'd done. Now all she needed to do was find out what Sara was up to. It may not be her place to, but now she was involved, whether she wanted to be or not. When the last of Sara's guards walked out of the room, she turned to Barnet, who had walked up next to her. "Barnet, I need you to find out everything you can about Sara. Where she goes, what she's been up to, when was the last time she left the city, and I need the information as fast as you can get it to me."

He didn't even blink at her request. "Of course, my Queen."

Vic was right; an adventure did await them, just not the type she had expected. She would have to be careful how she spent her time while she was here. There was too much at stake and she wouldn't be the one to upend things.

❧❧❧❧

"What just happened?" Elson asked, dragging the

body to the furthest wall away from them. "Is he even telling the truth?" He washed his hands in the bowl by the window, pulled the table away from the wall, then sat down in the chair the Jester had vacated.

Lanis pushed back from the table and stood. "We don't have a choice but to believe him." How could she have been so stupid to leave someone else in charge of Anya's protection? She ran her hands through her hair and fought the urge to pick up a chair and slam it against the wall. If Anya died because of her lack of judgement, she would never be able to forgive herself. "I have to find her."

Elson stood and pulled her into a quick hug before pushing her to arm's length. He waited until she made eye contact with him before speaking. "We will. She may be your love, but she is my High Priestess and I will do anything within my power to find her. You are not alone." He squeezed her shoulders, then moved back to his seat. "I'm not going anywhere."

"I know. It's just..." She bit her lip. "If I would have been by her side."

Elson threw his hand up. "Stop. Don't go there. It will eat you up inside. Trust me. I know. What's happened has already happened. Now, it's up to us to make it right."

She scrubbed her hands down her face. "You're right. No time for regrets."

He nodded. "Regrets will only eat you up."

He was right and she could see in his eyes the regrets he still carried with him. Anya needed her at her strongest. It was time to lay all her doubts, fears, and reservations to the side and figure everything out. "Once inside the Castle, it shouldn't be a problem to get around, but it's the getting in that will be the tricky part. The last time I had help, but what are the odds of that happening again?"

"Slim to none."

"Exactly." Lanis sat down opposite him. "We only have two weeks to find her and even on horseback who says we'll make it in time?"

Elson grabbed her hand. "Nia hasn't let us down yet and she won't. She is always with us."

How could he, after everything, still have such faith in her? She pulled her hand back and bit her tongue or risked saying something she would regret later. Where was Nia when Anya needed her? After everything that had happened, she wasn't feeling very faith filled at the moment. The idea of Anya being all alone and hurting was tearing her in two. She'd made it in time for Jalen; she could only hope the same fate held true for Anya. But first, she had to get into the Castle. Queen Isabel was a wild card and one she wasn't happy about playing. It didn't make any sense, but she would heed the Jester's words. The look in his eyes when he talked about Anya told her all she needed to know about him. He was in love with her and probably had been for some time. She had to believe his words; they were the only hope she had of finding Anya. "There is one good thing we don't have to worry about."

"What's that?"

"We don't have to get rid of the body."

"There is that, but I don't like the idea of you owing him. No offense, but what could he possibly want from you?"

Lanis laughed. "None taken." The fact was, she didn't want to think about what she would owe him. "We'll see when the time comes."

Elson smiled sadly. "Don't we always."

Lanis stood. "Okay. Here's what we know so far. The Holders have kidnapped Anya. We know where she is and we know how long we have to reach her. We also know I have to get in to see Queen Isabel. Then there's Rose. We don't know what happened to her or where she is."

Elson leaned back in his chair. "Your Protector mask is missing and we know Merek betrayed Anya. We still don't know who is behind this whole mess." He turned away from her, stood up, and started pacing.

"Elson, what is it?"

"I don't believe in coincidences. Do you?"

"No."

He leaned against the wall and slipped his hands in his pants pockets. "When High Priestess Anya called on me, it was for two Oaths. My first Oath, of course, was to keep you safe." He rounded his shoulders, pushed away from the wall, and motioned for her to join him at the table. "What I am about to tell you must never be repeated again."

"Okay."

"I belong to a secret organization within the Army of Malora. I am a Soliret. When called on, it is our duty to track down and kill any member of the Holders of the Spheres. Most people would be surprised how far their reach extends." He ran his hand down his beard. "The second Oath I took was as a Soliret. I never thought I would be called on for such a task. It was both a surprise and a gift. High Priestess Anya told me a name and that after I got you to Manight safely that I was to find him and kill him." He untied his hair and ran his hands through it, before putting it back up.

Lanis took that as a clear sign he was troubled. It didn't come as a surprise to her that the organization existed. In all her years as a mercenary, she ran into tons of people and groups that shouldn't exist, but did. Every country, army, and government had them, but they were never spoken of publicly. For him to tell her meant he trusted her, and also meant that what he was about to tell her probably wouldn't be good. She didn't know a lot about the Holders, but she knew there were seven spheres. What she didn't know, and what others didn't as well, was what the spheres would do when they were brought together. She, for one, wasn't looking forward to that day. Magic had a way of bringing like-minded people together, but it also had a way of alienating the masses. "Go on."

"The name High Priestess Anya gave me is of a very powerful and high ranking member of the Holders. He is said to have five of the seven spheres already and is actively looking for the other two. The thing is, no one knows where the original Book of Damrek is, not even this man." He shrugged. "I know there are seven indentions inside the front cover of the book that fits all seven spheres. I don't know how much you know about all of this, but the spheres, at one point, were said to have been spread across Adearian."

"I know that, but why weren't they found before now and destroyed? I am sure, that besides the Holders, other people have been looking for them."

"Yes, I am sure they have been. Damrek's magic was unlike anything anyone had ever known at the time. He obviously had something in mind when he created them and with the way magic has evolved since his time, who knows what will happen when brought together. For all we know, they could destroy all of Adearian."

That wasn't something she would think about

right now. No one should be allowed that kind of power. She pushed back in her seat and rubbed her neck. Everything was happening so fast, she had to remind herself to breathe. "How do members identity themselves?"

"Nobody knows, and those that do aren't telling."

"Okay. First things first. Who is your Oath to find?" This entire Oath, journey, whatever it was, was far bigger than any five-hundred-year old prophecy. Even Anya couldn't have seen all of this coming. Whatever was happening was far beyond their control and they were right in the middle of it. Anya had specifically told them not to enter into Laramore, but they'd disregarded her other orders; what would be one more?

"His name is Councilman Ramus and he is a member of the Queen's Court."

Lanis sat back and let that sink in for a minute. The man Elson was sent to kill was a member of one of the most respected Courts in the entire country. It would seem that everyone within the Castle had secrets. She leaned forward and clasped her hands together on the tabletop. "When that healer saved Rose in Vashta, it didn't come without its cost. I traded Rose's healing for an Oath of sorts. She wanted me to kill someone for her when we arrived here. I agreed." She held up her hand to ward off his questions. "It seems my Oaths are never ending these days." She laughed, then quickly sobered. "It wasn't until I read the name that I knew I was in way over my head. I may be a lot of things, but I could never, would never, kill the woman she wanted me to. For one, I would never get close enough to her and two, I think it would be nearly impossible to do. I do hope that stuff she made me drink didn't bind me to her in some way. In the future, I need to consider my choices before jumping in."

"Who?"

Lanis bit her lip. "Lady Sara."

He rested his hands behind his head. "What kind of mess have we gotten ourselves into?"

"But, we both know, there is more to Sara than she portrays to the public."

"I know, but our focus can't be on her right now, maybe not ever. Our main focus is High Priestess Anya."

"She's expecting me."

"And see you, she shall. One way or another, we will find her and bring her back."

"We haven't had time to talk about Rose."

"Right." He grinned. "It seems we are up to here in it, aren't we?" He held his hand above his head. "I don't have any answers for Rose. Sometimes it would be nice to have some magical abilities."

"The Mages might have saved her. We don't know. Her stuff is gone; someone took it. Don't get me wrong. I think it's weird, but what hasn't been weird this entire trip? Right now, we can't be concerned about her. Plain and simple, if I had to choose between her and you, I would choose you. We can always hire another sorceress, but." She turned away from him and stared at the wall. "I am kind of fond of you. I know in our line of work friendships aren't known to bloom but ours has and it would bother me if something happened to you." She ran her hands through her hair and turned to look at him. Being honest with someone other than Anya was new to her and she wasn't sure she liked it.

He nodded. "I completely agree. It would bother

me if something happened to you and that's not because of the Oath. I genuinely care for you."

She smirked and arched an eyebrow. "You do realize I am taken, don't you? Not that you aren't attractive, but— "

He held his hand up and grinned. "I understand." His smile vanished. "I would do anything for you. You know that, right?"

This is what she didn't want on this trip. She didn't want to get attached to someone, but that's exactly what happened. She couldn't deny the pull toward him. "As I would you."

He placed both of his hands on the table. "Good."

Lanis laughed. "Yes. Now that that's out of the way we have to figure out—" Her words were cut off when Elson jumped up from the bed and grabbed his sword. Lanis stood up and stared at the wall as a shadow started to appear. She pushed Elson back behind her when she realized what was happening. It only took a few seconds for a Veilshield to walk through the wall and appear before them.

"What the?" Elson said.

"Elson." Lanis patted his arm. "Lower the sword. I know who she is, or I hope it's the same person." Lanis breathed a sigh of relief when Mattea lowered the hood. Her features were even more striking in the light than she first thought. Her black hair was cut short and her bangs swept her forehead. She had a series of small tattoos that ran along her right cheek. Lanis could make out a scroll and a sword, but couldn't decipher the rest. The most distinguishing part was the fact that she wore all black, from her boots to her hood. Even the stitching in her clothes was black. The only color she could see, anywhere on her body, was one of the tattoos along her check was a pale blue. She tensed when Elson did and out of habit touched her whip. She looked between them and Mattea and, after a few moments, relaxed. "Elson, it really is okay. She's the one that helped me with Jalen." She couldn't make out the look on his face, but he never took his eyes off of Mattea.

"You know what she is, don't you?"

Lanis tensed and tried to cover her surprise. It was the first time she had ever heard something resembling hate in his voice. There was a story there and she would tread carefully. "Yes," she said softly.

"They are evil." He spit on the floor and Mattea took a step forward and let her hand, which held firmly to a black dagger, drop to her side.

Lanis stepped between them and forced Elson to look at her. "That may be the case, but whatever this is, we are not doing it now. I don't care what issues you have with them. Our only goal is to rescue Anya, who at this very moment, is waiting for us. I don't know why she's here, but I need her." She pleaded with him. He seemed to deflate before her eyes.

"Okay."

She nodded. "Okay." She turned and focused her attention on Mattea. She had already sheathed her dagger and looked relaxed. "Mattea, what brings you here?"

"I have come to fulfill a favor from an acquaintance." She pointed to the body on the floor.

Lanis blinked. "He really does seem to collect the favors, doesn't he?" Mattea ignored her, but kept her eyes glued on Elson. Lanis knew he wouldn't do anything, but Mattea didn't know that.

"Take the body and leave," Elson said.

Lanis glared at him when Mattea moved toward the body. "No, wait. I need your help."

"I don't make a habit out of helping people."

Lanis took a deep breath. What was one more? "I'll own you one." Mattea was her only way into the Castle.

"A favor?" Lanis nodded. "I will call upon you whenever I want and no matter the events, you will have to fulfill it."

She didn't have a choice but to agree to her terms. "Whenever and whatever you need me for."

"What do you need my help with?"

"I need to get into the Castle."

"Very well." She leaned over the body.

"Actually," Lanis said and Mattea straightened. "More specifically, I need to get into Queen Isabel's room."

Mattea pulled her hood up and easily lifted the body onto her shoulder, then walked back to the wall, with her back to Lanis. "Meet me at the same place as last time, before dawn. Don't be late."

Lanis felt a weight lift off of her as Mattea disappeared back through the wall, but she knew she had other things to worry about at the moment. Elson was rigid beside her. "Elson?"

"Don't." He held his hand up and frowned before setting his sword back on the bed. "I have issues with the Veilshield."

Lanis pulled up a seat at the table and waited until he sat across from her before going on. "Because of the army and Nia?"

"No." He laid his head back and stared at the ceiling. "The Veilshield killed my parents. My grandma never kept it a secret who killed them, she just never told me why."

"I understand."

"I know." He smiled, but it didn't reach his eyes. "I'm sorry for my behavior."

She waved him off. "Don't be. If it hadn't been for me needing her help, I wouldn't have stood in your way, but killing her wouldn't have made you feel better. That only works if you kill the person that has wronged you."

"I wouldn't have killed her. Her appearance just startled me."

"I get that a lot."

He looked pained. "I wasn't judging her because of what she can do; it was because of who she is. They're killers."

"So are we."

He turned to her sharply. "Not like them." He pointed to the wall.

"I don't know what they are. I don't listen to rumors. I go to the source, but I have a feeling she wouldn't tell me anything. Just as I would never tell my people's secrets to outsiders. I can remember every person I have ever killed. Their last words haunt my dreams and when I close my eyes, I relive their last moments over and over again. We all have our own demons we have to live with. Just as I am sure you've had to deal with persecution because of who you follow, I have had to deal with it because of what I am."

"I...you're right."

"Don't get me wrong. If your parents' killer or killers were in this room, I would help you kill them, but they aren't."

"No, they aren't." He scrubbed his hands down his face. "I need to stay focused. Tomorrow you meet

Queen Isabel. I have to tell you, I am glad it's you and not me."

"At this point," she said, standing and heading toward the door. "It can't be any different than what we've been up against thus far." She pulled open the door when Elson stopped her. "What? I figured we could get something to eat, then go to bed early. It's going to be a long two weeks."

"I agree." He grasped the hem of her shirt and pulled it out for her to see. "I thought you might like to change first. I don't think blood is the right color on you."

"See," she said. "What would I do without you?"

Lanis was startled, but relaxed, when he pulled her into a hug. "I pray we won't have to face that, but let me make it clear. I will do anything within my power to keep you safe, even if that means giving up my own life."

"I..."

"Change. I am hungry."

She watched him walk through the door and couldn't help the dread that settled in the pit of her stomach. She would do anything for him, but she would never fall on her sword for him. The only person that held that privilege was a long way away and tomorrow would be the first step in seeing that Anya made it home safely.

❧ ❧ ❧ ❧

Lanis knew it would be a losing battle, so she kept quiet when Elson insisted on accompanying her to meet up with Mattea. The night before, over dinner, he made it quite clear to her that if she wasn't back by nightfall, he would come looking for her. The closer they got to their destination, the more her anxiety spiked. It didn't take long for them to reach the meeting place and within moments, Mattea stepped out of the shadow of a large oak tree. Lanis patted Elson on the arm when he tensed beside her. She understood his reluctance and resistance to working with her, but knew he wouldn't do anything to disrupt their agreement.

"Morning," Mattea said.

"Good morning," Lanis said.

Mattea shrugged. "The good could be debated." Lanis flinched, but kept still when Elson stepped forward. She knew this was something he had to do.

"If anything, and I mean anything, happens to her," he said, pointing at Lanis. "I will hunt you down and kill you."

"Do not threaten me." Mattea sneered and took a step toward him. "I do not take threats lightly." She pulled her dagger. "If you know what I am, then you know what I am capable of."

Elson pulled his sword and held it out in front of him, his hands securely on the hilt. "I know what you are and I don't make threats lightly."

Lanis knew she had to stop this before it escalated. She touched his back. "Elson."

"Big man with a sword." Mattea snickered. "Pathetic." She slipped her dagger back into the sheath on her side, shook her head, and took a step back.

"You are nothing to me," Elson said. "Do not tempt me."

Mattea waved her hand in the air as if to wave off his words. "I've brought down bigger men. Besides, I have more important things to worry about than your threat." She turned to Lanis. "Ready?"

"Yes." She stepped in front of Elson. "I will be okay."

"You better be." He never took his eyes off of Mattea.

She squeezed his arm and waited for him to put his sword away. She clasped his hands between hers. "Wish me luck."

He pulled her to him and whispered in her ear. "I thought you said we didn't need luck?"

"Couldn't hurt." She pulled away from him.

He smiled, but it didn't reach his eyes. "Good luck."

She winked at him when Mattea pulled her close, then closed her eyes as Mattea pulled her backward. It wasn't an unpleasant feeling, but one she hoped wasn't a regular occurrence. She cracked open her eyes when Mattea released her.

Mattea didn't waste pleasantries. "Sun will be up shortly. We need to hurry."

Lanis nodded and followed behind her. They kept to the shadows and started on the same path as before, but before they reached the stadium, Mattea turned toward a small stone building that sat adjacent to the Castle. From Lanis's vantage point, dozens of guards were scattered around the grounds, but no one looked their way as they crept along the path.

"Give me your hand," Mattea said. "If we are not connected, this will not work properly." Lanis grasped her hand like a lifeline and felt somewhat reassured that Mattea's grip was strong and steady. "We will be walking through four or five walls fairly quickly. Stay plastered behind me." The first two walls they walked through happened so fast Lanis didn't have time to register what had happened, but as soon as they walked through the third one, the sweet smell of baking bread made her stomach grumble. Mattea tugged her hand and dragged her through the fourth, then the fifth wall.

They came to a complete stop inside a large office. A woman stood with her back to them, some five feet away. As the woman started to turn, Lanis grabbed Mattea and blended them both into the wall. The woman frowned in their direction and tightened the hold on the papers in her hand, but didn't make any sort of move toward them. After a few tense minutes, the woman walked to the large, wooden desk that sat adjacent to the door and sat down. Lanis sucked in a breath when she realized who the woman was. She had never met her, but she knew she was staring at Queen Abigail. Lanis, along with Abigail, swung their heads around when there was a knock on the door.

"Come in," Abigail said. She stood up, walked around the desk, and rested back against it. From the look on her face, Lanis felt sorry for whoever was about to walk through the door. Lanis kept her eyes glued to the door when it opened and four guards, including the one that beat Jalen, walked in. A short, stocky, female guard stepped away from the group, approached Abigail, and handed her the knife that she had strapped to her hip. Instead of rejoining the others, the guard took up position beside her Queen. Abigail ran her finger across the blade. "Have you found her yet, Douglass?" she asked, looking at the guard who beat Jalen.

"My Queen, no, but I am actively looking and have every available guard scouring the estate and the surrounding areas."

She nodded. "I see." She took a step forward and the guard on either side of Douglass grabbed his arms.

Douglass eyed the guards, then Abigail. "My Queen?"

Lanis cringed when Abigail stepped forward and without hesitating, ran her blade down his cheek. Lanis knew how excruciating the pain was, but Douglass never made a sound, even as blood dripped from his face onto the stone floor. "My daughter is missing. Your Princess is missing, and you can't tell me where she is, or why she was in the dungeon, or who put her there." She laughed. "Douglass, what good are you to me?" She shrugged. "People talk."

"Your Majesty, we are trying. We cannot find her. She has disappeared. Maybe it's like the first time she was attacked."

To Lanis, Abigail looked calm and reserved, which she found highly unnerving. Abigail took a step back, handed the knife to the guard, and leaned back against the desk. "I am a very patient Queen, but at this moment, I am not your Queen, I am Jalen's mother. My patience runs deep, but not when it comes to the welfare of my children."

Lanis bit her lip when a deep, rich laugh poured from his lips. A moment later, the guards knocked him to his knees. He turned hate-filled eyes to Abigail. "Kill me. I don't care." He snickered. "I hope she's dead." Lanis flinched when the female guard stepped forward and kicked him in the face so hard his head jerked backward and blood flew from his mouth, then the guard calmly stepped back to Abigail's side.

Abigail cocked her head, but Lanis didn't notice any crack in her demeanor. "Is that so," she said with such calm that Lanis felt her blood run cold.

His eyes darted around the room before focusing back on Abigail and for the first time, Lanis saw a smidge of uncertainty in his eyes. "Yes." She nodded and the female guard walked out of the room only to return a few minutes later with a young woman in tow.

"Dad?" the young woman said. Douglass whipped his head in her direction.

He spun around toward Abigail. "No." He shook his head and struggled against the guards. "This doesn't involve her. Please let her go."

He didn't sound the least bit sorry to Lanis's ears. "So, now you beg. Do you love her?"

"Of course I do. She's my daughter," he ground out.

"I see." Abigail pointed to the young woman. "Elizabeth, come here."

On shaky legs, Elizabeth stood in front of Abigail and bowed before her. "My Queen."

"Elizabeth, stand up and stand next to me."

"My Queen," Douglass said. "I will do anything."

Abigail ignored him and pulled Elizabeth to her side. "Are you aware that Princess Jalen is missing?"

"Yes," Elizabeth stuttered.

"Are you also aware that your father is the one that beat the Princess when she was in the dungeon?"

"What?" Elizabeth swung her head from Abigail to her dad. "Dad?"

He ignored her and focused on Abigail. "She has nothing to do with this. Let her go."

Abigail patted Elizabeth on the back. "Go and stand beside your father. Douglass, you beat my daughter and from everything I've heard, she was in poor shape, near death. You cannot believe I will let that go unpunished. An eye for an eye."

"Don't threaten me." He spat. "You have no idea what you're dealing with. You kill me and two more will take my place. Tell me, Queen Abigail, who can you really trust within your kingdom?"

"Exactly. Whom can I trust? That's one of the reasons every guard stationed under your care and every guard working in the dungeon, along with anyone that was associated with my daughter's care while she was in the dungeon, were taken care of this morning." She sighed. "Can't find good help anymore these days. Can you?"

He spit a mouthful of blood at her feet. "They were innocent."

"Really?" She shrugged and crossed her arms. "Just part of the process. Don't worry; their deaths were painless and quick. Now, you on the other hand, I have a better fate for. Elizabeth, you have your father to thank for your fate."

"No." Elizabeth hit her knees before Abigail. "My Queen, I didn't do anything. I have been faithful to the crown and you. His actions have no bearing on me. Please. I…I am pregnant."

"Elizabeth?" Douglass asked.

She wiped her cheek and sniffled. "We were going to tell you at dinner."

"Douglass, tell me what I want to know and I will let her go unharmed. Your daughter and your grandchild."

When he didn't say anything, Elizabeth forced him to look at her, but he jerked away from her. "Dad?"

He shook his head. "Elizabeth, I am sorry, but I can't."

"You mean you won't. You've disgraced your family, your Queen, and now you're leaving me to a fate that I don't deserve. How could you?"

He turned to Abagail and held his head high.

"You'll have to kill me because I am not talking."

"Fair enough. Guards, take him to the North Tower."

"No," he screamed, and lunged at Abigail, but the guards grabbed him and hauled him to his feet. Lanis didn't know what the North Tower was, but from his reaction, it couldn't be good. When they dragged him from the room, Abigail retook her seat. "Elizabeth, stand and come here." Abigail waited until she stood up before speaking. "You are free to go. I will send a formal note to your family concerning your father. Do not speak of anything that took place this morning. Do I make myself clear?"

She nodded franticly. "Yes. Thank you, your Highness."

"Get out."

When the door shut, the female guard spoke. "My Queen."

"Yes, Elisha." Lanis could see the faint traces of a smile grace Abigail's lips.

"Lady Sara wished me to inform you, she will be in the gardens when you are ready for breakfast."

Abigail smirked. "Did she now?"

"She did."

"Well then." Abigail stood and took Elisha's arm. "Let's not keep her waiting." Lanis waited a few minutes after the door shut behind them before she released Mattea and stepped away from the wall. To Lanis, Abigail looked like a woman on the verge of doing something drastic, and she was glad she wasn't on her bad side.

Mattea stretched her arms above her head. "You're really good at that."

"I know." She rubbed her neck. "Do you know

what happens at the North Tower?" Lanis couldn't decipher the look on Mattea's face.

"At the top of the tower there is a large opening around two feet by five feet. A few feet below the bottom of the opening is a smaller opening and a narrow ledge, about four inches wide and a foot long. They will strip him naked and make dozens of inch long, shallow cuts all over his body. The guards will bind his wrists, force him outside the opening, and lower him until his feet land on the small ledge. From inside the tower, they will tie a rope around his feet and secure them to the ledge. They will pull his arms behind his body, inside the tower, and stretch them up as far as they will go. His wrists will then be tied to a peg." Mattea shook her head. "Imagine. No food or water, the sun beating down on you all day, cracking and drying out the skin. The birds pecking at the skin and bugs crawling all over him and into the wounds." She shivered. "I've heard stories where the person lasted weeks, hanging there. When the person dies, they untie them and let the body fall to the rocks below." She rubbed her hands together. "Ready?"

Lanis couldn't imagine such a death. She always tried to make sure all the people she killed had a quick death. But, given the circumstance, if she were in Abigail's shoes, she wouldn't have hesitated to make that decision either. Her eyes darted around the room, then she grasped Mattea's hand. "I'm ready."

❧ ❧ ❧ ❧

Lanis held tight to Mattea's hand as they climbed up four flights of stairs. After leaving Abigail's office, Mattea had diverted them to the lesser used parts of the Castle. The dark, damp passageways were difficult even for her to navigate, but Mattea seemed to know exactly where she was going. Mattea stopped and pulled her hand away. "Wait here." Lanis leaned back against the stone wall. She was ready to get this over with and it hadn't even started yet. Mattea walked back to her, grabbed her hand, and dragged her ten or so feet down the hall. "This is our final stop." She pulled Lanis back against her chest and walked them through the wall. "I will collect that favor," she whispered in her ear.

Lanis shuddered and blended into the wall. The bedroom was massive. A huge four-poster bed sat in the middle of the room and dozens of pillows, in shades of blue and green, lay atop it. Multiple throw rugs were scattered throughout the room and a large fire blazed in the stone tiled fireplace. The only sign that the room was occupied was a trunk that rested at the foot of the bed. It was open and from her vantage point, she could see clothes and a few books poking out of the top.

She jerked her head around, and pushed back into her blend when the door opened and a woman entered the room. The woman could only be Queen Isabel, but she kept her back to her. Lanis sucked in a breath when the woman lifted the hood of her cape. That couldn't be a good sign. At this point, though, she didn't have much of a choice. Goosebumps covered her flesh and the beating of her heart drowned out her thinking when Isabel turned around, walked toward where her blend was, grabbed a chair from the table by the window, and sat down. She draped one leg casually over the other.

"I know you're there," Isabel said.

As far as Lanis knew, no one could detect a Ramden's blend. Her only hope had been to get the upper hand, but that wouldn't be the case. Hopefully, her trust in the Jester's love for Anya wasn't misplaced. He had to know that if he sent her to die, Anya would never be his. Lanis sucked in a breath and shook her head when the room started to lose focus. She closed her eyes to fight against the nausea, and quickly opened them when something wrapped around her body and started to tighten and tug her away from the wall. A blue shimmering rope was tied around her waist.

The woman lifted her hand and pushed the hood from her face. Lanis gasped. The resemblance was uncanny. Isabel smiled and waved her hand and the rope disappeared. Looking at her, Lanis knew why the Jester had sent her here. Isabel was Anya, only an older version. She could clearly remember Anya talking about her parents and she never once mentioned Isabel being her mother, but the resemblance was too much to deny. Isabel could only be her mother. It was the only explanation.

Isabel cocked her head and smiled. Anya's smile. "I don't do well with unwanted guests. Especially those that hide in my walls." She leaned forward in her chair. "What can I do for you?"

Lanis may have been looking at Anya's mother, but the voice was throwing her. Isabel had an unusual accent, nothing like Anya's. She didn't think lying would get her anywhere and this was, after all, for Anya. "A Jester sent me."

Isabel arched her eyebrow and cocked her head. "Really?" Her voice was skeptical.

"Really." She had to keep reminding herself this was for Anya. "My High Priestess is in trouble and I need your help. She's been kidnapped."

She scooted forward in her chair. "Why would I

help you? Who are you? Besides, she has a Protector," she said, waving her hand in the air.

Lanis wasn't sure if she was creating a spell or just waving her hand. She would have to be on top of things around her. She gulped and ran her hands through her hair, then pointed to a chair. When Isabel nodded, she walked over, and pulled it back to sit in front of Isabel's. "My name is Lanis and I didn't realize why he insisted I meet with you until I saw you."

"And why did seeing me change your mind?"

"Because you're my High Priestess's mother." Lanis noticed a brief break in her façade before it vanished.

"You have no idea what you're talking about."

"Don't deny it. She looks just like you. Just a younger version."

Isabel stood and crossed her arms. "What do you want from me?"

"I need your help." If she had to beg, she would. "My Oath has been anything but ordinary. I completed my Oath but my Oath bracelet," she said, pulling her shirt sleeve back, "Isn't gone and now I know why. Anya told me my Oath was to save a Princess. While I did save a Princess, it was the wrong one. It makes sense now."

Isabel sat back down and regarded Lanis. "So you're the one behind the mess surrounding Princess Jalen. Abigail is not happy. Do you know where Jalen is?"

Lanis shook her head. "No, I don't know where she is, and even if I did, I wouldn't tell you. Abigail should be happy; if it wasn't for me and an acquaintance, Jalen would be dead. I played my part and Anya needs me now."

"Fair enough. I won't ask any more about her. Now for your High Priestess."

"Anya."

"What?"

"Her name is Anya."

Lanis couldn't decipher the look on Isabel's face. "She has a Protector."

Lanis flinched and cast her gaze away. She finally worked up enough courage and looked back at her. "I'm her Protector."

"I see. What else are you to her or are you just that dedicated to your Goddess and her High Priestess?"

Lanis held her temper. "She's my love, but no one knows."

Isabel nodded. "A secret. They can get you into trouble."

"Sometimes trouble is worth it."

"You love her." She said it as more of a statement then a question.

"More than the air I breathe."

"Do you know where she is?"

"Yes."

"Do you know who kidnapped her?"

"Yes."

"Not much for talking, are you?" Isabel stood and slipped her cape off, then laid it on the bed. "I am going to need more if you expect my help."

"I know Anya is being held just inside Laramore's border inside of a cave. I also know I have two weeks to get to her or she is going to die. With or without your help, I will save her, but having your help would go a long way making that happen." This was a nightmare.

Isabel retook her seat. "I see." She seemed to choose her words carefully. "It is a bit unusual for a

Veilshield and a Ramden to work together."

Lanis wasn't sure how much to reveal, but it wasn't her place to mention Mattea. "That's irrelevant. You still haven't answered my question about Anya. Are you her mother?"

"Who kidnapped her?" Isabel said, ignoring the question.

Lanis hated feeling helpless, but the quicker they finished, the sooner she could get on her way. "All I know is that one of her advisers was in on her kidnapping. His name is Merek. Rest assured, though, that when I find him, I will kill him. One more death won't hurt my conscious."

"I wasn't worried about that. I would hate to be the one standing in your way. In order to help you, I will have to have answers. You do understand?"

"I do. I don't trust you, but I need you." Isabel acknowledged her remark with a nod. "My companion and I had another person traveling with us. A sorceress, but we lost her."

"Lost?"

Lanis nodded and rubbed her neck. "I'm not sure if you know about what happened at the edge of the Estate yesterday with the dead bodies."

"Wait," Isabel said, holding her hand up. For a brief moment, Lanis caught a glimpse of Anya. "You were behind that also. I have to tell you that if Abigail got a hold of you, you wouldn't be going anywhere. Like me, she doesn't take kindly to strangers invading her space. But," she said. "I won't tell her about you. What happened to your sorceress?"

"Rose, her name is Rose. All I know is when we were attacked, one of the bandits grabbed her, and they both fell over the side and over the cliff's edge, but when I looked, she wasn't there. We lost her."

"I guess you did lose her."

"When we got back to our room, Elson, he is my traveling companion, noticed all of her things were gone."

At that, Isabel sat forward in her chair. "Interesting. You have been busy."

"You are Anya's mother."

Isabel stood up. "I will only say I gave birth to her, but I am not her mother. That, my dear, is the only reason I am helping you." She walked to the door, then turned back to Lanis. "I will look into the disappearance of Rose, but I can't say I will get very far."

"I understand."

"Good." Isabel waved her hand and Lanis cringed when the same blue rope wrapped around her, securing her to the chair. "I can't take any chances, now can I? I will be back shortly with someone I think will be the best help you can ask for."

Lanis laid her head back and sighed when the door closed. She certainly hadn't expected this. Rose's magic didn't even compare to Queen Isabel's. She wiggled in the chair, but the rope just got tighter. Great. She hated feeling like a prisoner. She couldn't even imagine what Anya was going through. She would find her and kill anyone who stood in her way.

⚜ ⚜ ⚜ ⚜

Isabel closed the door behind her and cursed softly under her breath. What a nightmare. The last thing she wanted to do was get Vic involved, but that was her only option. Lanis would need the help of a sorceress. The only person she trusted enough to get involved was Vic. For the simple fact that Anya was involved. Her daughter and Victoria's sister. She wished that secret would never to come to the surface. She hoped Vic would understand. She leaned back against the door and closed her eyes. She should have never accepted the invitation to come here. She pinched the bridge of her nose. Anya, her first born, was the High Priestess of Goddess Nia. Unbelievable.

"My Queen?"

Isabel shook herself out of her stupor and opened her eyes. Trevor had been one of her personal guards for twenty years. She trusted him as much as someone in her position could. Tall and lean, with his uniform pressed to perfection, he always made a striking picture. "I am fine." She waved off the worry in his eyes and pushed off from the door. "Walk me to Vic's room," she said, slipping her hand through the crook of his arm.

He snapped his heels together and bowed his head in her direction. "My pleasure."

As they walked, doubts started to creep into her head. She knew what needed to be done, and she knew Vic would be the one that had to go. The thought of Anya dying because she was holding back would haunt her for the rest of her life. Vic would be an invaluable asset to Lanis. Sending her heir to save the daughter she didn't even know certainly wasn't in the plans for this trip. Life did have a way of revealing the unexpected. There was more going on in Manight and the surrounding countries then even she wanted to know about. Yet, here they were, getting involved. Rose must have been the one she saw fall over the cliff into a gray fog. She shook her head. So many questions. So few answers.

"My Queen, we are here." Trevor removed her hand, took a step away from her, and took up position beside the door.

She looked up and down the hall, but there wasn't any sign of Finley, Vic's personal guard, anywhere up or down the hallway. He should have been outside her room, guarding it, not inside. Victoria's one downfall was Finley. It was clear to anyone that saw them together that Finley was in love with her, but Vic never swayed one way or the other. If Vic agreed to help Lanis, Finley would accompany them, which could make matters worse. Finley didn't get along well with others. There wasn't a doubt in her mind that Finley would lay his life down for Vic, but she also knew he wouldn't do the same for anyone else.

She knocked twice on the door and it opened immediately. Finley held his finger to his lips, then moved away from the door to allow her in. His short brown hair contrasted nicely with his rich, green eyes. He didn't have any magical abilities, but his training in Candor's Elite Fighters gave him all the skills he needed to protect Vic. She patted him on the shoulder, then pointed to the hallway. He hesitated briefly before nodding in her direction and walking into the hall. She understood his urge to protect Vic, but Vic wasn't his Queen; she was. She would have a talk with him later. She smiled when she saw what Vic was doing.

Vic stood in the far corner of the room, waving her right hand in circles above her head. In her left hand, she held her ever-present maple and oak staff. A teacher gave the staff to her when she graduated University and she never let it out of her sight. The staff was enchanted and allowed her to channel her magic more effortlessly. Isabel straightened and watched in awe as Vic formed a small funnel cloud and grinned when Vic stilled her hand and the funnel burst into hundreds of colors and swirled in the center of the room. Vic kept her eyes on the funnel and walked up to it. She lifted her staff and brought it down hard in the middle of the funnel. Isabel held her breath when the colors shot out into the room and painted the walls. It was an amazing feat of patience and focus. Vic lifted her staff once again above her head, chanted, and within a matter of seconds, the colors had disappeared into the staff. Vic lowered the staff and tapped it twice on the floor.

"Well." Vic laughed. "That was fun. I am so glad we put our shields in place. I don't know what I would have done with myself otherwise." She leaned her staff against the wall and frowned when Isabel didn't answer her. "Mom?"

Isabel swallowed twice. This was going to be far harder than she imagined. She said the first thing that popped into her head. "You're very good at that."

"What's wrong and don't tell me nothing. I know that look. Is this about Finley? He was only watching."

"Have you thought anymore about his proposal?"

Vic rolled her eyes. "I'm not ready for marriage. There is so much to see and do."

Isabel pointed to the table and they both sat down. "Finley would be a willing participant."

"I know."

"Vic, what is it? If you don't feel the same way, I will relocate him."

"What?" Vic shook her head. "Don't be silly. That's not necessary."

"Do you love him?" Normally, she wouldn't have asked, but right now, she needed to know for her own peace of mind. "Do you love him?"

Vic rested back in her seat and crossed her arms across her chest. "Why all the questions? What's going on?"

Isabel knew a diversion tactic when she saw it. "It's a simple answer. Either you do or you don't. Do you really want to continue to lead him on?"

"I…" She sighed. "I don't want marriage to change me."

"What do you mean?"

Vic fidgeted in her seat then rested her hands on the table. She averted her gaze from Isabel, then after a moment, she lifted her head and locked onto Isabel's eyes. "I know you loved Dad, but he wasn't your true love. I don't want to give up who I am for someone else."

Isabel groaned. That certainly wasn't what she expected. "Vic."

"No, Mom." She held her hand up. "I know you loved him." She pleaded. "But, I don't know if you were ever *in* love with him. I had an amazing childhood and two wonderful parents. I'm not bitter about anything that happened. I know you were faithful to him and him to you. I don't want to settle."

The words stung more than Isabel wanted to admit, and Vic was far more observant than she ever gave her credit for. "I loved your father. Don't speak as if I didn't."

"Mom." Vic grabbed her hand. "My intention wasn't to hurt you. I know you loved him, but I am not blind, nor deaf." She shook her head. "The way you talk about Queen Abigail and the way your eyes light up."

"Vic." Isabel pulled her hand away. "We are not

talking about Abigail."

"Fine." Vic took a sip of her water. "When you're ready to talk about her, then I will be ready to talk about Finley." She smirked.

Isabel laughed. "Well played." When Vic got back, they would have a lot to talk about.

"I learned from the best. I love you, Mom."

"I love you too. More than you will ever know."

"Oh, I know, but I don't think you came here to discuss that, or Finley. What's going on?"

Isabel pushed back from the table and stood. She walked to the corner of the room and poured a glass of water. The glass felt heavy in her hand and she curled her fingers around it to keep her hands occupied. She started to pace, then after a few minutes retook her seat, and set her glass down. "There is something I should have told you about a long time ago. Honestly, I would have never told you if my hand hadn't been forced." She waved off Vic's question. "I will tell you about that after my story. Please don't interrupt me."

Vic nodded. "I won't."

Isabel smiled sadly. "Shortly after your father and I were married we found out I was pregnant. Your father was so happy." She licked her lips. "A few months into the pregnancy, I had a dream. I dreamt my daughter would grow into a leader. Someone that would change the fate of everyone around her. Not long after the dream, a stranger came to visit your father and me. She told us that our baby would grow up to do great things." She sobered. "Just not in Candor. She also told us that the baby wouldn't be magic inclined, but she would hold a power not many people ever would. Your father was just as amazed and troubled by everything as I was. Maybe more." She sighed. "She told us our daughter would one day be High Priestess to Nia. The only way our baby could be High Priestess to Nia was if she believed she grew up in Malora. The people of Malora would never accept a leader that wasn't born in the city. The woman told us she knew of a couple that would willingly take her in."

Isabel took a sip of water before continuing. "Your father was irate and firmly said no. I initially agreed with him, but the more I thought about it, the more I started to second-guess our decision. Think about it. Our daughter would grow up to be a great leader someday. She would change the fate of many." She slapped her hand on the table. "Who were we to stand in the way? In the end, we both agreed to give her up for the greater good. Your father never left my side through the pregnancy or the birth. He was by my side when we turned her over to the woman. We never heard back from her. Over the years, your father and I heard rumors, of course, but nothing concrete. That is, until a little while ago."

"What happened earlier?"

"When I got back to my room, I had a visitor. She was already in my room."

"What? How?"

"It's okay. I handled the situation. She is a Ramden, that's the how and it's what she had to tell me that changed things."

"Okay. I have another question."

Isabel ran her hands through bogh her hair. "Go ahead."

Vic leaned forward on the table. "What did you tell the people of Candor about the baby? I've never heard anything. Nothing." She swiped her hand across the table.

"Vic, we didn't tell the people of Candor anything.

At that time, I wasn't Queen. Your father and I travelled to a remote cabin where the baby was born."

"I see." Vic rounded her shoulders. "The woman that came to see you in your room. Was it her?"

"No, it wasn't." Isabel blew out the breath she was holding. "Vic, I wasn't. Your father and I weren't keeping anything from you. We just." She closed her eyes.

"It must have been hard to hand her over," Vic said quietly.

Isabel snapped her eyes open and held back the tears that threatened to fall. "It was, but time passed quickly and before we knew it, we found out I was pregnant with you. Your father told me that no matter what, we wouldn't give you up for anything. I didn't realize until that moment how much he regretted our decision." She squeezed Vic's hand. "The look on his face when he held you. I have never seen so much love before."

Vic caressed Isabel's palm and allowed her tears to fall. "I miss him."

"I do too. You look just like him. He was so proud of that fact. The baby we gave up had my features." She wiped Vic's tears away.

Vic took a deep breath. "What happened to her? Did she grow up to be a powerful leader?" She spat.

"Vic?"

"What?"

"Why the venom?"

"I am still your heir. I have trained all my life for this."

"She is not my heir. She never has been and never will be."

Vic stood up and stretched. "I was just saying."

She spun around. "I have a sister."

Isabel wasn't sure what to say to that. Vic did in fact have a sister, but it wasn't that simple. She didn't see them having any type of relationship together. "Vic?"

Vic frowned. "What?"

"Sit back down. Things are a bit more complicated than that."

"I see." Vic retook her seat.

"The woman that came to see me. Her name is Lanis. She asked for my help."

"You don't normally give help freely to a stranger. This is about her, isn't it? My sister."

"Yes. I am sure Lanis went to a lot of trouble to meet with me. She informed me her High Priestess had been kidnapped. She needed my help rescuing her. From everything that she found out, her High Priestess has, maybe, two weeks to live. Even without my help, she would go on her own. But, I fear she wouldn't be successful."

"I guess everything the woman told you was true, assuming that her High Priestess is the baby you gave up. Don't tell me." She cringed. "High Priestess Anya is my sister. They say she is the most respected and beloved leader of Nia's people ever." She sobered. "You do realize the impact she has had on everyone in her presence. If the people of Malora find out she has been kidnapped, there is no telling what would happen. I don't think in Adearian's history any of the Gods' chosen has ever been kidnapped."

Isabel knew and still couldn't believe that Anya was her daughter. The stranger had told her the truth. Her little girl grew up to be an amazing woman and a great leader. It was all so surreal. "I know the impact she's had on her followers and I also know that if her followers found out what has happened to her, it could be catastrophic. It had crossed my mind who my daughter was, but it wasn't confirmed until this morning that High Priestess Anya was the baby I gave up."

"How do you know she is the baby you gave up?"

"Lanis said when she saw me, she understood why the Jester had sent her to me. She said it was like looking at an older version of Anya."

"Wait a minute," Vic said, holding her hand up. "A Jester is involved in this?"

"Like I said. It seems there is a lot going on."

"What do you want from me? I mean, I can guess what you want, but I want to hear it from you."

Isabel pulled her ear. "On the ride here, the body that disappeared in the gray fog. Seems she was the sorceress Lanis hired to get her here." She tapped the table. "All this mess that's been happening around the Castle, Lanis has had a hand in it."

"All the dead bodies?"

"Yes."

Vic grinned. "Someone who doesn't play by the rules. A woman who is willing to do whatever is necessary. I think I am going to like working with her."

Isabel took several breaths to calm her racing heart. There was never a doubt in her mind that Vic would say no, but she hoped that she would. "Vic, thank you."

Vic stood and pulled Isabel up and into her arms. "Mom," she said, facing her. "You don't have to thank me. Besides, I know if there were another choice, you would have never come to me. Even though we don't know her, she is still family and I would never forgive myself if I didn't help her. As would you."

"That is the only reason I am helping Lanis, because of Anya."

"You trust Lanis?"

"I don't not trust her. I believe her."

Vic gave her one last squeeze then walked to the corner of the room and grabbed her staff. "Where is she now?"

Isabel snickered. "I have her in my room."

Vic laughed. "The blue rope?"

"It always worked with you."

Vic stopped with her hand on the doorknob. "Anya is thirty-five."

"Yes."

"Any more secrets you want to share with me?"

"Not right now." Maybe not ever.

"Fair enough. Let's see what Lanis has to say."

"Yes, let's." When they started on this trip, she didn't realize she would have to say goodbye to one daughter in order to save another one. She didn't intend for anything to happen to either one of them and would do anything to make sure nothing happened to them. The easy part would be making sure they made it out of the city safely. The hard part would be making sure they made it back alive.

ﷺﷺﷺ

Lanis rounded her neck and held her breath when the door opened and Queen Isabel walked in, followed closely by a young woman. Without introducing herself, the woman walked up to her and placed her staff on Lanis's chest. Lanis gritted her teeth as a warmth flooded her entire body, then quickly turned ice cold.

Isabel rolled her eyes. "Vic, we don't have time for your games."

"But, she's so helpless. A few games might be fun."

"I think we have more important things to discuss," Lanis said through clenched teeth. "All I need to know is if you're going to help me find Anya. If not, then let me go so I can find someone who can." Lanis relaxed into the chair and quit struggling against the rope.

Vic sat down in the chair Isabel had vacated and crossed her legs. "I'm surprised that you don't call her by her title. Who are you to use her name so informally?" She smirked.

She may not have looked like Isabel but she did act like her. "I am her lover."

"Really." Vic whistled and leaned forward in her chair, locking her clasped hands over her knees. "And you love her?"

"Yes." The last thing she wanted was twenty questions.

"Do you know what I love?"

"I don't care what or who you love. This isn't about you."

Vic ignored her. "I love magic." She tapped her staff on the ground and Lanis gripped the arms of the chair when it started to shake. Vic produced a small green light in her hand.

Lanis jerked in the chair to try and escape her restraints. "You're going to kill me? All I want is to save Anya."

Vic stood up and bobbed the globe in her hand, then laughed. "Oh dear. You have a lot to learn. This," she pointed at the orb "is Candor magic. It is very different than magic in other parts of Adearian. Green for us doesn't necessarily mean death." She waved her hand over the orb and it, along with the rope wrapped around Lanis, disappeared.

Lanis stood on shaky legs and touched her whip. "I am tired of your games. Are you going to help me or not?"

Vic glanced at Isabel, then back to Lanis. "I will help you, but only because of Anya."

"No one is to know that Anya is my birth child. No one," Isabel said.

Lanis couldn't believe any of this was happening. She ran her hands through her hair. "You do realize that Anya is set to read the Prophecy in two weeks' time, don't you?"

"What's your point?" Vic asked.

"My point is that once everyone sees them together, they will know Anya is her daughter."

"We'll deal with that when the time comes," Isabel said. "And Lanis, I will look into what happened with Rose."

Vic scrunched her nose. "Who's Rose?"

Lanis sat back down. "Rose is the sorceress we hired, but we lost her."

Vic retook her seat and Isabel pulled another one up to them. "Do you mean Ella Rose?"

"Ella Rose." Lanis searched her memory. She did recall seeing the initials E.R.R. carved into the side of Rose's bow. "Maybe. Why?"

"She is Councilman Ramus' daughter. He is on the Queen's Court."

Lanis groaned. Everything was starting to make sense and come full circle. Rose's dad was the man

Elson was sent to kill. That was some coincidence. "She fell over the side of a cliff and disappeared."

"Huh. No kidding," Vic said.

"I kid you not," Lanis said.

Vic turned to Isabel. "If we can put our own shields in place and no one detects them, the same could be said for someone else. Please be careful?"

Isabel patted her hand. "I will. Now, I think instead of Lanis sneaking out, you and Finley can escort her back to her room."

Vic stood and gripped her staff. "Sounds like a plan. That is as long as Lanis doesn't have any objections?"

"I don't, but I don't want you to go into this blind either. The last couple of months have been anything but smooth. I just wanted to warn you that going with us, you will probably see more action than you've ever seen in your life."

"You really don't know who you have on your team. I think my abilities will pleasantly surprise you. Maybe I am the one who should be worried. What do you have to offer?"

Lanis nodded. Turnabout was fair play. "I am Ramden."

"I know."

"You should know that death doesn't bother us, but senseless death does. I will stop at nothing to find her and save her."

Vic smiled. "You said us."

"Elson is my travelling companion. He is a Ranger in Malora's Army."

"Impressive."

Lanis stood up and rocked back on her heels. "What kind of sorceress are you?"

Vic laughed and reached for Lanis. "None like you've ever seen before."

Lanis brushed her hand away. "I'm only asking because, although Rose was what we needed at the time, I feel we will need more from you on our journey to find Anya, in Laramore." The last thing she would do was put her and Elson's lives in danger.

Vic rested her hands on her staff. "My, my, we are ambitious, aren't we?" She turned to Isabel. "Mom, what kind of sorceress am I?"

"She is one of the most focused sorceress Candor has ever seen. Lanis, you will not have to worry about her abilities on your journey."

Lanis frowned. "I've seen the Jester's parlor tricks and I've seen what Rose can do with her items, but you're a completely different story."

Vic shook her head. "Do you really want me to demonstrate my magic? Here?"

"Yes, I do." Isabel patted Lanis's arm and they moved to stand back against the wall.

Vic winked and started twirling her staff, then pounded it on the floor. The tornado she stored earlier poured out and landed beside her, spinning counter clockwise. It was gaining so much speed that Lanis couldn't tell the colors apart. They blurred in a synchronizing pattern. She pushed back into the wall when the tornado started getting bigger and bigger and seemed to fill the entire room. Vic stepped up to the tornado and blew on it. Lanis closed her eyes as the colors raced at her, then snapped her eyes open when something touched her arm. A multi-colored butterfly fluttered on her wrist, then took flight to join the thousands that were scattered throughout the room.

It was a cute showing, but Lanis wasn't all that

impressed. She turned her head and locked eyes with Vic. They might have been a different color than Anya's, but they were the same eyes. Vic lifted her hand and all the butterflies flew to the ceiling. Without breaking eye contact with Lanis, Vic dropped her hand and as the butterflies were falling, they turned into spikes and embedded themselves into the floor. Vic waved her hand and all the spikes shot up from the floor and floated in the air. Vic tapped her staff twice on the floor and Lanis watched her lips move, but couldn't make out what she was saying. She watched with interest as the spikes flew, one by one, toward the staff, collided with it, and disappeared on impact. Vic was much more powerful than Rose, and Lanis hated to admit it, but she would be an added bonus.

"Impressive," Lanis said.

Vic shrugged. "It's who you know."

"It would seem so. I am ready now."

"So am I," Vic said. Isabel smiled, then opened the door. Two men Lanis didn't know where waiting in the hallway. "Finley," Vic said to the taller of the two men. "This is Lanis. We are going to be accompanying her and her companion on a mission."

He looked skeptical, but hid it well. "Very well, my Lady." Lanis saw Vic roll her eyes and held back a laugh. It wasn't hard to tell he was gone on Vic. Lanis nodded at him and accepted the hand he held out.

"Good to meet you," he said, but Lanis knew he didn't mean it.

"Same," she said. He would be trouble.

"Now that we've got that out of the way," Vic said. "We are going to be escorting Lanis back to her room." She turned to Lanis. "I see you don't have your cloak with you."

She shrugged. "I...No. At the time I didn't think I would need it."

"Step back into the room, Lanis," Isabel said.

She followed Isabel and was about to protest when Isabel waved her hand in front of her and a brown cloak appeared upon Lanis's shoulders. The cool, sleek fabric was the finest she had ever seen. She was speechless.

Isabel spoke first. "Consider it a gift for saving Anya."

"I will. Thank you." Lanis lifted her hood and joined Vic and Finley in the hall.

Vic whistled. "Nice." She fingered the material. "Let's go." She grabbed Isabel in a hug. "We will see you later."

"You will." Vic let her go and started down the hallway. Lanis had to jog to catch up with her and took up position on her right side. When they reached the stairs, they took two flights down. They took a right and headed toward a door at the end of the hall. Lanis sucked in a breath when the door opened and Lady Sara walked through it, followed by two guards. Vic didn't seem bothered and kept walking. Lady Sara was a few feet from them when Vic nodded at her. Lanis kept her gaze averted, but felt compelled to look up. She caught Sara's eye, then quickly looked away, but not before Sara's eyes widened. When they reached the door and walked out, Lanis was never so happy to see the outside world. She prayed the entire way down the stairs and her heart rate returned to normal when they reached the gates. Only when they reached the marketplace did she allow herself to breathe.

"I have some business I have to attend to. We will join you later, along with Mom. I know you're eager to leave, but I am afraid we won't leave until tomorrow morning," Vic said.

"I figured as much. We are staying at the Green Dragon Inn Two, and we're in room seven."

Vic clasped Lanis's hand between hers. "We'll see you later."

Lanis hated to admit it but she liked her. She dropped her hood back and headed to her room. It was going to be a long day and an even longer night.

⚜ ⚜ ⚜ ⚜

Dimitri stifled a groan when Sara threw open his office door and hurried in. What did she want now? She was starting to be more trouble than he was willing to put up with. The day he was rid of this Castle and city couldn't come fast enough. "What do you want?"

"Do not look at me like that. I am Lady of this house and you best remember that."

"My Lady."

"Do you remember me telling you about that woman that saw me and my two riders on the way to our meeting?"

Dimitri lifted his head, but made sure to keep his face devoid of emotion. "Yes. I told you I have people on it."

Sara planted her hands on her hips. "Really. That's funny, because I just passed her in the hallway. Not fifteen minutes ago."

That wasn't possible. He stood and crossed his arms. "What?"

"I just saw her in the hallway. She looked right at me. Victoria and her guard were with her."

He smoothed his hand down his beard. Lanis

with Princess Victoria. It couldn't be a coincidence. It was time to get rid of her for good. "I will take care of it."

Sara laughed. "You mean like everything else you were supposed to take care of."

She might have held power outside of his office, but inside, he held all the cards. "Sara, tell me something. Do you know where Jalen is?"

"Bastard."

"Really. We are in the same boat. But, considering Jalen is your daughter and Lanis is merely a thorn in my side." He let the words hang in the air between them and it didn't take long for a frown to mar her pretty features. Her recklessness would be her downfall. He wouldn't lose all he had worked so hard for because of her, and now he had to also deal with Lantor. He leaned forward and grabbed her hand. "Don't come here again. We shouldn't be seen together. People will start to talk and I love my wife too much for her to hear such rumors. Do I make myself clear?"

Sara jerked her hand away and glared at him. "Crystal. Just handle things, because from what I'm seeing, you haven't been doing a very good job of it."

He walked around his desk and opened the door for her. "Lady Sara," he said, bowing before her. "You have a wonderful evening." At least now, he knew exactly where Lanis was. Now all he had to do was find her. The city was big, but it wasn't that big and on top of that, Victoria chwas traveling with her. He could take care of two problems at once. He motioned for one of his guards to come to him. "Do you know what Princess Victoria looks like?"

"I do, Sir."

"Find her and follow her. Find out where she

goes and who she's with."

"Very well."

His plans were looking up and if he could deal with the Ramden, it would go a long way in accomplishing his goals. The only kink in his plans was Victoria. From what he knew, she was well capable of taking care of herself. Whomever he sent after them would have to be just as accomplished and he knew just the man for the job.

⚝ ⚝ ⚝ ⚝

Isabel closed the book she was reading and set it on the nightstand beside her. She shivered the moment the air changed inside her room. A slight disturbance tickled just below the surface. Her room certainly was popular this morning. She relaxed back into her chair and watched with interest as a figure appeared out of the wall. A Veilshield. Probably the same one that helped Lanis. "What can I do for you?" She was intrigued. It wasn't every day that a Veilshield appeared in one's room. Victoria did a well enough job, but she would have to strengthen the shields after the Veilshield left.

Without dropping the hood, the figure spoke. "I have information you may be interested in."

A woman. Interesting. But, Isabel knew nothing came without a price. She reached across her book, picked up her cup, and took a sip of her tea. Her eyes traced the woman from her boots to her hood, all black. She lowered the cup and held it securely between her hands. The Veilshield weren't known to be any sort of help, so whatever information she had must have been very valuable. "What do you want in exchange for the information?"

"A favor."

Owing a Veilshield a favor didn't sit high on her priority list, but this woman had her attention and she was curious. "Do you want the favor now or later?" She set her cup down and rested her hands in her lap.

"Later."

She didn't feel any malice or any type of magic surrounding her. "I agree to your favor only if I deem the information worth me knowing and I am the one that will determine that."

The figure didn't hesitate. "Fair enough." She stepped back against the wall. "I don't normally stick around after a task is completed." She shrugged. "But, I was feeling restless today. What I have to tell you may very well shake the core of the Castle and everyone in it."

Isabel straightened and leaned forward in her chair. "In other words, the favor will be big."

"You are very perceptive."

"I am a Queen. I have to be." Isabel listened to her retell what she overheard between Sara and Dimitri. The Veilshield was right. It would rock the Castle and Abigail, who Sara's betrayal would devastate. Abigail wouldn't hear the news from her. Right now, Vic and what was happening with Anya were her main priorities. Everything else she would play out as the days wore on. Shortly, she would meet everybody at the Inn, but she would keep this new revelation to herself. "Call on me whenever you need me." The woman nodded and Isabel relaxed back into her chair. Circumstances were about to get a lot more interesting.

Lanis shifted in her seat and tried, but failed, not to stare at Isabel, who sat to her right. Vic sat across from her, while Elson and Finley sat on the edge of the bed. "I've already discussed matters with Elson." The stunned look on his face when she told him Rose was Councilman Ramus's daughter didn't compare to the look he gave her when she told him Anya was Isabel's daughter. The first thing out of his mouth was he didn't believe in coincidences. She agreed with him, because neither did she. The fact that Ramus was Rose's father didn't matter in the long run. Elson's Oath was to kill him and that's exactly what he planned to do. Lanis noticed he kept stealing glances at the three strangers and it confirmed to her that he was as alert as she was.

"I have a map," Isabel said, placing it on the table and smoothing the edges out. She looked up when Lanis and Elson both groaned. "Did I miss something?"

Elson laughed and shook his head. "I meant no disrespect. We," he said, pointing between him and Lanis, "have been through this before with High Priestess Anya. I would never talk against my High Priestess, and I have nothing but the utmost trust in her decision making, but the map she gave us didn't do us much good." He shrugged.

Lanis nodded in agreement. "I plan on having a talk with her when we get back home. I'm sure in the future the discrepancies could be worked out."

"Too right." Elson grinned.

Isabel's gaze stayed fixed on Elson. "You speak in such respect of her."

Elson startled everyone, except Lanis, when he stood and dropped to one knee before Isabel, with his arm across his chest and his head bowed in her direction. "I would fall on my sword for her, as I would for Nia and now Lanis."

"As would I," Lanis said. "But for completely different reasons."

Elson stood and took Lanis's hand. "And I respect you for that." He winked at her then sat back down beside Finley on the bed.

The room was silent until Vic spoke. "Good grief, Finley. Why don't you ever do that for me?"

His smile was strained. "If that's what it would take, my Lady."

Isabel shot Vic a glare, then pointed to the map. "I'm not going to give you a direct route, but I wouldn't go near Vashta or the Goddess Falls."

Elson and Lanis both burst out laughing. "I'm sorry, Queen Isabel," Lanis said. "Been there."

"Done that," Elson chimed in.

Vic held her hand up. "Wait a minute. You entered Vashta without an invitation and lived?"

"Barely," Elson said.

Lanis shook her head. "You can say that again."

"Barely." Lanis narrowed her eyes at him.

"I'm assuming you crossed into Vashta after climbing down the Falls?" Finley asked.

"Yes on both accounts," Lanis answered and waited for their questions.

Elson crossed his arms across his chest. "That's not taking into account the Black Brigade, the Ruins of Treko, the Jester, and the Rogue." He held each of their eyes before turning to Lanis. "Am I leaving anything out?"

If it were up to her, she wouldn't have disclosed everything they'd been through, but she understood his reasoning behind it. These people needed to know what they were capable of defeating and living to talk about it. "The Desert," she said softly. She would not soon forget that experience.

Vic stood, eyes wide, and started pacing. She spun around suddenly and ran her hand through her hair. "You crossed the Desert of Ram-Tar?"

Lanis and Elson exchanged worried glances. For the first time since they arrived, Lanis noticed Isabel stiffen. "Yes."

"I should have been writing all of this down," Vic muttered. "Okay, you crossed the Desert." She smoothed her skirt and sat back down. "Now I know what we could be facing. How did you get across?"

Lanis pulled back her shirtsleeve to reveal her Oath bracelet. "My best guess is the largest beast saw my bracelet and backed off long enough for us to get across." She rubbed her neck. "They let us go."

"That's not taking into account the Breeken," Elson happily added.

Lanis flinched when Isabel looked up at her sharply. "What?" Lanis said. "I told you our journey had been anything but routine. What did you expect?"

"Well, for one thing, I didn't expect Breeken or the Desert, but you're right. You did tell me that." She held up her hand when Vic started to speak. "We don't have time to discuss every aspect of your past journey now. Let's get back to the map." She pointed out a small area. "Your best bet would be to board the ferry, here. Then make your way adjacent to the Falls and finally cross through the Anolk Mountains. There is a remote village at the border of the mountains that I visited a handful of times when I was younger. Vic has a note that you can give to the guard that stops you at their border. It will explain why you're passing through. After you leave from there, I won't be able to help you."

"My Queen," Finley said. "I will not let anything happen to her."

Isabel nodded. "There is another matter we must discuss." She folded the map and handed it to Elson. "I will not reveal my source, but Lanis, someone is hell bent on finding and capturing you, and they know Vic and Finley are with you. I think our best option is a change in appearance."

"Hold on," Lanis said, when Isabel stood. "You can't expect to tell me something like that and not explain what you mean. I know someone is after Elson and me, but if you know who it is, you should tell us. What do you gain by keeping the information to yourself?"

Isabel cocked her head. "My dear, the information is mine and mine alone. If I thought it would help your cause, I would tell you. As it stands, it doesn't. When you get back, if you want to talk things through, I would be happy to. It seems to me that you have more important things to worry about."

Lanis stood with such force her chair toppled backward. Vic grabbed her staff and Elson jumped up from the bed and crossed the room to stand beside Lanis. "I know what I have to worry about, and don't think for a minute that she isn't always on my mind," she ground out.

"Lanis." Elson laid his hand on her shoulder. "Now isn't the time."

She threw his hand off and stepped back from the table. They didn't know what she was going through. If she could, she would make this trip by herself, but she knew that wasn't an option. She needed them. She sighed and ran her hands through her hair before turning back to Isabel. "I will hold you to that talk."

Isabel nodded. "Okay."

"Lanis, I understand you have the weight of the world on your shoulders right now, but if I ever hear you talk to my mother that way again, you will regret it," Vic added, her hand tightly wrapped her staff handle. Lanis held Vic's eyes until an understanding passed between them. "Now," Vic said. "About that spell."

Isabel patted Vic's shoulder. "I will need everyone in front of me."

"You can do the spell from here." Lanis bit her lip. "How?"

Isabel winked. "Secrets, Lanis."

"Secrets." Lanis nodded. "There seems to be a lot of those floating around."

"They do tend to make their rounds." Isabel placed everyone in a small circle. "Everyone, close your eyes and clear your mind." Lanis felt a touch to her arm then a warmth flooded her body. She took a deep breath and coughed when a strange, bitter taste filled her throat. "Okay, open your eyes," Isabel said.

Lanis cautiously opened one eye, then the other eye. Except for Isabel, she didn't recognize the other three people in the room. Elson's hair was a lighter shade and cut short and his beard was gone. Vic was the complete opposite of her original self. Instead of her short red hair, she now sported long brown hair, and the sprinkling of freckles that littered her nose were gone. It completely changed her appearance. If Lanis hadn't known her before, she wouldn't recognize her now. Finley was still clean-shaven, but his short hair was longer and a deeper shade of brown. She frowned when everyone continued staring at her. "What?" She knew her hair was longer and blond.

Elson reached his hand toward her then pulled it back. "Your scar is gone."

"I figured. It is my most noticeable feature." Lanis smiled and turned to Isabel. "How long will the spell last?"

"Until you drink the antidote."

"Okay." Lanis stepped back from the others and leaned against the window. So much had happened in so little time. Sooner or later, she knew, everything would come crashing down on her. But now was not that time.

"So," Elson said. "We leave in the morning."

"Yes," Lanis said.

"Sounds like a plan." Vic walked to Isabel and wrapped her arms around her. "I will be okay."

Isabel brushed the hair away from Vic's face. "I worry."

"I will be fine. Besides being able to take care of myself, I have Finley and I can't see Lanis or Elson leaving me for dead."

Isabel pulled her close and whispered something in Vic's ear, but Lanis couldn't make out what she said. Isabel pushed Vic away and headed to the door. She turned with her hand on the doorknob. "I bid all of you a safe journey. I will be eagerly awaiting your return."

"Queen Isabel," Lanis said, walking up to her. "We may have our differences, but I promise you, on my life and on Nia's, I will bring both of your girls home to you."

Isabel patted Lanis on the cheek. "I know you will. Good luck, Lanis."

Lanis closed the door and sank back against it. She didn't know if they stood a chance, but she knew at least two other people in the room who would stand and fight with her. Finley was an entirely different story. She didn't trust him and she would make sure to keep an eye on him at all times.

"Lanis, I don't like that look on your face," Elson said.

She shrugged and pushed away from the door. "Just mulling some things over in my head."

"That can get dangerous."

"What's a little danger between friends?"

He slapped her on the back. "I hear you."

"You know," Vic said. "I didn't ask before, but now I'm wondering." She bit her lip.

"What?" Lanis asked.

Vic pointed to several spots on the table and on the floor. "What are these spots?"

Elson cleared his throat. "Blood."

Vic's nose wrinkled. "That's what I thought."

Lanis accepted the cup Elson handed her and swallowed the water. Tomorrow would be the start of a very long couple of weeks. She didn't argue when everyone insisted on an early night. But really, how much worse could the next couple of weeks be after the last couple of months they just experienced?

✾ ✾ ✾ ✾

Lanis kept her eyes glued to the three people riding in front of her. Elson had earned her trust over the past few months and she felt lucky to be able to call him her friend. Vic and Finley were nothing more than a means to an end. Vic's abilities were impressive, but that alone wouldn't guarantee Lanis's trust. After waking early that morning, they had rented four horses for their trip to the border. Once in Biclin, they would make their way on foot to the water ferry and leave their horses at the guild. She trotted up next to the others when she realized she was lagging behind, and pulled up beside Vic. She didn't look much like a Princess in Lanis's view. However, her tight black leggings, coupled with the pale green tunic and brown leather vest she wore, would contrast nicely with her red hair when they reverted back to their original selves. She would be forever grateful for what Rose did for them, but Vic exemplified a confidence with her magic that could only be learned from years of training and experience.

She ran her finger along her face, quickly dropping her hand. It was eerie not to feel her scar. It had been a part of her life for so long, and it felt wrong for it not to be there. She liked who she was and didn't want to be anybody else. She frowned and gripped her reins tightly when they reached a congested part of the main road. Anya had been right; thousands of people were flooding in for the Festival. The Prophecy reading was going to be a bigger deal then she anticipated. Elson slowed until he was beside her and pointed to their left. They followed behind Vic and Finley until Vic entered the surrounding tree line and stopped.

"Once we're outside of the city limits, it will be harder for us to find a place to stable the horses. We can stable the horses now, at the guild house, or we can wait until we reach Biclin bond stable them at their guild house," Vic said.

It didn't make much of a difference to her, but she wasn't ready to go on foot yet. "I vote Biclin," Lanis said.

"Agreed," Elson said, after taking a drink of water.

"Very well," Vic said, and led them out of the trees back onto the main road.

By mid-morning, the sun was beating down on them and Lanis was constantly fanning herself and wiping her brow. The extreme heat only added to her increasingly bad mood. It felt like they weren't getting anywhere. When they reached the city limits and the guards stationed at the border allowed them to leave, it was a welcome relief. The difference in foot traffic was amazing. Only a few people were making their way to Manight via Biclin. After arriving at the guild house, everyone dismounted and Lanis and Elson waited outside while Vic and Finley went in and took care of their business.

Lanis leaned against the guild house. "Here we go again." She rubbed her neck and couldn't help but allow her eyes to sweep the surrounding areas. She was confident they weren't followed. "Instead of running from danger we're headed toward it."

Elson patted her shoulder, then leaned back beside her. "I'm confident we can handle anything in our path. Besides." He shrugged. "We don't have a choice."

Lanis stretched and sighed. "True, and we could use all the help we can get. I'm confident in our abilities, but at the same time, I've realized having help never hurts."

He laughed. "I hear that." He sobered and leaned closer to her. "I still can't believe High Priestess Anya is Queen Isabel's daughter."

"Me either. It wasn't at all what I expected when I met her."

"Surprises around every corner."

"It would seem so."

"All done," Vic said. Finley and another man walked behind her. "Stewart will take good care of the horses." She pointed to the stranger. Lanis made sure she had all her belongings and took off in the direction of the ferry. The walk was easy since they were the only ones headed in that direction. Vic motioned for them to follow her and they pulled off the main road. "Gather around." She pulled four small vials from her bag and handed them each one. "Bottoms up."

Lanis uncorked hers and hesitated before bringing it to her lips and swallowing the contents. She touched her face and was instantly at ease when her fingers traced her scar. "Ready?"

Elson took the lead. When they first started out together, it bothered her, but now she knew he was only doing what came naturally to him. He was a born leader. Once across the river, the real journey would begin. It wouldn't be easy and she didn't expect it to be, but she felt ready to tackle any obstacles in their way. Although, the closer they got to the ferry the more her stomach turned. From her vantage point, it didn't look like much. Four men stood beside the dock and three more men were aboard the ferry. The wood on the ferry was weather-beaten and cracked in several areas. In places, entire pieces of wood were missing. The span across the river wasn't vast, so surely it would make it across. The men didn't give her much hope either. By the looks of them, like the ferry, they had seen better days. From the unruly hair, to the long, unkempt beards, to their tattered clothes, everything about them put her on edge. She wasn't one to judge on first glance, but something was off about these men. The only bright side to this was the time of day. At least if the ferry went down, they would have plenty of daylight to swim across. She looked at Elson and he looked at her, then they both looked at the ferry. It wasn't as bad as the bridge in Vashta, but it was close. She tightened her whip and adjusted her bag.

"Well," Vic said. "I've been on worse." She shrugged. "No use in worrying over something we have to do anyway." She grinned and bounced on her feet. "Let's get it over with."

Vic sprinted across the road and Lanis had to jog to catch up with her. She scanned the shoreline as Vic explained what they needed. Two men stood on the opposite deck, awaiting the ferry. Farther down the shoreline, a fire was burning, but she didn't see anyone tending to it. She turned when Elson touched her hand and pointed to the ferry. A man stood at the entrance and stared at them. His beard hung down his chest and was as black as his short hair. He smiled, revealing cracked and crocked teeth, before speaking.

"My name is Vance and I will be escorting you across the Biclin River. Please refrain from putting any body parts outside the ferry. I am not sure if you are aware or not, but it is rumored the river is haunted. Only a few have ever seen the spirits." He clapped his hands together. "Watch your step, keep your mouth shut, and enjoy the ride." He stepped aside so everyone could board.

"Quite a friendly fellow, isn't he," Elson whispered in her ear.

"With our luck, we'll not only see the ghosts, but they will probably attack us," Lanis added.

"One could only hope," Vic chirped, walking past them. Once aboard, it did feel sturdier than it looked. Seats ran along the outer edges and there were two rows of seats in the middle of the ferry. She couldn't tell how the ferry operated, but wouldn't question it either. She took a seat beside Elson in the center. Vic sat beside her and Finley sat on Vic's right. By the set of Elson's jaw, something about all of this bothered him as well. The day had cooled considerably and the salty air stung her skin. The water was calm and the air was stale. Elson touched her hand and nodded. He felt it too.

Living and traveling on the water held no appeal to her. She loved walking the Malora Beach and was quite happy to have her feet on solid ground. She rubbed her neck, leaned forward in her seat, rested her elbows on her knees, and closed her eyes. The trip across was inevitable, but she didn't have to watch their progress. Her stomach lurched when the ferry was set into motion. This was her first, and if she had anything to say about it, her last ferry ride. She kept her eyes closed even when the air shifted and said a silent prayer to Nia to keep them safe. As the wind picked up around them, her eyes flew open. Something was wrong.

They were on the same ferry, on the same river, but everything was out of focus. She could see the wind. It, literally, danced in front of her like waves in the air. She closed her eyes then reopened them and everything looked normal again, but it still felt the same. In the future, she promised to keep her mouth shut. Off in the distance, moving at a steady pace, were four beings that floated above the water. She could see right through them. She looked to Elson, but he didn't seem concerned. He couldn't see them. She jumped in her seat when Vic touched her hand. Lanis pointed to the water and Vic nodded and smiled.

Lanis and Vic stood and walked to the railing, but

stopped a foot from it. Lanis ignored the Captain's and Elson's shouts. As the beings, or ghosts, got closer, she realized it was three women and one man. They floated within ten feet of the ferry and their bodies bobbed in the air. Two of the women wore similar plain, brown dresses, while the other woman and the man wore leather pants and a simple chest plate. The man's brown hair was cut short and he was clean-shaven. In his right hand, he held a battle axe. The woman's cloak was pulled over her armor and she held a short sword in her right hand. The other two women didn't seem to have any weapons on them.

The man smiled and inched closer to the ferry. Without warning, he laughed and lunged at the boat, only to come to a complete stop when Vic held up her hand. When Vic started chanting, the man floated closer to them. Lanis couldn't decipher the look on his face. It was a cross between sadness and hate. Lanis touched her whip when his hand twitched on his axe handle. Lanis jumped when Elson walked up to her and touched her arm. He frowned at her, then leaned against the railing. Lanis grabbed Elson's arm and pulled him away from the railing when the ghost winked at her and laughed at them. The motion of the ferry threw both of them to the deck and Lanis closed her eyes as the axe connected with the railing and sent wood shards flying in every direction.

"What the…" Elson said, helping her to stand. Vic stepped in front of them Harris and raised her staff into the air. Lanis tensed and her body temperature dropped when the man, once again, laughed at them, and held his axe up as if to strike out with it. Vic never flinched when she slapped the staff against the railing and held her hand against the wind. His smile instantly vanished and he floated back from the ferry several feet. The closer they got to port, the more agitated the spirits became. Without warning, all four spirits flew at them. Vic waited until they were close and she stomped her foot on the deck. When the spirits reached the ferry, they bounced backward as if they hit a force field. Vic lowered her hand when the ferry docked and the Captain walked up to them. Vance touched the railing where the missing wood was and frowned as he looked out over the water.

"You're a lively bunch, aren't you?" Vance scratched his beard and laughed.

"We try," Elson said, running his hands through his hair. Lanis took his arm and pulled him from the ferry.

"Thank you," Finley said and stepped off the dock, joining them. "So?" Finley said to Vic and Lanis. "Care to explain?"

Elson shook his head. "I'm not even going to ask." He put his hair back up. "I don't think I want to know the answer." Lanis laughed and watched with interest as Vic pulled a leather bound notebook out of her bag and started writing.

"If I knew this was going to be such an educational experience, I would have brought another notebook with me," Vic said. "Who knew I would be able to practice my spirit magic on this trip? To think one of my professors, Professor Moran, said it was a waste of time to learn it. What did she know?" Vic made a check mark in the air with her finger. "One thing I can mark off my list."

Lanis couldn't help but be amused with her. Her smile vanished and she touched her whip when a stern looking older man dressed in military garb walked up to them. Elson stiffened beside her.

"Good afternoon. I am Commander Razen. I wanted to inform you that there is a small village just up the road." He pointed to a small ridge. "They have food and lodging."

Lanis turned around when Vic pointed behind her. There was a man off in the distance staring in their direction. By his position, Lanis guessed that he was standing where she had seen the fire on the shore when they were on the ferry. "Who's that?" she asked the commander.

He snarled. "You will want to steer clear of him, I am afraid."

Lanis turned around and faced him. "That's not what I asked. I asked who he was."

Razen spit on the ground and glared at her. Elson took a step toward him, but Lanis held her hand out. Vic and Finley joined them. "He's crazy," Razen said. "Calls himself a water Shaman. Like I said. Your best bet is the village."

"Water Shaman." Vic smiled. "Really?"

"Yes. Steer clear of him."

Lanis knew it was already too late. By the look in Vic's eyes, she knew that wouldn't be the case. She was curious about the man, but in this instance, she agreed with the commander. The village was their best bet.

"Thank you," Vic said. "I think we will take our chances with him." She pointed to the old man. Not waiting for the others to join her, she headed in his direction. Lanis groaned and turned to follow her. It didn't take long for them to reach Vic and the man. He was old, very old, and his clothes barely fit his slim frame. His long hair and beard were solid white. Lanis inhaled when a sweet smell she didn't recognize reached her nose.

"Come," the water Shaman said, leading them farther along the shoreline and into a clearing where a large fire burned. A woman stood up when they approached the fire. She was young and wore a loose fitting blue and brown dress. She smiled and waved when everyone entered the camp. Vic readily walked up to her and sat down on a bench that encircled the fire. She accepted the cup the woman offered her. Finley sat to Vic's left and Elson and Lanis sat down at her right. Lanis and Elson both refused the cups the woman offered them. The old man sat down across from them and the young woman sat down beside him. "We have been expecting you," he said, looking at Lanis.

❧❧❧❧

Lanis watched, her unease spiking, when the Shaman picked a rock up off the ground and threw it into the fire. The flames grew gradually, then without warning, shot upward toward the sky. Lanis coughed into her arm as smoke bellowed out of the fire and she squinted into the haze as the young woman reached her hands heavenward. Out of the corner of her eye, she noticed Vic writing frantically in her notebook when the woman started muttering, what sounded like to Lanis's ears, complete nonsense.

Out of instinct, she slid backward off the bench when Elson and Finley fell forward and landed on the ground, motionless. By this time, Vic had put her notebook away and her eyes were fixed firmly on the woman in front of them. The instant the woman dropped her hands, an intense pressure started to build in Lanis's head. With each second that passed, the pressure intensified and the flames grew higher and hotter. Lanis's eyes widened and she scrambled away from the bench when the flames licked out in all directions. She accepted Vic's outstretched hand and stood on unsteady feet. The pounding of her heart drowned out the woman's words and her entire body popped out in a cold sweat as her eyes adjusted and a figure begin to materialize within the flames. The figure flickered a few times, faded, then reappeared again. Before her eyes, the same water spirit from the river stood in the fire, clasping an axe firmly in his hand. The cold, cruel smile plastered on his lips spoke volumes about what kind of spirit he was.

The woman stopped talking and walked into the fire and through the man, stopping in front of Lanis. Her words were clipped and the accent she spoke with wasn't like anything Lanis had ever heard before. "The journey will be laced with red. Time will not stand still for anyone. Destruction lies in your wake. Do not underestimate the value of a friend and do not hesitate to give up something close to you." The woman laughed and walked backward into the fire. She took a deep breath and sucked in the flames. Her chest heaved a few times, then she lunged forward, toward Lanis.

Lanis stepped back only for Vic's hand on the small of her back to stop her. The face hovering in front of her was unrecognizable as any one person and Lanis turned away from the grotesque image as an intense heat washed over her. She relaxed somewhat when Vic squeezed her waist. She took a deep breath, said a silent prayer, and faced the figure. The moment her eyes locked onto its, it nodded, and walked back into the flames. After a few seconds, the woman walked back out and held a small, black book in her hand. Lanis hesitated when she offered it to her, but still reached out and grasped it. The cool leather felt refreshing, compared to the raging fire in front of them. Her fingers trembled when she realized what she was holding. It took every ounce of her self-control not to throw it back into the fire. When she lifted her eyes from the book, the fire had returned to normal and the woman and the Shaman sat side by side on the bench across from them. Although she would never heed the woman, the Seer's words, she wouldn't dismiss them entirely either.

Vic squeezed her waist. "Let's sit down."

After sitting, the Shaman handed them both a cup full of a murky brown substance. Vic shrugged then downed hers. Lanis hesitated, but swallowed hers as well. She wiped her mouth, then handed the cup back.

The Seer's smile was tentative. "Things aren't always clear at first, but as time progresses, it will all make sense."

Vic raised her hand. "Can I ask a question?"

"You can, but I may not answer it."

"What kind of spirit was in the fire?"

At the Shaman's nod, the woman answered. "He was a water spirit."

"Does that mean he died on the water?"

The Seer smiled. "It means he either died on the water or his body landed in water after death."

"So," Lanis said. "Is his being here coincidental or does it have something specific to do with our journey?"

The Seer hesitated before she spoke. "It could be coincidental, but in your case, I don't believe it was. He was speaking directly to me. I can't tell you what it all means or who the spirit was. Someone could have sent him." She shrugged. "Or, he could have sent himself. I don't know." She cocked her head and stared at them. "You saw him on the water?"

Lanis rubbed her neck. "We did."

Vic nodded her head vigorously. "Yes! I didn't think I would get to use my spirit magic, but I did, and it worked."

"Would you be willing to explain it to me?" The Seer looked just as excited as Vic.

Vic jumped up from her seat, her bag firmly in hand. "Of course." She turned back to Lanis and touched her hand. "You will be fine. I wouldn't have let anything happen to you."

"I know." She watched them until they settled down at a table a good ten feet away, then turned to the old man and pointed to Elson and Finley.

"They are only sleeping," he answered.

Lanis picked up the book and held it stiffly in her hands. After everything she'd been through and the little faith she now held for Nia, it felt like a betrayal to her to hold such a book. She slid her thumb across the words written in bold strokes across the front, The Book of Damrek. With trembling fingers, she opened the cover of the book. The first half of the book was blank and a small hole had been cut into the center of the paper, where the sphere would have been. She flipped further back and read.

Heed my words. False Priest and Priestess will rise up and fool you. Do not believe their lies. I will guide you. Believe my words, for they are the truth. There are no Gods or Goddesses, only magic. Magic will prevail long after time is no more and the world has gone to ashes. Magic will prevail long after they are no more.

Lanis slammed the book shut and threw it on the ground. To believe such lies was utter nonsense. It left her feeling dirty even to touch the book. Nia was with her always and although, in the past, her faith was tested and still was, she would never worship another. It made no sense that a water spirit they had never met would give them the book. Something else had to be at work here and the only two people that could be involved were the Shaman and the Seer. She took a few deep breaths, then calmed her breathing to a slow, even pace. It wasn't like her to get so worked up over a book. A simple, black book.

She leaned down and picked it up, turning it over in her hands. It didn't look like anyone had ever read it. The pages were crisp and the binding was still intact. Such a small book to make such a big uproar and to cause so much bloodshed. She needed answers. She turned and headed in the direction of Vic and the Seer. She spared a quick glance at Elson and Finley, who were still out. Stepping around the benches, she walked up to the table, and laid the book down. "What is the meaning of this?"

The Seer picked the book up, read the cover, then set it back down. "I honestly don't know. And before you ask, I don't know why I gave it to you. The spirit gave it to me to give to you. I think that is something you will have to figure out. I do know that there are a lot of people who would love to have this book. Maybe it would be best if you held onto it." Her eyes held a wisdom that spoke more than her words ever could.

"I don't understand. I serve Nia and would never believe such lies. Damrek is a false prophet. I don't know how anyone could believe in this book and I don't know what help it could possible give me on this journey."

The Seer picked it up and handed it back to Lanis. "You don't have to believe in it, but there might be something inside its pages that will help you. Don't discount it just because of what it is. It could help you."

"Lanis," Vic said, grabbing her arm. "Just because you have this book doesn't mean that anyone of us believe that you would ever take to heart the words written inside. Use it for what it could be. A tool, given to you for a reason."

She let the book slide from her fingers into her pack, then closed the clasp. She walked away from them and past the fire. Her feet came to a stop as the water lapped onto the shoreline. Looking up at the moon, she hadn't realized how late it had gotten until now. All she wanted was to get to Anya in order to save her in time. If not, at least, she would be able to bring her body back home. She could never, would never, leave her where she lay. It didn't make any sense that the Book of Damrek would play a part in that. She ran her hands through her hair, turned, and walked back toward Elson. She shook him until he started to come around.

He squinted at her, then jumped up when he saw the expression on her face. "What happened? What did I miss?" He grabbed her arm. "What's wrong?" Without saying a word, she reached in her pack, pulled the book out, and handed it to him. He read the title. "Where did you get this? I know I haven't been out that long."

Lanis bit her lip, then pointed to the Seer. "You've missed quite a bit while you were out. She gave it to me. She said she didn't know why she gave it to me, only that the spirit from the water wanted me to have it. She said it could possibly help me on our journey."

His eyes were glued to the title. It took him a few moments to answer. "Maybe it will," he said softly.

Lanis snatched the book back from him and put it back in her pack. "How could you say that? You of all people." She turned and walked back to the water. It didn't take long for her to hear his approaching footsteps.

"Nia has never once let me down, or you, for that matter. What's to say this isn't part of her plan? I am not saying read it and believe its lies, but the Seer is right. There might be something in there that might help you. The Holders do have High Priestess Anya and we all know they worship Damrek. This book could be of some use."

She rubbed her neck and frowned. What was wrong with her? That should have been the first thought that entered her mind. She had to get her focus off of Anya and back to who she was. She was her Protector and as such, she would use all the resources available to her, no matter where they came from, to aid her. Her thoughts had stayed jumbled since she found out Anya had been kidnapped. That had to change. "You're right. I don't know what's wrong with me."

He laughed and pulled her to his side. "Everyone is allowed one moment of weakness of not being themselves. This was yours. We have been through a lot, but you especially. I won't even pretend to know what you're feeling. I can only guarantee that I will be by your side no matter what happens. We know every word in that book is a lie. You're not going to be reading it for enlightenment. You're going to be reading it for some clue or some bit of information that would have otherwise not been given to us. Nia is always with us."

He tapped her pack. "She works in mysterious ways."

Lanis sighed and ran her hand down her face, squeezed his waist, then stepped away from him. "I know. It's late and we need to get some sleep. I guess we will have to stay here considering it is so late, although that wouldn't be my first choice."

"I hear you, but I think that staying here, if they will let us, will be our best choice."

"I was afraid you would say that."

"Lanis, this was only a moment of distraction for you. Don't let it eat you up. We all have them."

"It's just so weird. I have never let anything hinder my judgement so much. It bothers me, but now that I have identified what the cause was, I know how to fix it. Don't worry, I am still the same Lanis as before."

"Oh, I know. I wasn't worried. I know when the time comes, you will do whatever you have to, to see that what needs to be done is done, and I will be right there beside you."

"How about we get some sleep? I have a feeling tomorrow will come all too quickly. Besides, after today how bad can tomorrow be?" She smiled and slipped her arm through his.

He smirked. "You do realize you just cursed us. Probably cursed us for the rest of the journey."

"What fun would it be if everything ran smoothly? You know that's not our style."

He laughed. "Not our style at all."

❧❧❧❧

Isabel walked to Abigail's private office with more confidence than she felt. The clicking of her heels upon the stone floor echoed off the empty hallway and only added to her anxiety. Would seeing her again be like old times or would she be looking at a complete stranger? She was only lying to herself if she said she didn't still carry some feelings for Abigail. After all, she was her first love. Seeing her again, she knew, after all this time, would bring her feelings back to the surface and she wasn't sure she was prepared for that. But, she couldn't say no to the meeting; Abigail had requested it. Hopefully, it went better than her meeting with Sara. Her heart raced when the ornate wood carved doors to Abigail's office came into view. When she got close, the guard at the door nodded at her and opened it.

"Queen Isabel," the guard said. "She's expecting you."

Isabel shook her hands out, smoothed her skirt, nodded at the guard, and walked through the open door. As soon as her eyes locked with Abigail's, all of her long buried emotions started to surface. Abigail looked the same, albeit a bit older. Grey sprinkled her long black hair and her blue eyes still had the same sparkle she remembered. She was, in a word, breathtaking. She did not look like a woman in her fifties. Isabel took a deep breath, steadied her nerves, and walked into the room. Her heart sank when Abigail pointed at the chairs in front of the desk she was sitting behind. So that was how she was going to play it. It had been a long time; she couldn't fault her for that. Isabel bowed her head in her direction before sitting down. "Queen Abigail."

Abigail rested her elbows on top of her desk and smiled. "Really, Izzy, why so formal?"

Izzy-she hadn't heard that name in a long time. Isabel grinned back. "You were the one that directed me to sit. I at least expected a hug." She rested back in her seat. "It is really good to see you, Abigail. The years have been very kind to you."

Abigail waved off her words. "Nonsense. I have good genes, that's all. Others aren't so lucky. You, my dear, are one of the lucky ones."

"Thank you." She was just as charming as ever.

Abigail leaned back in her chair. "I hear you met with Sara yesterday."

"She requested the meeting."

"Sara told me about it. Or rather, her version of it. She always was jealous of you."

"I assured her there was no reason for her to be jealous. We both got what we wanted, Abigail. I wouldn't trade the years I have lived or the way I have lived them for anything or anyone."

"I agree. I have three wonderful children that I would lay my life down for."

"As I would for my Victoria." Abigail nodded and looked thoughtful. Here it comes, Isabel thought, the real reason she sent the invitation.

"Isabel, I have a problem and I need your help."

"I assume that is the reason you asked me here and not for the reading of the Prophecy. To be quite frank, I had made my mind up to turn the invitation down."

"What changed it?"

"Victoria was curious to see the city. I agreed for her."

Abigail grinned. "Our children do tend to have a strong pull over our decisions, don't they? Nevertheless, I am glad you came and I would love to meet your daughter."

"I would also love to meet your children, but you will have to wait to meet Vic. She met up with some friends and, as she would say, went on an adventure.

Don't worry, though, she will be back in time for the Festival and the reading. We are both looking forward to it."

"Why don't we agree to meet before the reading?"

"I think that's a great idea, but back to business. What do you need me for?" Abigail didn't say anything, only slid a folder across the desk toward her. Isabel opened it and skimmed through several pieces of paper. She frowned and picked up a page, then another, and another. The discrepancies in the accounting of the magic detected varied, a lot. Some of the spikes shouldn't have been detected, while others should have been caught and taken care of quickly. The same spikes showed up on several different pages. Someone was slacking in their duties. She arranged the papers, closed the file, and slid it back across the desk. "What do you need me for? You, obviously, have someone on the inside that you trust gathering this information."

"I want you to visit with my Mages. I know you, Izzy. I know what you're capable of. Hell, when we were kids, what you had already accomplished was far beyond even the most seasoned sorceress. I have to know what's going on. The people of this country count on me. I can't do this myself. I trust you."

"Even after all these years."

Abigail didn't hesitate to answer. "Yes."

She certainly hadn't expected anything like this. "It is unorthodox for anyone to visit or talk to another country's Mages, or to study their shields." Abigail had to know that if she visited them it would throw up red flags to anyone monitoring the magic.

"I am not asking you to steal our secrets." Abigail laughed. "But I have to know. Someone is betraying me and I have to know who that is so I can deal with them swiftly. On top of that, I have the Festival to contend with." She sneered.

"Do I detect a bit of annoyance in you?"

"A bit. It is more of a hassle than in years past. We had to open one of fields adjacent to the marketplace to accommodate those that are going to be camping out. It is more trouble than the Prophecy warrants."

There was a grain of truth to Abigail's words, but Isabel could see the mischief behind her eyes. "You aren't a bit curious as to what the Prophecy says?"

"You know me too well, Izzy. Of course I am."

If Isabel was to do what Abigail wanted, there was a lot to prepare for. "I know one of your current Mages was born in Candor. So I can use that as pretext to visit their workspace. I am sure that won't curtail the situation, but it will give me somewhat of an excuse to be there. As for them telling me anything of value, I think that is out of the question. They will not welcome my presence; however, I have ways of finding out things myself. I am sure I will find something that will be of use to you." Abigail stood and pointed to the door. She always was direct.

"I think that's a fantastic idea. I will send word that I am allowing you this brief visit."

"Thank you."

"No, thank you. I wanted to ask you to join Sara and me for dinner tomorrow evening?"

That was the last thing she wanted, but she knew it wasn't a suggestion. "I would love to." She stopped with her hand on the door handle. "It really is good to see you again, Abigail."

"I look forward to finding out what you discover."

Isabel knew when she was being dismissed. "Tomorrow night then."

"Yes."

It wasn't until she was halfway down the hallway that she remembered to breathe. Abigail was the same woman she remembered all those years ago. She couldn't let Abigail distract her right now; she had to focus on the task at hand. She had to prepare for her meeting with the Mages. On their own, none of them would be able to beat her, but combined, she wasn't so sure. What had she gotten herself into?

⁂

Dimitri halted his horse, jumped off, and tied the reins to the nearest tree. He straightened the cuffs on his shirt and walked to the remote cabin he used for these types of meetings. He opened the door and shut it behind him. The Jester was already seated and waiting for him. "I appreciate you meeting me on such short notice."

"I was intrigued."

"It has recently come to my attention that Lanis is in Manight and was seen in the Castle."

The Jester tapped his fingers on the arm of the chair. "Is that so?" He stood, walked to the far wall, picked up three oranges, and started juggling. "She does get around, doesn't she?"

He wished he could figure out what the Jester was up to. It would solve a lot of his problems. Truth be told, he needed his help, and he had been somewhat helpful thus far, and Treg was busy taking care of other matters for him. "I think I am more concerned about who she was seen with."

He stopped juggling. "And who, pray tell, was she with?"

"Princess Victoria and that dog that follows her around. I need you to track them down and take Lanis out once and for all. Quit playing games with her. Also, you should know, Victoria is the one that shielded Jalen from her first attack."

"The first time I tried to take Lanis out, it didn't exactly go as planned, and the fact that Victoria shielded Jalen is quite disturbing."

"It is. Have you found out why Lanis didn't die when you hit her with the green orb?"

"I have a pretty good idea."

"How much is the information going to cost me?" It would bring him great pleasure to bring him to his knees. They both jumped when a man suddenly appeared in the middle of the room. "Treg, what are you doing here?"

"I am sorry, Dimitri, for leaving my post, but I have some information I thought you would want to hear right away. It is disturbing," he said, glancing at the Jester.

Dimitri noticed the look between the two men. "Go on, Treg."

"It would seem that our lovely High Priestess isn't dead yet."

Dimitri groaned and leaned back against the wall. "I thought you took care of her?"

"I did." The Jester started juggling again.

"The room she is in is enchanted. No one can enter," Treg said.

"What was the meaning of this?" He slapped the oranges out of the Jester's hand. "She was supposed to be dead by now."

"She will be. I only gave her enough food and water to last two weeks."

"You what?" Dimitri shouted.

"I think," the Jester said, poking Dimitri in the chest. "You need to remember who you're talking to. I did you a service."

"How?"

"You want to get rid of Merek and Lanis?"

"Yes."

"Now you can. You just have to give it some time. I know for a fact that, at this very moment, Lanis is headed to rescue Anya."

Dimitri narrowed his eyes at him. It seemed too good to be true. "And how do you know that?"

"In order to get rid of Merek, all you need to do is send him along with Treg when he goes back to Anya. Once Lanis gets there, she will kill Merek, then Treg can do what he wants with her." He waved his hand in the air and produced a single card. He handed it to Dimitri.

"It's blank."

"Turn it over." The Jester laughed.

Dimitri flipped the card and it depicted a Protector. "What is this?"

"Isn't it quite clear? Lanis is Anya's Protector. If you want to get her Protector, all you have to do is wait."

This was too good to be true. "How do you know this?"

The Jester shrugged. "I see things. I hear things. All you have to do is wait for her to get within distance of Anya and you can capture her. As I said, Anya only has enough food and water for two weeks. It makes a kill more satisfying when it lingers."

"Treg, there is an unforeseen power behind Lanis. Take a quarter of the Brigade and station them at the outpost. When Lanis gets there, she will have quite the surprise."

"Very well," Treg said. He waved his hand in the air and vanished.

"How long have you known she was her Protector?"

"Does it really matter?"

It did, but he knew he wouldn't be getting any answers from him. "It would be nice to stop them before they made it to Anya. Can you stop them?"

"I can try, but I have to be honest. Victoria is a very powerful sorceress. If it came down to me or her, I choose me every time."

"Try and I will make it worth your while."

"I can try. By the way, how is Rose doing?"

"She's fine. Why?" He knew the moment the words left his mouth, the Jester had played him. The Jester smiled and disappeared. He would have to watch what he said in the future. He fell into the closest chair and ran his hands through his hair. The Jester had answered one question about Lanis. He groaned when he realized why Lanis was in the Castle. The guard had said Jalen had disappeared and only one group of people could do that: Ramdens. Lanis had taken Jalen, but why and where? He stood and walked out of the cabin, untied his horse, mounted him, and turned back toward home. At least there was one answered question. Sometime in the next two weeks, he would hold a Protector's mask in his hand.

Isabel took a deep breath, concentrated on her surroundings, and pushed her senses to their limit. Magic vibrated inside the room, but there was a slight disturbance in the air. She couldn't pinpoint what the cause was; however, it was strong enough that she couldn't ignore it. Squeezing her eyes tighter, she focused all of her attention on the disturbance. Hundreds of colors danced behind her vision and clouded her mind, dancing in numerous patterns, making it hard for her to decipher one from the other. Pushing the primary colors out of her line of sight, she caught a glimpse of one element that stood out among the rest. It was stationary, cutting a line across the rest, and it was slightly out of focus. She grasped it with her mind and sealed it within her memory. Changing the elements of time was never her strong suit, but she had the link and would hold onto it until she figured out what was causing it. She opened her eyes and accepted the hand her guard held out to her and stood. Now all she had to do was pinpoint the culprit and for that, she would have to visit Abigail's Mages.

Outside of her room, one of Abigail's guards waited for her and when she shut the door behind her, he led the way down the corridor. As they walked, he informed her that Abigail had already advised the Mages of her visit. Which in turn would give the Mages time to build up their hate toward her, but with each step, her confidence soared. She knew who she was and what she was capable of. At the end of the hallway, they turned left, toward a small, wooden staircase, and as soon as her foot touched the first step, she felt it: magic. Powerful magic. The higher they climbed, the stronger the magic became. She stopped when the guard ahead of her bent over, gasping for breath. Not bothering to check on him, she stepped around him and continued up until she stepped onto a small landing that led to the only door on the floor. She calmed her senses and opened up her mind to whatever she would face inside the room. When she lifted her hand to knock, she felt the disturbance. She stepped back when the door was opened and Leland, the Mage from Candor, allowed her in.

The room was larger than she had expected from Abigail's description. Three solid brick walls surrounded her and one large wall of windows looked out onto the cliffs and the ocean below. It was a breathtaking sight. No wonder the Mages rarely left this room. On one side of the main room was a seating and dining area. On the other side was a large table, at least five feet long and three feet wide, with an intricate map of Hadmore laid atop it. Without breaking control of the link or her emotions, she turned to Leland and smiled. From the frown on the others' faces, she knew they weren't happy about her appearance. She also knew this was their territory and if this was Candor, she wouldn't have liked the intrusion either, but this wasn't Candor. Her intention wasn't to disrupt their environment, but she wouldn't walk on eggshells around them either. She had to remember these people protected Hadmore's borders. They were powerful in their own right. "Leland, how are you? May we sit and talk?" She pointed to the chairs behind her.

He bowed in her direction and clasped his arm across his chest. "Of course, my Queen." He led the way across the room and sat only when she indicated he could. The four years he had been in Manight hadn't changed him much. His wavy black hair still hung around his eyes and he still wore the same pale, green robe she had awarded him when he left. He fidgeted under her gaze.

"How have you been?"

He nodded. "Good." He looked around the room before bringing his sky blue eyes back to hers. "I have learned quite a bit here. Things are different, but good."

She could feel the penetrating gazes of the two men and two women staring at them and she knew he was censoring his words. She smiled as he explained about his experiences and nodded at the appropriate times. A deep relief flooded her when she grasped his energy and realized he wasn't the one behind what was happening within Hadmore's shields. She shifted in her seat when her mind hit a roadblock. A roadblock that had been deliberately set up for her as soon as she entered the room. When Leland stopped talking, she pointed around the room. "Show me around."

"I..."

"Actually," a man said, coming up from behind her. "We have allowed you this far and that is as far as you will get." He was tall, broad shouldered, cocky, and exuded an extreme amount of magic ability. When she smiled and stood, he blinked at her, and took a step back.

"If I am not mistaken, Queen Abigail has already agreed to my being here. In fact, I believe, it was by her request. If you don't mind, I will look around whether I am escorted or not." He crossed his arms and after a few moments of silence, he stepped away from her. "Do I make myself clear?"

He let his arms fall to his sides and sighed. "Your presence here is quite unorthodox."

"It is and I can understand your reluctance, but I am here."

"Fine." He grunted and walked off, slamming a door behind him. She allowed her mind to follow his as it faded. It wasn't him. Passing the other four, she walked up to the table and leaned over it, without touching it. The borders of Manight were sparkled with yellow dots and Hadmore's borders with green dots. Thousands of dots littered the map. For five Mages to keep that many shields in place was a remarkable feat. She glanced at their wrists and saw all white bands. Abigail had always employed only the best in their fields. "This is amazing."

One of the women walked up beside her. "Yes. It takes a lot, but we are all quite capable in handling whatever is needed."

"Eleanor," one of the other men said.

"What?" she said, glaring at him. "Queen Abigail told us to cooperate with her. I am not going to disobey a direct order from our Queen."

"Thank you." Isabel leaned over the map, pretending to study it, but instead reached out with her mind and latched onto the element. She tugged on it until she had a secure hold. When she knew she had it, she raised up, and turned around to face everyone. "Again, thank you for your time. This has been an enlightening experience." She smiled and tugged on the element and watched for a break in one of their armor. It didn't take long until the other woman flinched. It was almost undetectable, but she had seen it. "Eleanor," Isabel said, reaching her hand out. "I will tell Queen Abigail how helpful and nice you have been."

"So," the man who had confronted her earlier said, "Did you find what you were looking for?"

"Raleigh," Eleanor said.

"Eleanor, it's okay, and Raleigh, is it?" Isabel asked. "I didn't come here looking for anything. I was only curious as to how Leland was fairing and Queen

Abigail, graciously, allowed me to see where he works. That's all."

"Raleigh, what did you expect her to do? No offense, Queen Isabel, but you're only a yellow band," the other woman said.

"Sadie," Leland said. "You have got to be kidding me. She's from Candor."

"So, what does that have to do with anything? So are you." Sadie looked at everyone. "What?"

Isabel smiled. "Sadie, in Candor we don't follow the rest of Adearian when it comes to sanctioning our magic. When everyone is of age we are all banded with a yellow band, but that is where it ends for us. We do not put limits on what our magic inclined can accomplish. We do not brand with other types of bands. Leland was because he chose to work and live in Manight. If I was to be branded in Manight, I would be well past a white band stage." Isabel grinned when Sadie paled. "It was nice meeting all of you." She held her hand out to the remaining Mage. His long blond hair hung around his shoulders. "And you are?"

He smiled and took her hand. "I am Norris, Queen Isabel."

Sadie may have been the one to create the element, but Norris was the mastermind behind it. His entire essence was guarded. "I do appreciate your time." She pulled her hand away, walked past him to the open door, and walked through, followed by her guard. She didn't allow herself to relax until she was back in the safety of her room. Something was definitely going on with those two and whatever it was, it wasn't good. She walked to the corner table and poured a glass of water. The cool liquid felt refreshing sliding down her throat. At the knock on the door, she motioned for her guard to open it.

"You wanted to see me," Harrison said.

He had been her personal assistant for thirty years and she trusted him with her life. "Yes. I need you to find out everything you can about two of Abigail's Mages, Sadie and Norris."

"It would be my pleasure." He bowed and walked out of the room. For a Mage to throw away what they had worked so long and hard for was unthinkable. Harrison would get her all the information she needed. He always did.

❧❧❧❧

After leaving the camp, they bought four horses at the village as Commander Razen had directed them to the night before. Lanis trotted up beside Elson and thought over last night. She still felt funny about the whole episode and it didn't help that the Seer had warned her, yet again, this morning. Her dreams the night before felt more like nightmares. She dreamt that the road they traveled on would fall out from under them. It was silly, but she kept glancing at the road to make sure it was still there. When Elson had asked her what she was doing, she explained about her dream, and he laughed and told her there wouldn't be anything they could do about it if the road suddenly vanished.

"It's a bit eerie being back here so soon," Elson said. He accepted the apple she handed him and took a bite.

"I was just thinking the same thing." They were making good time, and she knew that tomorrow they would be traveling adjacent to the Goddess Falls. That wasn't something she was looking forward to. She was on high alert and tried not to jump in her saddle every time a noise caught her attention. "Vic, Finley, I thought I should tell you, it was about a week ago that we were attacked close to here. Tomorrow we will be near the Falls. It was there that we had to climb down then we were taken by the Berrocka."

Elson laughed and threw his apple core into the trees. "Good times."

Vic nodded. Not long after the words left Elson's mouth, Vic's horse reared up and eight men stepped out of the shadows of the trees and into the pathway. The men didn't look familiar, probably just bandits, wanting a payday. Vic had a grin plastered on her face and Lanis was beginning to learn that that grin meant that something intrigued Vic. Her fears were confirmed when a man pushed through the others to stand in front of them. Lanis's horse reared back when a fireball appeared in the man's hand, and a second later, he threw it in Vic's direction. Vic stood up in the saddle, caught the ball, jumped from the horse, threw it back in his direction, and crouched on the ground. She slipped her staff from the saddle and stood up. Lanis, Elson, and Finley dismounted and joined her.

As the men advanced, Elson ran past them, ran his sword through the closest one, and engaged another. Lanis uncurled her whip and let it slide down her leg. She stepped to her right and flicked her wrist, feeling a deep satisfaction when it wrapped around one of the men's foot and she pulled on it, bringing him to his knees. She dropped her whip, grabbed her knife, and threw it at a man advancing on Elson. She fell backward to the ground when a blue orb sailed past her head. She jumped up just as a bandit swung at her, barely missing her ribs. She grabbed his arm, twisted, and cringed at the audible crack. He fell to the ground and she kicked him in the face. She slid across the road and plucked her knife out of the chest it had embedded itself into. There were only three men left standing. They backed away from them, then turned and ran in the opposite direction they had come from.

Vic laughed and lifted her hand in the air, making a twirling motion, and a purple lasso appeared. She threw her hand out and the lasso flew through the air and encircled the three men. She pulled her hand back and the lasso tightened around the men, imprisoning them. Vic dropped the rope, crooked her finger, and the rope started moving back to her. Lanis took the opportunity to walk back to the man whose arm she broke and slit his throat. She cleaned her knife, then joined the others.

"You okay?" Lanis asked.

Elson grinned. "Never better. You?"

"Same." Lanis walked up to the three men and touched the rope and it tightened even more at her touch. The men couldn't move, even if they wanted to.

"Now," Vic said. "We have a few questions for you."

"Who are you?" one of the men stuttered.

"You mean little ole me?" Vic laughed. "I can be your worst nightmare or just a bad dream. It all depends on the answers you give us. Lanis, Elson, be my guest." She pointed to the men.

"Who do you work for?" Lanis asked.

"No one. We work for ourselves."

Elson grabbed one of men's faces. "Why did you attack us?"

"Honestly, it was the horses. We can get a pretty penny for them."

"Are you serious?" Lanis and Elson exchanged looks. There had to be more to this than the horses.

"We need the money."

"You're only telling us part of the truth," Elson said. "Now. Tell us the rest."

The man looked between all of them before turning back to Lanis. "I recognized the scar. We would have turned you in for the bounty."

"That's more like it," Lanis said. She had wondered if it was still in play. "Do you have the paper on you?"

"My pocket."

Lanis reached into his pocket and withdrew a folded up piece of paper. She unfolded it. "It's blank."

"It wasn't, I swear," one of the other men said. "Please don't kill us."

"You know what? I am getting tired of people begging me for their lives." Lanis handed the paper to Vic.

"Too true," Elson added.

Vic flipped the paper through her hands several times. "It was done by a spell. I can't bring it back." She crumbled the paper in her hand and it burst into flames. "What do you want to do with them?"

Elson cocked his head. "Did you have something in mind?"

"I could wipe their memories."

"Really?" Lanis said.

"I can, but it will weaken me. We would have to make camp now for me to rest. I know there is still plenty of daylight left, but we wouldn't have to kill them."

Elson nodded. "It would also put us behind in getting to High Priestess Anya." He picked up his sword and ran it through each of the men. He wiped the blade clean and sheathed it. "The only thing that matters to me is her safety. No matter how many men I have to kill in the process. Understand?" He directed the question to Vic.

"Yes," she said quietly.

Lanis joined Elson and mounted their horses. Vic waved her hand and the rope disappeared. Lanis couldn't decipher the look on her face. When they were on their way, she rode up next to Vic. "We didn't have a choice."

Vic smiled sadly. "Lanis, there is always a choice."

❧ ❧ ❧ ❧

Isabel tightened her hold on the book in her hand before sliding it back on the shelf in front of her. She inhaled as a familiar, sweet fragrance drifted her way. Being back here wasn't supposed to be this hard. After settling her nerves and masking her emotions, she slowly turned around. If she was being honest with herself, she never expected to feel this way. The woman standing across the room from her opened feelings she thought she had buried long ago. It would seem the past really did have a way of coming back to haunt you.

Abigail sat down on the couch, set in the middle of the room, and motioned for Isabel to join her. "Have you found out anything yet?"

Isabel sat down at the opposite end of the couch. It was best, at this point, to keep her distance. Abigail's black hair was put up off her neck, and her cream-colored blouse contrasted nicely with her black trousers. Isabel knew George, Abigail's only son, made the leather belt she wore. The only difference between Sara and Abigail wearing their wealth was that Abigail didn't flaunt who she was and Sara did. Isabel calmed her beating heart and took a deep breath before speaking. "I sensed something was amiss, but I couldn't pinpoint what exactly it was. There was a continual disturbance in the elemental flow of your shields." Isabel relaxed back into the cushions and rested her hands in her lap. "Most of your Mages seem quite happy with their positions, but Norris and Sadie exhibited guilt over something. I feel Norris is at the root of the problem, but Sadie isn't far behind. I don't know what they've done, but the disturbance is in the shields that protect Hadmore. It may, or may not, be the cause of your problems. You will need to have someone look into it more closely and that can't be me."

Abigail ran her hand along the back of the couch. "Thank you. I will."

"I would act quickly. None of them trusted me, and I am sure they suspect something."

Abigail snapped her fingers and a guard left the room. "As you know, my eldest daughter, Jalen, is missing. No one I employ can find her."

The jagged edge to Abigail's words sent chills down Isabel's spine. "I do know that she is missing."

Abigail leaned forward and grasped Isabel's hand. "I need Jalen found. No matter what that takes. I don't know where she is, obviously. I have never let pride get in the way of my dealings concerning my children and I won't start now. Please, can you help me find her? She is my heir."

Isabel knew this was a slippery slope, but if it were her daughter, she would hope someone would help her. She caressed the skin on Abigail's palm and considered her words. "I will try." She released Abigail's hand and stood. "I cannot guarantee anything."

Abigail stood. "Good." She bit her lip. "Do you have any plans for the rest of the day?"

For the first time since being back, Abigail actually looked unsure of herself. Isabel would love to have spent all day with her, but that would only cause more problems. It would be best to stick to her original plan. Abigail, after all, wasn't hers. "Actually, I do. After I leave here, I am going to take in the preparations for the Festival. Then, maybe take a stroll through the marketplace."

Abigail smiled, but it didn't reach her eyes. "Well then, I hope you have a wonderful afternoon."

"Abigail, you have a good day also." She grasped Trevor's arm and let him escort her out the door, down the hall, and through the Castle doors leading outside. She wasn't sure how to go about finding Jalen, but she would put feelers out and see if anything surfaced. She would have to do a better job of keeping her feelings in check. Now was not the time to fall apart. As she walked out the Castle doors, an onslaught of chaos greeted her. She stopped at the top of the stairs and watched the workers in the courtyard adding decorations to the already immaculate space. It seemed such a waste for a Festival that only lasted a week, but Abigail had never spared an expense. Why would she start now? From her vantage point, she could clearly make out the basic layout of the marketplace, just beyond the Castle gates. She inhaled as a wave of cinnamon caught on the breeze and engulfed her. Her smile vanished as she spied Sara hurrying toward her. At the bottom of the steps, Sara stopped in front of her on the cobbled walkway.

"Why are you out here?"

Isabel didn't think it was possible, but Sara was

even more stressed today then the last time she saw her. "I wanted to see the preparations. Are they keeping you busy?"

Sara nodded and smiled at the workers that passed by her. She slipped her hand through Isabel's arm and led her away from the steps. "Are you checking up on me, Isabel?"

Isabel slipped out of Sara's grasp. "Don't touch me." She made it a point to keep her voice low. "I have no reason to check up on you. Should I be? You think too highly of yourself, Sara. Not everything revolves around you."

Sara shrugged, but kept her smile on her face. "Most things do." She pointed at the people around her. "All these people are here to do my bidding. I would say that would make me pretty important."

"You will never learn, will you? Even when we were younger, you thought you were better than everyone else." She smiled. "Trust me, Sara, you're not."

Sara grabbed Isabel's hand and squeezed. "Do you have any idea who you're talking to? I will not allow anyone to speak to me in that matter."

The hate in Sara's eyes only gave Isabel pause for a second. "Do you hear yourself?" She stepped closer to Sara and squeezed her hand, digging her fingernails into Sara's palm. "Do you know who you're talking to? I didn't come here to fight with you." She stepped away from Sara and let her hand drop. "I came here by invitation of the Queen."

Sara clasped her hands in front of her and smiled. "You have not heard the last of this."

"My Queen?" Trevor asked when Sara was out of earshot.

"I am fine." In truth, the entire episode only

added to the fact that Sara was up to something and closer to stepping over the edge. What edge, she didn't know. She needed to find out what she was up to and fast. She slipped her arm back through his. "Let's check out the marketplace."

"Of course."

They walked down the long, narrow, cobbled path and through the gates. The marketplace was much more crowded than she was used to and much more hectic. People were scattered like ants as far as she could see. It did seem well organized, though, and well guarded. After scouting out the area, she pointed to the path to their right and they started down it. The cinnamon rolls tempted her, but she walked past them and instead stopped at a fabric vendor's stall. The cool, sleek fabric felt refreshing sliding through her fingertips and the cream color would pair well with Vic's complexion. While she waited for the merchant to bag her material, she spied a familiar face off to her left; the description she had received was spot on. She did a double take, but the woman was gone. She handed Trevor her package and headed through the maze of merchants. After an hour, she glimpsed the woman again. Isabel followed at a discrete distance, keeping the woman within eyesight. When the woman turned down a small path, Isabel slipped her arms around her and led her farther away from the crowds. When Isabel released the woman, she turned and shocked eyes bore into hers. "My dear," Isabel said. "There are a lot of people looking for you."

"I..."

Isabel held her hand up. "Don't, not here. I know somewhere we can talk." The woman's eyes darted around the marketplace before settling back onto

Isabel's. "I wouldn't even try to escape," Isabel urged. This would certainly be a turning point in how things played out in the future. Now all she had to figure out was how to use the woman in front of her to her advantage.

⚘⚘⚘⚘

Vic's reaction still troubled Lanis later that night when they made camp. She had to know that people would die in the process. If Elson hadn't killed them, she would have. They couldn't afford to let people go and they couldn't afford for Vic to become weak. There were too many unknowns to be at a disadvantage. She and Elson sat on one side of the fire and Vic and Finley the other side. She accepted the cup of tea he offered her. Everyone had been quiet since the attack, but she had questions and she needed answers, and the only person that she knew could answer them was Vic. "Vic, can I ask you a question?" She settled the cup in her hands. Vic hesitated before nodding. "Can you tell us about the Desert of Ram-Tar? You seemed intrigued when we mentioned it."

Vic seemed to consider her words carefully. She picked at the fabric of her shirt. "It is said that the Desert appears without warning and without reason. Many men and women have died by its hands."

Elson sat forward. "What about the beasts?"

"From what I've been told, the beasts weren't created to wreak havoc or kill. A powerful sorceress created them foremost as an experiment. She only created one at first, but over time, they multiplied."

Lanis nodded. "When Rose traveled with us, she mentioned the creator was a woman."

"All mention of her was wiped from the history books, even in Candor. Many people, especially the ones in charge, saw her work as betrayal of magic. I believe her punishment was harsh, given out of their fear of what she had become. People do a lot of things out of fear. Hers is a sad tale and not one for me to tell."

Lanis drank the last of her tea and set her cup on the ground. "She must have been very powerful to create what she did and have so many fear her."

Vic's entire face lit up. "Oh, she was. Only one accomplished in many different areas of magic could have created the Desert and the beasts that roam it." She bit her lip. "What was the Desert like?"

"Hot." Lanis ran her hands through her hair.

Viv waved her hand in the air. "I know that, but what was it like?"

"She's telling the truth," Elson said. "It was hot."

"The heat burned my skin. It felt like mine was on fire."

"Rose," Elson said. "The sorceress that was with us, told us it was all an illusion, but I tell you the sweat was not an illusion. My clothes were drenched."

"What of the beasts?" Finley asked.

"They were massive…"

"Wait," Vic said, reaching for her notebook. "I should have been writing all of this down. Give me a second." After she grabbed her notebook, she motioned for Lanis to continue.

Lanis sighed. "Like I was saying. They were massive. At least four feet wide and tall. Their heads were huge and their teeth were razor sharp. Spikes encompassed their heads and when one of them drooled on my arm, it burned and left a scar."

Vic leaned forward. "Can I see it?" Lanis held her arm out and showed them both.

"One of the beasts had two heads."

Vic clasped her notebook in her hands. "How did you get across? You said something about your bracelet."

"When one of the beasts charged at Rose, I wrapped my arms around her and the beast saw my bracelet and backed off. We ran, and that was when the Breeken decided to make their presence known."

Elson ran his hand down his beard. "I didn't think we were ever going to get across."

"How did you?"

"I took a chance with the beasts. I pleaded with them to distract the Breeken and they did. We ran for the forest and made it. As soon as our feet touched the grass the desert disappeared."

Vic snapped her fingers. "Just like that?"

"Well," Elson said. "It wasn't quite that easy."

"Vic, I have another question."

"Go on."

"Why is green magic different in Candor than in other parts of Adearian?"

Vic licked her lips. "I can't tell you why they are different in specifics. Magic in Candor doesn't have the same restrictions that it does on the mainland. We let our people learn at their full capacity." She lifted her wrist up. "As you can see, I have a yellow band, indicating I have magic ability, but that's as far as we go. We don't label our people with other types of bracelets. When one is found to have an ability, they can choose to stay in Candor or they can learn from the teachers on the mainland. But once they reach the mainland, they have restrictions put on them. That's why most choose not to leave Candor. They have more freedom there."

Vic sighed and waved her hand in the air. "Green in Candor can mean death, but not necessarily. In all other parts of Adearian, it is widely known to cause death. I don't know about the Pona Islands. To tell you the truth, not many people know much about the Pona. When magic is created," She held her palm out. "You call on your specific talent. If you had items, you would use those." She took her other hand and started circling her palm. A small funnel appeared. "I don't have those type of restrictions. I call on a lot of different forms of magic." She moved both hands and the funnel hovered in the air. "I am by no means an expert. I am learning as I go. Case in point, the spirit magic. But, if you don't ask the questions, how will you learn?" She waved her hand, the funnel turned into a green orb, and she let it rest in her palm. "This is a parlor trick. The real reason green kills is because of the intent behind it. You can kill with any color, but here green is meant to kill." She shrugged and waved her hand over the orb and it disappeared. "I can't really explain it. It just is." She looked between them both. "Why did you want to know?"

Lanis fidgeted and Elson looked at her funny. "Lanis?"

She stood and ran her hands through her hair and looked down at him. "Do you remember when we first ran into the Jester?"

"Yes." He stood up, slowly.

"He threw a green orb at me."

Vic and Finley both stood up. "Lanis," Vic said. "Are you sure?"

"Yes. Rose couldn't explain it either. She was just

as freaked out as I was."

"Why didn't you say something?" Elson pleaded with her.

"Elson, I was scared. I survived a green orb. Who does that? I couldn't even understand it then. Rose said only one other person had also survived one, but she would not tell me who it was."

Elson turned to Vic. "Do you know who?"

"Yes, I know who. The same woman that created the Desert also survived not one, but three green orb attacks."

Lanis hadn't expected that. "How is that possible? So you know who it is, but you're not going to tell us."

"Would you tell me the secrets of your people?"

"No." She shook her head. "I wouldn't."

"Then don't ask me."

"I have another question," Lanis said. Vic nodded. "When we arrived at our first Oath house, it was destroyed and everyone was dead, but it's what we found behind the Oath house that was disturbing. Twelve bodies lay side by side. Their feet were tied together and their ankles were crossed. They were lined up tallest to shortest and their heads were cut off. When we woke up the next morning, the bodies were gone."

"What do you mean gone?" Vic asked.

"They were gone. Vanished," Elson said.

"Wow," Vic said. "You don't have any idea why?"

Lanis didn't like the look on her face. "No."

"Well, it seems to me that what you encountered was the work of a Shadow Sorcerer. Do you know what that is?" Lanis and Elson shook their heads. "A Shadow Sorcerer is someone who practices dark magic. They are recorded throughout history, but when one is found out, they are dealt with swiftly. The last known recording was sixty years ago and it was a teenage boy that was dabbling in stuff he shouldn't have been."

Lanis rubbed her neck. Rose never mentioned anything about a Shadow Sorcerer. "Do you mean someone who practices Damrek's magic?"

"No. What you all witnessed was evil and I am not sure I would call Damrek's magic evil. Destructive, yes, evil, no. Shadow Sorcerers have taken their God-given gifts and twisted them until they are unrecognizable. My professors only touched on the subject once while I was at university. But, in our home library, my dad had several books dealing with dark magic." She licked her lips. "Let me just say that dark magic is hard to detect within someone, and it's very hard to accomplish. In order to give yourself over to it, you must first sacrifice a part of yourself in the process, a part of your soul. Most people that mess with it don't survive because it feeds off you and most people's bodies can't handle that. You both were very lucky to get there after the deed was done."

"What about the bodies?" Elson asked.

"They were probably enchanted and when the Shadow Sorcerer called for them, they came. What happened to them after that, I don't know."

"Yes," Lanis said. "But they were dead. They didn't have any heads. What could they do?"

"I honestly don't know. I read one book on dark magic and it drained me. I promised myself I wouldn't pick one up again, and I haven't. I think your questions would be better answered by my mom when we get back." Lanis nodded.

"I think, and I think Finley would agree, that we should all get some sleep. I'll take first watch," Elson said.

"No." Lanis shook her head. "I will take first watch. Don't argue with me, Elson."

He held his hands up and backed away. "Okay."

Lanis stepped away from them and walked the perimeter. She only came away with more questions than answers. Why didn't she die? Or the better question was how is she still alive? After a few more passes around, she walked back to camp. Elson and Finley were asleep, but Vic was sitting on a stump, warming her hands over the fire. She handed Lanis a cup of tea when she sat down beside her. "I thought you could use this."

"Thank you."

"I didn't want to say this in front of them, but there were rumors why the woman survived the green orbs."

"This didn't take place in Candor, did it?"

"No."

Lanis took a sip of the tea. "Rumors are mostly lies."

"At times, but at others, they are the truth loosely veiled."

Lanis wasn't sure she wanted to know, but she asked anyway. "How did she survive?"

Vic didn't mince words. "You must not tell anyone this."

"I won't."

"It is said she survived because she carried one of Damrek's spheres somewhere on her body."

She couldn't have heard her right. "I don't have a sphere. Don't you think I would have known if I did?"

"All I am saying is that is the rumor." Vic shrugged and bid her goodnight.

That was ridiculous. She didn't have a sphere. There had to be another reasonable explanation for why she didn't die and she wouldn't quit asking questions until she got the answers she was looking for. She set her cup down and slipped the book out of her bag. With shaking fingers, she turned to a random page.

Others will tell you their lies. Do not believe them. They are sent here to distract you from your true purpose: magic. All can practice it, but it does take time and effort. Believe in magic. Believe in yourself and most of all believe in me. I am Damrek.

Lanis closed the book. So many people believed such lies. Magic was a powerful motivator, but it wasn't anything to worship. It didn't make sense for so many to worship him because of it. But, she could see it as an incentive. Magic, though, wouldn't be easy for someone who wasn't magic bound to learn. Maybe that's what drew everyone to him. The thought of being able to practice something only few ever mastered. She turned to a page further in the back and opened it.

Hold tight to my teachings, for they will lead you in your path and guide your future. Deep in the recesses of day, you will find my dwelling. Follow it and you shall know all my secrets. They will be given freely to those that willingly make the journey. But, beware, only true followers of our faith will be allowed to enter. Those unfit will be struck down. Take heart that I will be with you. Enter and you shall know all my knowledge.

Lanis slipped the book back into her bag and stood up. So there really was a hiding place, but it necessarily wasn't a cave. No wonder so many people were looking for it. If Nia ever spoke such words, her followers would look for it too. She took one last look around, but didn't see or hear anything out of the ordinary. She patted her pocket, content when she felt the stone the old women had given her. It was a comfort to know that at least one thing, when the time came, would be taken care of.

❧ ❧ ❧ ❧

Dimitri slammed his hand on his desk and took several deep breaths. Nothing was going according to his plans. He scrubbed his hands down his face and sighed. Lately, he didn't know whom to trust. Everyone had their own agenda. One day, everything would run smoothly, and the next, everything would fall apart. He needed more answers than anyone could give him and he still needed the last two spheres. The spies he had inside the Castle had searched Jalen's room countless times, but had come up empty-handed every time. They were getting sloppy and he hated lazy people. A bit of fresh air would do him some good.

He straightened the cuffs on his sleeves, stepped into the hallway, and walked down the long corridor. He rounded the corner only to come to a complete stop when he got a good look at the woman coming toward him. He smiled when he heard one of the men that accompanied her refer to her as Queen Isabel. So this woman had the Castle and Sara in an uproar. He couldn't blame Sara for being jealous. Isabel was a beautiful woman. If Abigail were so inclined, he would understand, but Sara was delusional; Abigail was faithful to a fault. His heart started pounding in his chest as she got closer and turned to face him. The woman in front of him was the spitting image of Anya, albeit an older version. It didn't seem logical that that was an option. The only explanation was that she was Anya's mother. But how?

Isabel stopped in her tracks, cocked her head, and regarded the man in front of her. "Can I help you?" The two guards beside her stiffened.

"Queen Isabel, I don't believe we have ever meet. I am Councilman Ramus of the Queen's court."

Isabel nodded. "I don't believe we have either. It is a pleasure to meet you." She pointed behind her. "Quite the spectacle outside."

"Yes, the preparations are almost finished. It is a great time of celebration. That, coupled with the reading, is going to make it quite the show."

"I agree. I am looking forward to it."

"As am I. I am also looking forward to seeing High Priestess Anya. I have never had the pleasure of meeting her before."

"Neither have I. It will be a pleasure to hear the reading from her. It is quite the treat." She motioned to one of her guards. "If you will excuse me, I have a meeting I must get to."

"Of course, your Majesty." After talking to her, he was confident; she was Anya's mother. He was also quite certain nothing got past her. He turned and walked back to his office with hundreds of questions racing through his mind. After shutting the door, he addressed one of his guards. "I need you to find out everything you can about Queen Isabel and do so quickly."

"Of course, sir."

Dimitri walked to the window and looked down at the people working feverishly on the courtyard. He couldn't help the smile that graced his lips. This day was turning out to be far better than he anticipated.

The next morning, by everyone's agreement, Elson took the lead and guided them past the Goddess Falls. Lanis breathed a sigh of relief when they were clear of the entire area. It held nothing but bad memories and if given the choice, she would never return there. She kicked her mount and trotted up next to Elson. For the next hour, they rode in silence until Lanis held her hand up, bringing everyone to a halt.

"I hear them too," Elson said, handing her the water.

She took a long pull then handed it back to him, wiping her hand across her lips. She squinted into the distance and blocked out the others around her. It started gradual, then she picked up the sound of chatter. "Four, maybe five." By the way they were making themselves known, it was unlikely they were bandits. Their track record with strangers on the road wasn't exactly stellar.

"How could you possibly know there are five of them?" Finley asked.

Lanis rolled her eyes and ignored his question. "I thought we should be prepared, that's all."

"Nothing wrong with being prepared." Vic added. "We can handle four."

Elson turned on his saddle and faced her. "Or five." He grinned.

Vic smiled. "Everyone is quite capable of keeping themselves alive. What are we waiting for?"

"Indeed." Lanis laughed. She couldn't help it; she liked her. She was Anya's sister, after all. Vic didn't seem to be afraid of much, but she knew if she were anything like Anya, she would hold her fears close to her chest. Elson took the lead again, followed by Vic and Finley, and Lanis took up the rear.

Finley, on the other hand, was a completely different story. It was a relief when you could rely on those around you, but Finley only cared about Vic. She could respect that to a certain degree, but these were unusual circumstance and he would have to learn to play fair.

Lanis sat up straighter in her saddle when she caught sight of the strangers ahead of them. She had been wrong. There weren't five of them; there were seven. Five of them wore long, brown robes with the hoods pulled up. Elson kept them at a slow, but steady pace, and when they were a good thirty feet from them, the man and woman without a robe on turned and looked at them.

Vic slowed her pace and allowed Lanis to ride up next to her. "He's a sorcerer."

Lanis groaned. Figured. Her eyes locked onto the woman. Even from this distance, the woman didn't look like anyone Lanis had ever seen before. Her dark hair was braided and hung down her back, her skin looked to be deeply tanned, and her sharp features stood in stark comparison to the man walking beside her. "The woman's look is unusual."

"It is," Vic agreed. "But, then again, there are a lot of different tribes I've never seen before."

"True." As they approached them, the group moved from the middle of the road to the side. Lanis nodded at the woman as they passed by. She smiled and nodded back. She was young, probably still in her teens. She wasn't bound in anyway and was walking freely on her own.

The people in the robes didn't look up at them. She kept her face devoid of emotion when she caught sight of the crest on their robes. She'd never meet any before, but the crest, depicting a tree and tornado intertwined, was the symbol for worshippers of God Acker. The sorcerer traveling with them must be a nature sorcerer. They were rare. In Adearian's history, only a handful of nature sorcerers were recorded. They could manipulate nature along with weather patterns. They were the most managed group of sorcerers because of what they were capable of creating. There was only one rebellion in the history books concerning two nature sorcerers. They wiped out an entire village with what they considered to be experimenting. The next day they were captured and killed, according to God Acker's doctrine. When they were clear of the group, she touched Vic's arm. "The young woman seemed to be walking freely on her own."

"I was just thinking the same thing." Vic scrunched her nose up. "Do you know who they serve?" She bit her lip.

Lanis nodded. "I do. I've never actually met a missionary of Acker's before, nor have I ever meet a nature sorcerer. The young woman doesn't fit with them, though."

"No, she doesn't. I have never met any of them either. They intrigue me. I can do a minimal amount of magic involved with manipulating nature, but nothing compared to what he crould do."

From the excitement in her voice, Lanis knew what she wanted, but they didn't have time to stop and talk with them. "Vic?"

She held her hand up. "I know." She shrugged.

After a few hours, they decided to make camp.

Night was fast approaching and the terrain they would have to travel the next day would be challenging enough by the light. Vic and Finley went out hunting and returned shortly with a good size rabbit. Lanis loved the taste of rabbit, but if she was honest with herself, she could never actually kill one. When she was younger, she went hunting with her father and she struck one. As it lay dying in her arms, she vowed she would never do it again. Taking a human life was much easier to her than an animal's life.

She stopped with the cup halfway to her lips, lowered it, then slipped her knife from her boot. Elson stood and pulled his sword. Without saying a word, Vic grabbed her staff and Finley took up position beside her. Lanis's fingers felt heavy on the knife handle, but her grip was sure when the first person broke through the trees and entered their camp. The other six weren't far behind. She had a feeling they hadn't seen the last of them.

"Is there something we can help you with?" Elson asked. "We don't take kindly to people, unwelcome people, invading our space. There is plenty of forest out there."

As if their strings were being pulled, all five missionaries lifted their hands and pushed the hoods off their faces. Three women and two men. The oldest woman took a step forward and clasped her hands in front of her. "We mean no disrespect. We only wanted to join you for the evening and partake in your fire."

Lanis eyed each one of them, ending with the sorcerer. "Really, because it would seem to me that we were travelling in opposite directions. You had to backtrack to follow us."

The woman only smiled. "I am Doloris and I am

the leader of our small band of missionaries. We would be quite humbled if you let us join you."

"No offense, but why?" Elson questioned.

"No offense taken. We are tasked with teaching the word of our God, Acker. We enjoy talking about him with whoever will listen. We take great pride in the task our God has given us. It would be our honor to tell all of you about him."

Elson tightened his grip on his hilt. "We serve Goddess Nia and that won't be changing anytime soon."

Doloris smiled. "Please, may we join you?"

"Sure," Vic said, surprising everyone. Lanis rolled her eyes and slipped her knife back in her boot. All five missionaries took a seat on the ground around the fire on the opposite side of them. The sorcerer stood behind them and the young woman sat on a stump a few feet away from where Elson stood. She was out of place with the group; that was clear seeing everyone up close. Lanis sat back down, followed by the rest. She picked up her cup, took a sip of her tea, and cringed when Vic slipped her notebook out of her bag.

Vic addressed the sorcerer. "Would it be okay if I asked you a few questions?"

He snarled. "No, it would not be okay."

Doloris jerked her head in his direction. "Sani, that is uncalled for. She is obviously a sorceress. I am sure all she wanted was to learn something from you."

He bowed his head in her direction. "I am sorry," he said to Vic. "I will answer your questions as long as they do not go against my code, but I won't answer them here. We can talk away from the group. That would be ideal."

"Sure." Vic jumped up, her notebook clutched in

her hand.

"Vic," Lanis said and stood up. She spoke low enough that the others couldn't hear her. "We don't even know them. This is a bad idea."

"I will be fine." She kissed Lanis on the cheek and instructed Finley to stay where he was.

Lanis shook her head, sat back down, and motioned to the young woman. "Are you hungry?" She pointed to the pot hanging over the fire. "Rabbit stew."

"You don't mind?" she said. "I am a bit hungry."

Her voice held a slight tilt that Lanis had never heard before. She liked it. "We don't mind. Everyone else has already eaten. It's not much, but it will fill you up." She addressed the others. "After she gets some, you're welcome to what's left."

"Actually," Doloris said. "I would love a cup of whatever it is you're drinking."

Elson smoothed his hand down his beard. "What we are drinking," Elson pointed between him and Lanis. "Is for us, but I do have some other tea leaves that I would be happy to share with you."

Doloris nodded. "Fair enough, although, it has been ages since I have had any Maldorna tea."

He shrugged. "Like I said. We have other tea leaves."

"Of course."

Lanis held his cup while he dug in his bag for the other leaves and handed them over. When he took his cup back, he pointed to the girl. "Don't be shy. Come on and get something to eat." He picked his bowl up. "You can use my bowl. It's clean." She accepted it and scooped out enough to fill the bowl.

"This is good."

Lanis nodded and held her hand out. "I am Lanis."

"Pash," she said, shaking the offered hand.

Lanis pointed to her left. "That's Elson."

"Good to meet you."

"Same," Pash said. Lanis patted the log beside her and Pash sat down.

"Where are you headed?" Elson said, directing his question at the missionaries.

Doloris cocked her head. "Here. There. Where are you headed?"

"Same." He drank the last of his tea, wiped the cup clean, and slipped it back in his bag.

Lanis directed her question at Pash. "Where are you headed?"

Pash smiled, showing off deep dimples and her brown eyes lit up. "I'm headed to the Festival. It's my first time."

Her excitement bubbled over and Lanis couldn't help but be excited for her. "In order to make it on time, you'll need to rent a horse. On foot, you won't make it. The Festival will be here before you know it."

Pash grinned and took another bite of her stew. After she swallowed, she answered Lanis. "I'm not worried about that. I am confident I will make it in time."

"Fair enough."

Elson winked. "A word of warning. The ferry in Biclin has seen better days, but we made it safely across."

"Steer clear of old men," Lanis added. Elson slapped her on the back and laughed. She couldn't decipher the look on Pash's face.

"I'll keep that in mind." Pash stood up, cleaned the bowl, and handed it back to Elson. She leaned forward and whispered in Lanis's ear. "Eyes are everywhere. Be vigilant." She straightened and sat back down on the stump. She pulled a notebook out of her bag and started to write. Lanis noticed only Doloris was staring at her.

"Elson," Lanis said. "I am going to walk the perimeter. I'll take first watch."

"You sure? It's my turn for first watch."

"I'm sure." She stood and slipped her bag over her head. She pulled her knife and stepped into the forest. After walking the perimeter, she kept her ears, and eyes open. She circled the camp several times before coming to a stop beside a tree, some hundred feet from camp, and settled back against it. She opened her bag, slipped the Book of Damrek out, and opened it.

Do not turn your back on others. Everyone is out for themselves. No one is above taking what they deem as theirs. No one. Do not fall prey to pretty words and flowery prose. Words only matter if the person speaking them has your complete trust. Have faith in what you know and believe. Lies lie on the tips of the tongues of the righteous. Follow not those that seek you out. You go and seek what calls to you. Do not blindly follow a God. They deem to squash your true calling and make you theirs. Your true calling lies within you. Seek it, grasp it, and fulfill it. Hang on to it with your complete being. It lingers near the surface. Do not stomp it out. Water it, nourish it, and embrace it. Heed my words. You are more than a follower. You are a leader in the grandest form. I do not ask for blind obedience. I want you to be all that you were called to be. Read my words and take them to heart. Life is too short to waste it on a life spent on your knees before a false God made of stone.

Lanis's hand gripped the book, and she let it drop to her side when a stick snapped to her right. She stayed blended for a good amount of time, then felt confident enough to step away from the tree. After slipping the book back in her bag, she uncurled her whip, and circled the area but didn't see or hear anything. Everything was calm and quiet. When she stepped into camp, everyone was asleep. Elson, Vic, and Finley lay on one side of the fire and the missionaries and Sani lay on the other. Pash was gone. She could have heard her, but in her gut, she knew that wasn't the case. Lanis knelt and pushed Elson on the shoulder. He rubbed his eyes, stood, and stretched.

"Everything okay?"

"I think so, but I heard some sticks break when I was on watch. I circled the area, but didn't see or hear anything. Pash is gone."

He nodded and looked around camp. "Do you think she's trouble? I didn't get that vibe from her."

"No. She didn't belong with these people. I have a feeling she knows exactly what she's doing. I don't think she's the one that I heard. Keep your ears open. Something is going on."

"Okay." He squeezed her shoulder. "I'll stick close to camp. Get some sleep. I won't let anything happen."

"Wake me up if you hear anything. I'll try, but I am not sure I will be able to sleep."

"I need you at your best tomorrow."

She lay down on the bedroll he abandoned and closed her eyes. Things had been going so well.

☙ ☙ ☙ ☙

Lanis ate the last of her biscuit, stood, and kicked dirt over the fire, never taking her eyes off their guests.

They were tenser this morning, more reserved. Doloris had spoken to Sani earlier, but none one of them had looked her way. She would have shrugged it off if not for the nagging feeling that something was wrong. After repacking her bag, she slipped it over her head, tightened her whip, and adjusted her boot knife. A chill still lingered in the air so she slipped her cloak on and loosely tied it around her neck. The sweet smell of honeysuckle invaded her senses and washed over her. It brought her a sense of calm in an otherwise tense situation. She looked at Elson and nodded as the others followed suit. Hers eyes swept the camp before coming to rest on Vic, who held her staff firmly in her left hand. Considering she usually left it attached to her horse, Lanis knew Vic also felt the shift in the air. Elson walked up to her and patted her on the shoulder. Lanis smiled stiffly. "I'm ready."

"Me too," he said. "I don't trust them."

"I know. We should leave. I'll get Vic."

He squeezed her shoulder. "I'll get your horse ready."

Lanis was halfway to Vic when Doloris cut her off. She rocked back on her heels and crossed her arms across her chest. "Is there something I can do for you?" She felt, rather than saw, Elson come up behind her and out of the corner of her eyes caught a glimpse of Vic and Finley step up to her right side.

"Liar." Doloris sneered. "Deceiver."

Lanis stiffened and took a step back at the venom in her voice. Elson pulled his sword when Vic held her staff out in front of her body. Lanis touched her whip as the rest of the missionaries stepped up next to Doloris and Sani, who, by this time, had taken up his place beside her. "What gives you the right to speak to me that way? You don't know me."

"I know you worship Damrek, a false god."

"What?" Elson said. "No, she doesn't."

Lanis groaned and dropped her arms to her sides when she realized what Doloris was talking about. One of them must have seen her reading from the book the previous night. What a mess. "Look, I realize what you think you saw." She clamped her mouth shut and covered her eyes with her hands when the wind picked up and debris started to fly around and at them. She grabbed her head and dropped to her knees as a tightness filled her mind. A thousand thoughts fought for control.

Keeping her eyes shut, Lanis rose onto her knees, but fell backward when the ground beneath her started to grumble and shake. With a calm she didn't feel, she opened her eyes, but quickly shut them when dirt engulfed her, and threw her sideways onto the ground. She slapped her hands over her ears when Vic screamed from behind her, then the ground rumbled and dropped out from under them. Lanis screamed and flung her arms out to the sides as her body fell. She grabbed onto the nearest body and held on tightly. Without warning, her body slammed to a halt inches from the ground.

After taking several deep breaths, she opened her eyes and sucked in a breath as she took in their surroundings. The hole they had fallen into had to have been a hundred feet deep and ten feet wide. She looked to Vic, who nodded at her, and their bodies slowly fell the rest of the way to the ground. Lanis pushed up onto her knees and looked up, quickly closing her eyes and dropping her head when dirt started pouring in on them. Sani was burying them alive. Heart pounding in her chest, she swung her head to Vic, who stood on unsteady feet, and raised her staff above her head. Without muttering a word, Vic lowered her staff and pounded it on the ground three times. Lanis looked up when she didn't feel the dirt falling anymore. Instead of piling on top of them, it was piling on top of what looked to be some sort of force shield. Vic had saved them, but for how long? She wouldn't be able to hold the shield up indefinitely.

Lanis clasped Vic's hand and allowed her to help her to her feet. Lanis wiped the dirt off of her hair and helped Vic get it out of hers. She then reached her hand toward the top of the shield, but Vic swatted it away. The shield was at least ten feet wide and eight feet high. Her happiness at not dying quickly vanished when the enormity of the situation hit her. They were at least a hundred feet under the ground, with no way out. Sani had, essentially, succeeded in burying them alive. "How long will it last?"

Vic ran her hand through her hair and bit her lip. "I don't know." She leaned back against one side of the wall. "I...I didn't know what else to do. I didn't have many options available. I'm confident I can hold the shield, but I don't know what good that's going to do. We're trapped inside the earth." She laughed. "It's funny. I would normally be able to transport us out of here, but creating the shield weakened me. So I prolonged our lives so we could see our deaths coming, instead of letting death take us."

Lanis understood her fear and frustration; she felt it too, but she was glad they weren't dead. "Thank you. I would rather take my chances now, rather than die without fighting." This was certainly nothing she had ever experienced before. "Well," she said. "This is certainly something for you to write in your notebook. I mean, really, how often does this sort of thing happen?"

"That's for sure."

"Can you write in your notebook or do you need to concentrate on the shield?"

"I can do both." Vic still looked uncertain. "I do have a lot to write about. Number one being Sani. If I ever see him again, I will kill him."

"I second that. If you can do both, then do both. I'll check on the boys." Vic nodded and rummaged in her bag, pulled out her well-worn notebook, and started writing. Lanis checked Finley first, then Elson, relaxing only when she saw them both take breaths. She slumped on the ground beside Elson, wiped the dirt from his face, then buried her face in her hands. Dirt literally surrounded them.

She sat back and surveyed their prison. It should have been dark, but the shield seemed to be putting of a soft, warm light. Anya was waiting for her. If something happened and they didn't make it out alive, she could at least die with the knowledge that Anya would soon join her. She rubbed her neck. What a mess they had gotten themselves into. All over that stupid book. This was one situation she had no idea how to get them out of.

When Elson moaned from beside her, she leaned over him. "Elson." She touched his check. Warm. He slowly opened his eyes when she said his name again. He accepted her help, leaned back against the wall, and shook the dirt from his hair.

"What happened this time?"

"Doloris accused me of worshipping Damrek, then Sani attacked us."

He laughed. "Obviously he didn't succeed. We're a little bit banged up, and dirty, but alive." His smile vanished when he saw the look on Lanis's face. "What?"

Lanis waved her hand in the air. "Look around. He may have killed us yet." His body stiffened when he took in their surroundings. "Vic says she can keep the shield in place, but only for a short period."

He nodded and rubbed his hand down his cheek. "That's good." They both turned their heads toward Vic when Finley moaned, then sat up. Lanis watched the different emotions cross his face when Vic whispered in his ear. "So," Elson said. "What do we do now? What's our game plan?"

Vic put her notebook away and grasped her staff. "Well, I've been thinking. I know I won't be able to transport all of us out of here, but I believe I could get two of us out safely."

Finley jumped up, surprising everyone, and took Vic's hand. "I promised Queen Isabel I would get you back to her safely. I failed. I will gladly lay my life down to keep you alive." He clasped his arms to his sides and bowed slightly. "I am ready to die."

Vic shook her head. "Finley, it was only a suggestion."

Elson also stood and helped Lanis up. "I agree with Finley. If you can get yourself and Lanis out of here safely, then do it. I am also ready to die."

"No." Lanis threw his hand off of her shoulder and took a step back from him. "No," she said to Vic. "We still have a little time before the shield fails, don't we?"

Vic took her time in answering. "If I am going to get us both out alive, it will have to be soon. After that, I won't have enough energy left to do it safely."

Lanis glared at each of them. "I, for one, am not going to sacrifice them to save our lives. I would never be able to live with myself if I did, and I can't believe you could either."

"Lanis," Elson said. "I do not matter. The only thing that matters is High Priestess Anya. She is waiting for you. I vowed long ago to give my life up if I needed to. I am willing and able to do this."

Lanis turned her back on them and ran her fingers through her hair. The stone the old ladies gave her rested neatly in her pocket and the thought had crossed her mind to use it, but deep down she knew this wasn't the time. That had to be a good sign that they would make it out of this alive. She wasn't ready to give up on everyone yet. "There has to be another way. Think, everybody. Vic, is there anything else you can do? If we can't come up with any viable solutions, I will agree with the plan."

"The shield will protect us, but I cannot produce any other type of magic while the shield is in place."

After a long silence, Finley spoke. "If we could walk, with the shield in place, we might run into an open space."

"What do you mean?" Elson asked, already taking the map out of his pack.

Finley walked up beside him and pointed to the map. "We weren't far from an underground cave system. There are tons of them under the road that we were going to be walking on today."

Elson snapped his fingers. "You're right, there were. Okay, this is where we were headed." He pointed to a spot on the map. "And I am confident in saying this is where we camped last night. Vic, is there any way we can walk with the shield in place?"

Vic hesitated before answering. "It is possible, but I will have to make the shield smaller and I am not sure how far we would be able to get before my strength and concentration began to fade."

"From the map," Elson said, folding the map back up and slipping it into his bag, "we are at least a mile from the rocks themselves. That's not to say the actual cave system."

"It is a chance, and not one I think we should take," Finley said.

Lanis gathered her things. "It is a gamble, I know that, but if we don't do something we are going to die and we are not leaving the two of you behind."

Vic laughed. "Who knew when we started this journey we would be facing certain death?"

"What else did you expect from us?" Elson grabbed her by the waist and pulled her to his side.

Vic patted his hand. "I'm ready if everyone else is."

"Excellent," Elson said, letting her go, and slipping his arm around Lanis's waist.

"Me too," Lanis said.

"I never had a doubt." Elson turned to Finley. "What do you say?"

"I don't like it. I would rather have Vic get out now, but I can see I am outvoted. I will go along with it, only because I have to."

"Fantastic," Elson said. "What do we do now, Vic?"

"Give me a few minutes to get everything in order."

Lanis turned to Elson. "Pray with me." He nodded and bowed his head. She stayed quiet as he prayed softly. Her faith was strained, almost to the breaking point. Nia had been with them, but it seemed when they needed her the most, she was never there. Her ideal way to die would not be buried beneath a ton of dirt and she was sure whatever Anya was going through didn't sit well with her either. When he grew quiet, she raised her head and smiled at him.

He released her hands and leaned back against the wall. "This is new even for us."

"I know. I didn't think things could get any worse. I was wrong. It can always get worse."

"It is eerie being down here. I am not a fan of tight spaces. Especially tight spaces you can't get out of."

"I thought my biggest fear was heights. I was wrong. It's taking everything within me to keep my bearings." That was an understatement, but she wouldn't let on how frightened she really was. It wouldn't do anyone any good for her to lose it. Elson, she was sure, knew how badly she was fighting her fear.

His smile was tense when he answered. "That's all we need, for both of us to go crazy." His eyes held a tension she had never seen before. With that one look, he conveyed more to her than words ever could. He was really scared. She knew she couldn't lose it now.

"Elson, it's one thing to be afraid and quite another to let that fear overtake you. You are stronger than this and so am I. We've got this."

"Yes, we do."

"I'm ready," Vic said. "I need everyone to gather around me and make sure all of your belongings are somewhere on your body. When the shield closes in, it will be a tight fit. I will have to shrink it by at least half. I will walk in front."

"I will walk beside you," Finley said.

"Very well. Elson, Lanis, stay right behind me."

"Just for kicks. What would happen if one of us fell? Would we just fall back into the shield or would we fall out of it?"

"Elson, you wouldn't fall out. You would be fine."

"Good to know."

"Ready?" Vic asked. Everyone gathered close.

"Wait," Elson said. "Does anyone know if anything or anyone dwells in this particular cave system? I know we don't have a choice. I just wondered what we were getting ready to walk into. I know of other cave systems where tribes live, but I don't know about this one."

"You hear things," Lanis said. "But I don't know anything about this one."

"Finley," Vic said. "I know you study cave dwellers. Do you know anything?"

"I don't know anything concrete, but I know of one group. The Fenaks. They are said to be a peaceful people that dwell in the cave systems. I don't know if it is these caves, though."

Lanis blew out a breath and rocked back on her heels. "I've never heard of them."

Elson shook his head. "Neither have I. Finley, you said they were a peaceful people?"

"Well, everyone is peaceful until you show up unannounced in their home. I don't know how they will react, or even if it is the same group."

"Let's be alert," Lanis said. "Let's keep our focus when we do break through into the caves."

"Optimistic. I like that," Elson said.

"It's hard not to be around you."

Elson turned to Vic. "We're ready."

"All right."

Lanis tried to recall anything she had ever heard about cave dwellers, but couldn't recall anything about the Fenaks. It was not a welcome feeling to be venturing into someone else's home. It almost got them killed with the Berrocka. She grasped her whip and held her breath as the shield started to shrink around them. To keep her wits, she closed her eyes. When Elson's grip on her hand tightened, she turned to him, opened her eyes, and noticed his breathing had increased significantly and sweat dotted his forehead. She slipped her hand though his arm and squeezed.

"Thanks," he whispered.

They walked at a steady pace for over an hour, but didn't come upon anything that indicated they were close to the caves. The earth around them was still dirt packed, and by the slump of her shoulders and her increased breathing, Lanis knew Vic wouldn't be able to hold on much longer. Finley had his arm securely wrapped around her shoulder, helping her to stay on her feet. Elson hadn't let go of Lanis's hand since they started. If something didn't change soon, they wouldn't live through this. They were all tired. Lanis wasn't even sure how much time had passed.

"I don't know how long I can keep this up," Vic said.

"I think we should turn left and walk for a few minutes. Let's see if the dirt around us shows any signs of rocks or anything to indicate we are getting close," Elson said, with more confidence in his voice then Lanis felt.

"I agree," Lanis added.

Vic smiled sadly. "Okay." After a half an hour, the dirt around them started to change. Rocks appeared more frequently within the dirt, starting off small then gradually increasing in size. "You were right," Vic said. "It's a good thing too because I am going to lose the ability to hold the shield up pretty soon. I think it would be a good idea if we took our chances and ran for it."

Elson let go of Lanis's arm. "I have an idea. Vic, why don't you climb on Finley's back, that way you won't have to worry about keeping up?"

Finley nodded. "It's a good idea." He knelt and allowed Vic to climb on his back. She wrapped her arms around his neck and closed her eyes. When Vic nodded, they started to run. It didn't take long before the rocks started shifting and cracks started to from in the dirt around them. Lanis also noticed, to her dismay, that the shield was shrinking. She said a silent prayer when Vic raised her head and looked back at her.

"I'm fading."

"Just a little farther," Elson said.

"I'm sorry." With one final sprint and a final prayer, Finley jumped into a boulder, followed by Elson and Lanis. Lanis closed her eyes and smiled as the air shifted. Without warning, her body slammed into the ground and knocked the breath from her chest. She rose to her knees and gulped in several deep breaths before she was able to get it under control. Vic grabbed her arm and pointed behind them. Lanis stood, afraid to look where Vic was pointing, but turned around anyway.

They were standing in a huge cavern that had been carved into the rocks. The ceiling was at least two hundred feet tall and there were holes carved into the walls around them. Water dripped from different points of the ceiling, falling to the ground, where a small pond collected the drops. Lanis could hear rushing water somewhere in the distance. It was surreal and breathtaking at the same time. The only downside she could see were the twenty or so men and women that stood across from them. It seemed they had interrupted some sort of gathering that was taking place. Lanis held up her hand to speak when she grabbed her neck and pulled a small dart out that had imbedded itself into the flesh. She stumbled back and fell to the ground when people rushed at her and grabbed her arms, hauling her to her feet. She fought, but quickly lost the battle when her limbs gave out and a man picked her up and threw her over his shoulder. The last thing she saw before she closed her eyes was Finley and Elson being tied up and dragged away.

❧ ❧ ❧ ❧

The cell Lanis and Vic had been thrown into was just a smaller cave, inside of the larger cave system. Solid rock surrounded them on three sides. The wall that held the door had a small, round hole at the top of it, but besides that, Lanis couldn't see any other openings. The only advantage they would have was to blend, but that would only be possible if these cave dwellers didn't know who she was. Lanis glanced at Vic for the fifth time to make sure she was still breathing. The magic she performed had drained her, and she had been out for hours. Lanis settled onto the floor beside Vic, and waited for her to wake up. Then there was Elson and Finley. She wouldn't even speculate to where they were being kept or if they were even alive.

She rubbed her neck where the dart had been and winced when she felt a small knot had already formed. It was sore, but considering she had woken fairly quickly after the initial attack, she was confident the affects had worn off completely. She jumped up when someone walked by their door. She looked out the hole, but didn't see anybody down either side of the hallway. They needed to act quickly, but they also needed to be at their best. She wasn't sure she should wake Vic up or not. The decision was made for her when she heard Vic groan from behind her. She helped her sit up against the wall. "How are you feeling?"

Vic frowned and felt her neck. "I've felt better. What did they shoot us with?" She rounded her shoulders and closed her eyes.

"I don't know, but it worked fast. It had more of an effect on you then me. I've been up for what seems like hours. I don't know where they took Elson and Finley."

Vic opened her eyes. "Help me stand?" She staggered and leaned against Lanis until the nausea passed. "What a mess. I feel all right, just give me a few minutes to get my bearings. Is that the only opening?" She pointed at the door.

"Yes." Lanis leaned in close to her and whispered in her ear. "Our best bet would be for us to blend with the wall until someone comes for us."

"You can walk when you're blended?"

"Yes, but you will have to stay plastered against me. Emotions can affect my blend, so keep yourself calm. How is your magic? Have you gotten your strength back?"

"I'm ready, but I won't be a hundred percent until, probably, tomorrow. I can perform magic, just not as strongly as in the past." She ran her hands through her hair and looked at the floor. "They didn't take our stuff? That's surprising."

"I thought so too. Maybe that's a good sign. If they wanted us dead, we would already be dead. I have no clue what they want with us." She picked up her bag and slipped it over her head, tightened her whip, and secured her knife between the folds of her whip.

"When are we doing this?"

"Well, there aren't many open spaces, so when we hear someone coming we can blend with the wall by the door." She shrugged. "We'll need to keep our ears open in case we hear anything about the guys. I am grateful we aren't still in the ground, but I am not sure how this is going to play out."

Vic patted her on the arm. "No worries. We made it this far, we'll make it out of here."

"Yes, we will." Lanis stretched and tried to shake her unease. It wasn't an impossible situation, but it was an unpredictable one.

"It's not as dark in here as I would expect."

"No, it's not." The room wasn't well lit, but there was enough light for them to make out all the shadows around them. Lanis swung her head around when voices drifted their way. She wrapped her arms around Vic and pushed back into the wall. "Relax." She took a deep breath and concentrated. When the door started to open, she blended, as two guards walked into the cell.

"Where are they? This is the cell, right?"

"Yes. I don't know where they are. Who knows where they are. They did come here through the side of our cave."

Lanis knew she would only have one shot to get out. She inched them closer to the door and waited for one of the men to move away from it.

"What do we do?"

"I don't know." The guard ran his hands down his face. "Go get Tegan."

The man nodded. "Good idea."

Lanis saw her chance when they both walked into the hallway. She slipped out the door and held her breath when he moved toward them. When he leaned against the opposite wall, she took her chance and slipped farther out of the cell and into the hallway. She pushed further into her blend and continued down the hallway. She was almost to the end when the other guard appeared again, followed by a woman. Lanis stopped.

"Well," Tegan said. "Where are they?" She cocked her head and crossed her arms. Lanis didn't see any weapons visible on her, or for that matter, she didn't see any on the other two guards either.

"I don't know. They were here."

"Did you check the other cells? That was the right one, wasn't it?" Tegan pointed down the hall.

"Tegan, of course it is. They are gone."

She laughed. "No, they aren't. We know where they're going. Make sure everyone knows what happened. I am going to the chamber to talk to the Elders. Both of the men haven't given them any information about what happened. From the looks of it, we should have interrogated the women first." She grinned. "Maybe the men will cooperate when they find out we lost both women."

"Why don't we just kill the men? They don't belong here."

"So that's what it's come to," Tegan said. "Kill anyone that ventures into our lands. We would be no better than everyone else."

"What are we doing now? We threw them into

a cell and we have the others tied up. What does that make us?"

"Cautious. It makes us cautious," Tegan said. She stormed off down the hall and passed Lanis and Vic. Lanis kept the blend and followed along the wall behind her. When she made it to the corner where Tegan had turned, she stopped short. Tegan was gone and they could go down four different paths. But which one should she take? Lanis bit her lip and headed to the one on the far left.

They walked for ages, and just when Lanis thought it was the wrong tunnel, she heard voices. At the end of the tunnel was a large cavern. Finley and Elson sat in two chairs, back-to-back in the middle of the large open space. The wall on their right was solid stone. The wall on their left was carved out and at least a hundred people were gathered. Above the opening was a balcony where a crowd had gathered as well. Tegan stood next to an older man on the balcony. Lanis counted six archers perched at all four corners of the cavern.

Lanis turned and walked back the way they had come. When they entered into a narrow hallway, and she was sure they were alone, she unblended. "Here's what I propose." She explained her plan to Vic and she nodded and grinned.

"Let's go get the guys and get out of here."

"Yes." Lanis pulled her back against her, blended, and headed back the way they had come. Lanis entered the cavern and kept to the right so they were standing on the opposite wall as the people gathered. She was directly in front of Elson. By this point, four guards were standing in a circle around Finley and Elson. They could do this. She relaxed back into the wall and released her hold, and Vic walked away from the wall. The guards stiffened as Vic walked up to them. Lanis stayed blended and continued along the wall, until she was directly across from Finley.

"Well," someone said from above them, "You are full of surprises, aren't you?"

"If you would have allowed us the opportunity to explain ourselves, instead of attacking us, and throwing us in a cell, we might be more willing to cooperate," Vic said, holding tight to her staff. "What choice did you leave us? We are peaceful, but we will defend ourselves."

"I understand," the man said. "Tegan." Lanis tensed, but kept her blend when Tegan jumped from the upper balcony and landed a few feet in front of Finley. Lanis flicked her wrist, and the whip glided from the wall, and wrapped around Tegan's throat. Lanis pulled on it and brought Tegan to her knees, as she stepped away from the wall. She walked to Tegan, confident Vic had her back, and pulled on the whip. As Tegan clawed at the whip, Lanis kicked her to the ground, and rested her boot on Tegan's chest.

"The whip isn't tight enough to kill her, but that can easily be remedied. You caught us in a weak moment before. We are not weak anymore." Lanis held her ground when the man raised his arm.

"Gentlemen, step away from them and stand back."

Lanis tightened her hold on the whip and addressed Vic. "Vic, untie them."

"Already on it."

She relaxed when Elson stepped up next to her, with his sword drawn. "The stuff we get ourselves into," he said.

She nodded at Vic when she touched her on the back. "We would like to leave, unharmed. If you will allow us to leave and show us the way out, we will not harm anyone. It would be in your best interest for you to allow us that convenience."

"Is that so? Seeing as you have my granddaughter under your feet, why should I do that?"

"Because I could have easily killed her."

"We don't want any trouble," Elson said. "All we want to do is leave. We won't be back, that I can promise you."

The man turned to the woman next to him and spoke to her. He frowned and shook his head. "I will allow you to leave if you would explain to us how you got here. How did you come through the earth, and land in our weekly chamber meeting?"

"Vic," Lanis said.

"One minute we were being accused of something by someone and the next we were some hundred feet under the ground. My quick reflexes allowed me to create a barrier that shielded us from the earth around us. We figured we could wait until I couldn't hold the shield in place and die, or take our chances and try to walk out. The only reason we crashed through the wall was because my energy levels were fading and, in turn, the shield was failing." She clapped her hands together. "Here we are." Lanis flinched, but stood firm when Vic threw her hand up and several darts bounced off the force field she had created. Lanis uncurled her whip from around Tegan's neck, and hauled her to her feet.

"If that's how you want to play this," Lanis said. "I have no problem killing her. If you do not allow us to leave, unharmed, we will do whatever is necessary to fight our way out."

The man stood up, waved the guards away, and spoke to Lanis. "You have someone with you who can get you out of here safely. Take her with you. For her to get captured so easily is a disgrace to our people. She is useless."

Tegan slumped in Lanis's arms. "Grandfather. Why?"

He sneered. "You are no longer a part of this tribe. Do not speak to me. Lead them out and never step foot in here again."

Lanis let go of her and pushed her forward. "Walk us out of here and if you do anything other than led us out, I will kill you and as many people as need be in order to get out of here alive."

Tegan glared at her. "Fine."

Lanis followed behind her and didn't look back as they continued down the hall and through several different passages. When they reached a crossroads with several different routes, Tegan took one to the left and it felt like they were going down. Lanis kept her mouth shut and waited to see where she was leading them.

Tegan stopped. "From here we will come to a ladder and climb out. We will not be able to climb up as a group. It will have to be single file."

Lanis nodded. "Lead the way. When we get there, Elson will go first and you can follow behind him, then me, Vic, and Finley."

"Sounds good," Elson said.

After two more turns, the ladder came into view. When it was Lanis's turn, she slipped her knife in her boot and climbed up. Her heart pounded as Elson reached the surface and he helped each of them out of the cave. She scanned the area, but they were alone.

"Tegan, where are we in relation to where we entered the chamber?"

She shrugged. "Probably three or four hundred feet that way." She pointed to the west. "That should get you back to where you were."

"Everyone ready?" Lanis asked.

Tegan spun around. "You are taking me with you, aren't you? You can't leave me here. They won't take me back, not now. Where am I supposed to go? All of you got me into this mess. You will take me with you."

Lanis laughed. "We don't have to do anything. I don't care what happens to you." She pointed to the west and started walking.

Vic caught up with her. "Lanis, I think we should take her with us."

"They are playing us. They sent her with us for a reason."

"I know. But we might be able to learn something from her. How often do we get to learn from a secret tribe? It's a thought."

Lanis rubbed her neck. She hated to admit it, but Vic did have a point. But was it really worth the risk? The book did say the original Book of Damrek was in a cave. What if his cave was within theirs? "I guess it couldn't hurt, at least for a little while. Keep in mind, though, that if she gets out of control, I will have to do something about her."

"Noted."

Lanis stopped walking and grabbed Tegan's arm. "You can stay with us for a short time, until you get your bearings, and figure out where to go."

"Really?" Elson asked. Lanis nodded.

"Thank you," Tegan said.

"Now, we need to make our way back to our camp and see if our horses are still there. Be vigilant. If we run into the missionaries again, don't hesitate to take them out. They didn't when it came to us," Elson said.

Vic ran her hand through her hair. "Sounds like a plan." It didn't take them very long to make it back to their last camp and to notice that their four horses were still tied.

Lanis called everyone to a stop and handed her bag to Elson. "I am going to check things out. Stay here and stay as hidden as possible."

"Be careful," Elson said.

Lanis squeezed his hand and slipped into the woods. When she was confident the others couldn't see her, she blended with the nearest tree. No need for Tegan to know of her ability. For all she knew, Tegan could think Vic made them disappear back at the caves. The only sounds she heard were the wind and the occasional chirp of a bird. She creeped along from tree to tree until the horses were within arm's reach. Out of the corner of her eye, she caught movement to her right. After a few minutes, she felt confident and moved forward.

As she pushed away from the tree, a white orb flew at her. She ducked and it hit the tree behind her, splitting it in two. She hurried out of the way as the tree fell, and squatted when Vic ran past her. Vic threw her hands out and spikes shot out from her fingertips toward Sani. Lanis uncurled her whip and jumped up. When she caught movement to her left, she threw her whip out. She pulled on her whip and the missionary fell to the ground. She ran to him, pulled her knife, and slit his throat. She accepted Elson's hand and stood up.

Vic was still fighting it out with Sani. Finley and Tegan were nowhere to be seen.

Lanis scanned the area, but didn't see any other missionaries. "Ready?" They were somewhere.

"Since Vic is taking care of Sani, let's look around. I'll go to the left, if you go to the right."

"Sure thing." Lanis turned toward Vic and Vic winked and smiled at her. Lanis slipped into the forest, closed her eyes, and listened. The air turned hot and the wind picked up, but she ignored it. Her knees hit the dirt, and she opened her eyes. A missionary stood a few yards from her. At the same time Doloris smiled, Lanis threw her knife. Doloris's smile froze on her lips when the knife embedded itself into her chest. Lanis stood up, and ran to her when her body hit the ground. Doloris reached for her, but Lanis pushed her hand away. "You should have been willing to listen to my explanation. Instead, you just assumed you knew what was going on. Pity." Lanis shook her head. "I am a true worshipper of Nia." She gripped her knife and pulled it from her chest. She wiped the blood splatter from her face. What a waste.

As she walked back to the others, she stayed alert, but didn't see or hear anything out of the ordinary. When she got back, Vic and Sani were still engaged. Lanis caught her eye and nodded. Vic raised her staff and held it above her head. She smiled and swung her staff in a downward arc. Sani grabbed his chest and turned disbelieving eyes on Vic, before falling to the ground. When he lifted his hand, Vic brought her staff down and struck him in the chest. As if in slow motion, his body jerked off the ground then stilled.

"Is he dead?" Elson asked.

"No. You need to finish it." Vic's breathing was

erratic and her hand shook on her staff.

"How?" Lanis asked.

"Cut his head off."

Elson shrugged, picked Sani's body up, and threw it over a stump. He lifted his sword and cut his head off.

Lanis felt a bit of satisfaction when his head hit the ground and rolled away from her. "How many did you kill?" She smiled at Elson.

"Two."

"I killed two also. One of them was Doloris, so that leaves one missionary."

"Let's hope the other one doesn't cause any trouble."

"Yes, let's."

Lanis wiped the blood off her knife and slipped it back in her boot. "I guess we should set up camp here for tonight and get started in the morning."

"Looks that way," Vic said, breathing back under control, as Finley and Tegan walked up to them.

"You're quiet." She directed her comment at Tegan.

Tegan bit her lip. "I am not use to so much killing. You killed a sorcerer without a second thought. I don't think I could do that." She fidgeted. "We are a peaceful people."

"You weren't that peaceful toward us," Elson said, dragging the sorcerer's body away from camp. He walked back shand kicked his head into the trees. "If you're going to be traveling with us, you should get used to it." He sat down by the fire that Lanis had started.

Lanis handed him a cup of tea. "You can leave if you want to."

Tegan sat down and buried her hands in her face. "Where am I supposed to go? My tribe kicked me out. My grandfather disowned me. I have nothing. Literally, nothing. What am I supposed to do? This is all your fault." She pointed at Lanis.

"It's not my fault. If you hadn't captured us and forced our hand, and if you would have given us the chance to explain, none of this would have happened." By the look on Tegan's face and the way she was behaving, Lanis was starting to believe she wasn't a plant. Could her Grandfather really have disowned her? Just like that. It didn't make any sense. She took a sip of her tea. "The first thing you're going to have to start doing is quit blaming everyone else for your problems. Every one of us has countless issues to deal with. Get over yourself. You can come with us, for a short time, but if you don't like the bloodshed, I don't think you will appreciate where we are going."

Tegan smoothed her hands down her pant legs. "I am a quite accomplished hunter. I can survive. I am just not used to doing it alone. I will do everything I can to prove myself to you and to hold my own."

Finley stood up, startling them all. "I'm taking first watch."

"Tegan," Lanis said. "I get it. I really do. But, you won't be going the whole way with us." She held her hand up to ward off her questions. "I am sure we can find an acceptable place for you. There will be quite a few stops along the way. I am confident, you will fit in somewhere." Tegan nodded and turned away from them. Lanis leaned back against a tree and kicked her legs out in front of her. She hoped they found somewhere to dump her. The thought of killing her wasn't foreign, but at this point, if that's what it came down to, she would do it. They would figure it out when the time came. The only downside she could see was that Tegan would have to ride with one of them. Whatever she had to do in order to ensure it wasn't her, she would.

⁂

Lanis halted her horse when Vic stopped in front of her. Considering everything that had transpired the last few days, she had somewhat of a good night's rest. She woke determined to face whatever they came across today and the days that followed. She took a drink of her water and eyed Tegan, who rode with Elson. She had been quiet all morning, but she would keep an eye on her. The morning ride, since leaving camp, had been peaceful and easy, but the sight in front of her threatened to sour her mood. The Anolk Mountains lay stretched out in front of them, as far as she could see. The snow-capped peaks rose high into the sky and some disappeared into the clouds. They were impressive and a bit intimidating. She shuddered, thinking about what they were about to cross into. The cold held no appeal to her and it would affect her blend. Isabel had told them it would be safe to stop and she had to trust that she wouldn't send her daughter into any type of danger.

The boundary between the mountains and where they stood was breathtaking. It was an incredible sight and a clear marker between the two separate regions. On their side, everything was green and a lush forest grew with bright leaves in a multitude of colors. On the other side, a blanket of snow covered everything and it *looked* cold. She would never get used to magic and what it could accomplish. She tightened her hold on the reins and focused on Vic when she turned toward them.

"Okay," Vic said, rubbing her hands together. "Finley and I both have our cloaks. Elson, do you have anything warmer than what you have on? Tegan, I know you don't."

"No," Tegan said. "I don't have anything. As you are all aware, what I have on is all I have."

Elson frowned and touched his armor. "What I have is all I've got. I didn't pack for cold weather."

"Elson, that's not true. I don't know how much they will help, but you have the leather gloves Anya gave you."

He snapped his fingers. "You're right. I do." He rummaged in his bag, pulled them out, and slipped them on.

Lanis shrugged. "I don't have anything either."

"Lanis," Vic said. "You have the cloak my mom gave you."

"I do, but it won't keep out the cold I see over there." She pointed to the mountains.

Vic smiled. "She gave both me and Finley ours too. When you wear the cloak, you won't have to worry about the cold. It will keep you warm."

"Seriously?"

"Yes." Vic laughed.

Lanis slipped her cloak on and caught Elson's eye. "Sorry, friend."

"The cold doesn't bother me anyway."

Lanis slipped her gloves out of her bag and handed them to Tegan. "It's all I have to offer."

"Thank you."

Vic bit her lip. "I want everybody's full attention.

Just so we are clear, crossing the boundary between here and the mountains will be intense. If you're not prepared, you may not survive. Once we cross over, make sure that you exhale instead of inhaling. All right." She smiled and turned around. "Ready?"

Lanis and Elson exchanged looks. "I guess," Lanis said.

"What do you mean not survive?" Tegan questioned. "I'm not used to cold weather. I have never traveled this far from my home before. What should I expect?"

"The boundary, as you can see, is a separation between the Anolk Mountains and the surrounding area. It has been this way as long as scholars have been recording history. You will feel an immense coldness that will settle into your core. It will fill every fiber in your soul. But do not dwell on the cold. Let it fill you, then imagine it floating away. Take even breaths, through your nose, until you get used to the cold."

Tegan eyed her gloves, then Vic. "Sure. Sure."

"Not to worry," Elson said. "I'm sure we will be fine."

Tegan snorted. "That's easy for you to say. I will be blocking quite a bit of the wind from you."

"Too true."

"I'll lead," Finley said, lifting his hood. Lanis and Vic lifted their hoods as well. Lanis was prepared, but nothing could have prepared her for the surge of energy she received when they crossed over the border. Her breath floated out in front of her, but even though cold surrounded them, she didn't feel any of it. The cloak not only warmed her arms and upper body, it seemed to encase her entire body in a comfortable warmth. Elson and Tegan were both shivering, but when he caught her looking, he winked and gave her a thumb's up. He was always in good spirits, but even he wasn't strong enough to handle this type of cold for very long and Tegan would fare even worse. Maybe this would be a perfect spot for Tegan to stay. She would ask around and see if it was a possibility. After a few hours, Lanis sat up higher in her saddle and noticed three men headed their way on foot. Vic broke away from the rest of them and trotted up to the men. Vic was too far ahead of them for Lanis to hear what she was saying, but the men started laughing when Vic pointed behind her.

Lanis rode up to Vic when she motioned for them to come forward. "What did you say to them?"

"I told the truth."

"Why did he laugh?"

Vic had a silly smile on her face. "Why wouldn't he?" She huffed. "I am quite funny." She rode up next to Finley.

Lanis stayed back with Elson and Tegan. The same man that had laughed at Vic moved away from a large opening and directed them to pass through. He mounted his horse and instructed everyone to follow him. An hour into the ride, they reached a crossroads. Their guide instructed them to stop when he talked with a young boy and the boy waved them through. Vic hadn't taken her eyes off the man since she talked with him earlier. That couldn't bode well for Finley and when she turned to him, his clenched jaw told her all she needed to know. She only hoped he didn't cause them any trouble; they were only going to be here a night. They entered into what Lanis could only describe as a well-oiled machine. People were scattered everywhere doing one task or another. Large fires were set in several locations throughout the large village. Once inside, they were directed to the stables and their guide had assured them their horses would be well taken care of.

"Oh," Vic said, pushing her hood back. "We're not worried." She bit her lip and he smiled.

Lanis could see what attracted her to him. He wasn't as tall as Elson, but the way he held himself, you wouldn't know it. His shoulder length, wavy brown hair and short, well-groomed beard only added to his appeal. His clothes were what one would expect in such a region, black wool pants and a large overcoat. He wore a scabbard on his left hip. She looked at her boots, then his. On his feet, he wore a thick-soled pair of black leather boots, with thick laces. When she looked up, he was smiling at her.

He pointed to her boots. "I can see if we have a pair to fit you."

"Really? You don't even know me."

He cut his eyes toward Vic, who was talking to Elson and Tegan at one of the large fires, where they were warming up. "I know all I need to."

"I would gladly pay for a pair, but at the moment, I don't have any extra money. I am sure, though, that we could come up with a trade of some sort."

"No need for that." He waved her off and walked closer to her. "Are Vic and the skinny fellow together?" He fidgeted.

Lanis kept her laughter in check. That was the last thing that she expected him to ask. It wasn't her place to say, but the way Vic was acting, she didn't see any harm in answering his question. "Finley, the skinny guy, is Vic's personal guard." Lanis pointed to Elson. "The other one, Elson, is with me. Tegan is an add on and we don't know much about her."

He gulped. "Good to know." He ran his hands through his hair and nodded. "I'll see about those boots." With one last look at Vic, he walked off.

Lanis slipped her cloak off and put it back in her bag. She shivered for a moment, but the feeling quickly passed. There was a chill in the air, but with all the fires set, it quickly passed. She joined the others and leaned in close to Vic. "He's nice. I like him."

"I don't trust him," Finley said.

"I have been around a lot of people in my life and I trust him," Lanis said. "I'm pretty good at reading people."

Finley laughed. "Really? You didn't do such a good job of picking a replacement Protector." Before anyone could move, Lanis picked him up and slammed him against the mountain.

"I don't care who you are or what position you hold. Do not ever talk to me that way again."

He struggled against her. "Let me go."

Vic squeezed Lanis's shoulder. "Let him go. People are starting to notice"

Lanis slammed him against the mountain again, then let him go. "Do not ever say that to me again. Next time, she won't be able to save you."

Finley shoved her away. "It's not my problem you can't handle the truth."

Lanis snickered and walked up to him. She spoke low enough that he was the only one that could hear her. "And it's not my problem that the woman you're in love with is taken with another." He pushed her back and Elson grabbed his arm.

"Do not touch her like that."

Finley put his hands up. "Whatever."

Their guide walked back to them. "Is there a problem?"

"Finley," Vic said. "Cut the attitude. Next time you won't have to deal with them, you will deal with me. I won't stand for your insolence. You forget your place."

Finley bowed on one knee. "My Lady, I am sorry. It won't happen again."

"It better not. Stand up and go cool off."

Their guide clasped his hands behind his back. "I didn't get to properly introduce myself to everyone. I am Mitchell."

Lanis held her hand out. "I'm Lanis and I am sorry about all of that."

"Don't worry about it. I just wouldn't make a habit out of it. We extend our hospitality, but we will not put up with a real disturbance within our village."

"I understand," Lanis said. "I don't speak for everyone, but I wouldn't turn down a bite to eat."

"Hear, hear," Elson added. "And a nice cup of hot tea."

Mitchell laughed. "Follow me."

Vic and Mitchell walked in front of them, talking. Lanis slowed down so they would be out of earshot of them. "Finley's going to be trouble."

"He is, at least while we are here. Let's hope that when we leave, so will the tension," Elson said.

Tegan bit her lip. "Who are you people?"

"We are who we are," Lanis said.

"You know, Lanis," Tegan said. "You don't have to be so evasive. I am not your enemy."

Lanis stopped walking and faced her. "I don't know you. Everyone is my enemy until they are my friend. You are not my friend. I will not let anyone, or anything, deter us from our final goal. Do not get comfortable with us. You are not coming."

"We'll see." Tegan ran to catch up with Vic.

Lanis sighed. "I hope she's not trouble."

"Me too." He pointed in front of them. "Vic likes Mitchell."

"She's does. I feel for her. It only took one meeting with Anya for me to fall in love with her."

"You coming?" Vic hollered back at them.

They both nodded. "Let's get something to eat. Later we can deal with everything else," Elson said.

"I couldn't agree more."

They settled on benches around a large fire that burned in a stone pit. Lanis ate the last of her biscuit and set her plate on the ground in front of her. She took a sip of her tea and looked around the area. Elson and Vic were relaxed, Finley was tense, and Tegan seemed indifferent to everything and everyone. After every bite of food, a grin would cross Vic's face. It wasn't hard to figure out whom she was thinking about. She knew that look, and was sure it had crossed her face more than once when she thought about Anya. She longed for the day when she could hold Anya in her arms again. When Tegan set her plate down, Lanis knew it was time. "Tegan, would you mind if I asked you a few questions?"

Tegan narrowed her eyes and licked her lips. "I guess it all depends on the questions."

"Fair enough," Lanis said. "I was wondering about all of the underground cave systems."

"What do you want to know about them?"

"The cave system you lived in was enormous. Do you know if there are a lot that size in Adearian?"

Tegan leaned back against the building behind

her. "I can't speak for all of Adearian, and I can't say for sure how many there are, but I know of at least four that are either as big as the one I lived at, or bigger. Is there something specific you wanted to know?"

Lanis wasn't sure how much she should ask and how she should phrase her question. There was always the chance of giving too much information away. "Well."

Tegan frowned at her. "What exactly do you want to know?"

"I am sure you've heard of Damrek's Cave. Do you know where it's located?" Lanis rolled her eyes when Vic pulled her notebook out of her bag.

Tegan whistled. "You don't pull any punches, do you?" She rubbed her hands along her pants. "I know what you want to know, but it's not that simple. My people protect the caves around the area where you were captured. They are tasked with keeping them safe and keeping unwanted visitors out. I have never seen Damrek's Cave. I have heard about it. I don't know who hasn't. Before I answer your question, I have one of my own."

"Go ahead," Lanis said.

"Why do you want to know? I know you don't worship Damrek, so what do you have to gain from such knowledge?"

Lanis hesitated before answering. "If you're asking if I want the spheres, I don't. The knowledge of where the Cave is located could help out in future events. That is the only reason I want to know. I speak for everyone here when I say that none of us wants the spheres."

Tegan ran her fingers through her long, black hair. "I see. You don't trust me, but you expect me to trust you?"

"Your people held us in a cell and had them tied up." Vic smirked. "Can you blame us for not trusting you?"

"Besides," Elson said. "If we didn't trust you, even a little bit, you would already be dead."

"Okay," Tegan said, and reached her hands toward the fire. "If you want to know an exact location, you will be disappointed. I don't know it, but I will say this. I know where it isn't. It is not in the cave you were in, or in any of the surrounding cave systems. They have been searched. To be honest, I don't think anyone really knows where it is."

"You're holding something back," Lanis said. "Go on."

Tegan bit her lip. "Look. Every time I brought this up with my people, they laughed at me."

"We won't laugh," Vic said.

Tegan scooted forward. "I don't think there is a cave. At least I don't think Damrek was talking about a cave at all."

Lanis rubbed her neck. "Have you read the book?"

"I have. I don't worship Damrek, but my elders have every one of my people read others' views to be better prepared in the world."

"What do you think he was talking about?" Elson asked.

"I think he was talking about ruins. They can be dark and damp, and have twists and turns. My people didn't give it a single thought."

Tegan was confirming what Lanis had already figured out. Damrek's Cave wasn't a cave at all. "Do you have any idea what ruins the book talked about?"

Tegan arched her eyebrow. "You believe me?"

Lanis nodded. "I do."

"Really," Elson said. "Why?"

Lanis turned to him. "A cave, while it would be hard to find, just doesn't make sense. Damrek didn't strike me as the type to hide away in a cave. He was smart and he knew what he was doing."

"I don't know where the ruins would be located. Though, I don't believe, with his level of talent, he would allow just anyone to locate them."

"You believe they're hidden?" Vic asked, writing in her notebook.

"I do. I also know they would have to be someplace close to both Malora, and Manight. For such an explosion to take place, and where it took place, had to be between the two. I think if you are looking for them, your best bet would be to look for ruins between the two." Tegan stood up. "I am going for a walk before turning in. I do hope I have been of some help to you, even though you all haven't been any sort of help to me."

"She's crazy," Finley muttered after she left. "There aren't any ruins between Malora and Manight." He stood up, threw the rest of his tea in the fire, and walked off.

Lanis stared into the fire. She knew that wasn't the case. She had clearly seen a set of ruins below the bridge in Vashta. Damrek certainly hadn't made them easy to find, if they could disappear on a whim. It wouldn't be easy to reach them, and she didn't know if she even wanted to try after what happened the last time. At least she had the information. For now, she would keep the information to herself. It was still unclear if she would even need to share it. Her number one priority, right now, was Anya. Everything else could wait.

☙ ☙ ☙ ☙

Lanis picked up her teacup and scooted back as an older woman collected their plates. Tegan sat at a small, square table, talking to a girl around her age, and Finley sat off by himself. He was far enough away that he wouldn't have to participate with them, but close enough that if Vic needed him he would be there for her. Lanis leaned back on the stone bench and rested her head against the building behind them. She turned toward Elson when he elbowed her. Mitchell was walking their way with a young boy in tow.

"Excuse me," Mitchell said. "I hope I am not interrupting?"

"Of course not," Vic said, smiling.

"Excellent. I had a request, Victoria?"

Lanis snickered and Vic shot her a dirty look when she smoothed her shirt and stood up. "What can I do for you?"

He pushed the boy forward. "This is my son, Steven. He has had a bit of trouble grasping how to use his magic." Steven fidgeted with the hem of his shirt.

"I see." Vic knelt down next to him. "Steven, look at me." He raised his head. "What sort of trouble are you having?"

"I don't understand what my teachers are telling me to do. It's hard. Everyone laughs at me."

Lanis pushed off the wall, entranced with what was about to happen. She completely understood what he was going through. He couldn't be more than seven or eight years old. When she was younger, her peers picked on her relentlessly because she was smaller than they were, but with the help of amazing instructors, she was able to overcome that. They had the same look in their eyes when they taught her that Vic had in her eyes now. She took a sip of her tea. Seeing Vic teach would be a nice change of pace and keep her thoughts off Anya, at least for a little while.

"Okay." Vic nodded. "You are not grasping what your teachers are telling you, but the other students are?"

"Yes."

Vic raised her head. "Mitchell, is his mother around?"

"His mother died in childbirth."

"Oh, I am so sorry."

"In time, wounds heal."

Vic nodded and turned her full attention on Steven. "Hold your hands out, Steven." He did as she instructed and as soon as she grabbed his hands, he screamed and fell to his knees. Vic let go of his hands, but everyone around them had stopped what they were doing and turned their attention to what was happening. Lanis touched her whip, but relaxed when Mitchell held his hand up to ward everyone off.

"That," Vic said, "was lesson number one. Do not, and I cannot stress this enough, do not allow anyone to touch you in such a manner." She held her own hands out. "For most magic inclined, these are their only weapons. The most powerful way to harm or fully engage your power is by touch." Vic raised up and settled back on her knees. "Do you understand?"

Steven picked himself up and stood to his full height. He didn't bother to wipe the dirt from his pants. "I do."

Vic clapped and grinned. "Now, lesson two. Are

you ready?"

"Yes," he said. As soon as the words left his mouth, Vic formed two small light orbs in her hand, and threw them at Mitchell. She waved her hand and they stopped an inch from his body. Mitchell, to his credit, didn't blink or even move.

"How did you do that so quickly?" Steven grinned.

Without answering him, Vic drew the orbs back to her, waved her hand over them, and they disappeared. "Can you make a plain, clear orb?"

He looked uncertain, but held his hand out. His smile vanished when nothing happened.

"Okay." Vic reached out, and without touching his hands, repositioned them, palm up. "Imagine in your mind a clear orb in your hand. Concentrate. It will get easier." She scooted closer to him. "Concentrate. Picture it. Think on it. See it. Create it," she stressed. Lanis moved across the table so she could more clearly see what was happening. Steven's face lit up when a small, clear orb appeared in his palm. "Now," Vic said. "Don't let go of the image in your mind. Set the image of the clear orb in the background, but always keep it there. You still have to focus on it, but it shouldn't be your entire focus. Do you understand?"

"I do, but why is my orb so much smaller than yours?"

"It mostly has to do with your experience level. Your classmates' orbs will probably be bigger, but that shouldn't discourage you in the least. And I've had a lot of practice. Now, take your other hand and lay it palm up as well. Good. I want you to picture a clear, pink orb in it."

He scrunched up his nose and snickered. "Pink?"

"Yes, pink," she said sternly, not leaving a trace of doubt that she was upset. "Do not ever see the color of an orb and think it isn't dangerous or in some way any less because of its color. Look at me, Steven. Many foolish sorcerers and sorceresses have died for such nonsense."

He shook his head and disappointment was written across his face. "I will not forget. I am sorry."

"Don't be sorry, but magic isn't something to be played with lightly. Magic is life and death, literally. There are times for you to have fun with it, but first you must master it. Magic is an unforgiving foe that will turn on you in the blink of an eye. Never forget that." He nodded. "Picture a small pink orb. It needs to be smaller than the first one." By this time, a small crowd had gathered to watch what was happening. Lanis couldn't wait to see what would happen next. Vic was a fantastic teacher. It was rare for someone who wasn't magic bound to see such a lesson being taught.

"Picture it," Vic said and a small, dark, pink orb flickered in his hand, almost red in color. "That's too dark. In your mind, picture the color fading. That's good. Some more. Excellent." As the pink faded to the correct shade, the orb had solidified in his hand. "That's the color you want." She stood up. "Lesson three. Always make sure your prominent orb, in your case that will be the clear one, is bigger than the secondary one. Here comes the fun part. The clear orb will expand and contain whatever your secondary orb is. So with your smaller orb, you need to be explicit in your needs for it. Do not falter in your mind once you set it to do something. The results could be disastrous. In your mind, place the pink orb into the background, but place it beside the clear one."

It took him a few minutes to answer. "Done." She leaned over and whispered in his ear and he giggled. "Really?"

"Yes, but remember you took an Oath. Signed a binding contract not to ever harm yourself or do harm to others with your magic when you started school. With the gift of magic also comes great responsibility."

He looked offended and Lanis snickered. "I would never use my magic for such things."

"Good. Turn toward your father. Raise your head, but keep the orbs in your mind, and look him in the eyes. I cannot stress enough to keep everything else firmly in mind. Concentrate and remember what I told you and I want you to throw both orbs toward him and midway I want you to combine them in your mind. That is much easier said than done. Picture what will happen. Can you see it?"

"Yes, but I don't want something to go wrong. I don't want to hurt him."

"Steven, I am your teacher. I will not let anything happen to him. I can see when something has gone wrong. Let me take that burden from you. Trust me. Okay?" He nodded. "Focus on your father and throw them out." Steven let them go, but something looked wrong and at the last second Vic waved her hand and they disappeared. "Create them. Throw them again." At the last second, she diverted them. "Again." The same thing happened and she winked at Mitchell. "Concentrate. Picture it." She diverted them. "Picture it. Concentrate." She diverted them. "Again. Again. Again. Again." Lanis stood up when a different look crossed Steven's face and Vic smiled. The orbs flew at Mitchell and combined at the halfway point. The orb shimmered, then slammed into Mitchell and exploded.

A small cloud formed above his head and it started snowing on him. Everyone gathered looked stunned, then laughed. "Excellent," Vic said. "Do you know the exact moment it changed?"

"I felt different. My dad," he said excitedly, "gave me a puzzle game and all the pieces have a certain place they have to go in order for everything to click into place. That's what I did in my mind."

"Lesson four. Do not ever think for one moment that the spell I just showed you is some kind of parlor trick. It is not a game or a toy." She turned and faced Mitchell, who smiled at her, and licked at the snow. Lanis wasn't sure what was about to happen, but Vic looked different. Lanis flinched when Vic threw her hand out and waved it back and forth. The snow, which started out as flurries, picked up quickly and whirled around Mitchell like a funnel. His smile vanished. He tried to step away from the funnel, but it kept pulling him back in. Vic twirled her finger and the snow was coming down so fast Mitchell was a blur. He fell to his knees and covered his face with his hands. "Steven, I want you to stop it."

"How?" He was almost in tears by this point. Lanis understood the lesson she was teaching him and she also knew it would be best for him to learn that lesson now.

"Think about what you want to happen in your mind. Then wave your hand and make it vanish." He looked more determined than he was before and, after a moment, he waved his hand in the air and everything vanished. Mitchell looked up and a few men helped him to stand.

"That was wicked. How?" Lanis cringed at the excitement in his voice.

Vic narrowed her eyes at him and he took a step back. She pointed to Mitchell. "I just said this wasn't a game. I could have done a lot worse to him. Stand up straight and listen to me." She knelt in front of him. "I could have turned the snow into rain, sleet, or ice and it would have covered him. Essentially burying him alive. A simple, stationary spell can go from funny to deadly in a matter of seconds. Look at me, Steven. I don't care if your classmates make fun of you. Do not ever give into peer pressure to mess around with spells. Even the slightest spells are to be taken seriously. I am not getting on to you, but you have to realize that just because you, or anyone else, wears that yellow band doesn't mean you will ever excel in magic. Not everyone who is gifted with magic abilities gets to use them."

"I didn't know that."

"It takes years to learn the art of magic and if a teacher, somewhere down the line, doesn't feel that a particular student is excelling or using their abilities the way they should, they will be deemed unworthy and stripped of their abilities. I don't want that to happen to you. You caught on very quickly. Okay."

"Thank you." He threw his arms around her neck and kissed her cheek. "I won't." He ran to his dad, who picked him up and squeezed him before setting him back on the ground. Lanis looked around and everyone looked pleased and patted Steven on the back. Finley had left halfway through the teaching. Lanis and Elson walked up to her.

"Well," Elson said. "That was amazing."

"You're a born teacher." Lanis said.

Vic grinned. "That's because I am a teacher. I teach the youngsters the basics of magic in Candor.

What I don't understand," she said to Mitchell, who had made his way over to them, "is why his teachers didn't explain it the way I did?"

"They're hard on him," Mitchell said. "He's smaller than his classmates so he shies away from everyone. It's hard to stand back and watch him go through that, so thank you. He's smart. He just needs someone to bring it out of him. I believe you may have given him the confidence to do just that."

"I agree. He is smart." Vic bit her lip.

Mitchell fidgeted like a little boy. "That was very impressive. I saw the change in him the moment it clicked. It's a great feeling."

Lanis leaned back on her heels. "I saw the change too. At that moment, everything started to make sense." She knew that feeling all too well.

Mitchell pointed to Lanis's feet. "Your new boots will be ready before you leave in the morning." Mitchell was talking to her, but his eyes never left Vic.

"That's great. Thank you." Lanis rolled her eyes and Elson laughed. Neither Vic nor Mitchell were paying any attention to them.

"Vic, would you like a cup of tea?" Mitchell said.

"I would love one."

Lanis shook her head and she and Elson walked back to the fire and sat back down.

Elson looked at the boots on his feet, then Lanis's "How did you get him to give you a pair of boots?"

Lanis shrugged. "He saw me looking at his."

"For real."

She laughed. "For real." They both settled into a comfortable silence. Even though night was upon them, the villagers were still running about, making sure everything was taken care of and in its right place.

Lanis leaned forward and rested her head in her hands. Until this moment, she hadn't realized how tired she was. She was pulled from her own thoughts when Elson spoke.

"Vic is smitten."

"I know," she said quietly.

"What are we going to do about Finley?"

Lanis raised up and accepted the cup he offered her. "Keep an eye on him. I think that at this point that's all we can do. I am not going to put up with him causing trouble."

"Me either and if he ever talks to you the way he did earlier, I will kill him myself."

She sipped her tea. She didn't doubt he would either. Lanis didn't want to think about Elson not being around. It would be weird not to see him at least once a day. But, when they got home, they would each have their own lives to lead. She shook her head to clear her thoughts. She sighed and drank the last of her tea. That's why you shouldn't get attached to anyone. Nine times out of ten, you would never see them again.

"I've never seen magic taught before." Elson swallowed the last of his tea and slipped his cup into his bag.

"Me either. It was pretty special to see when everything clicked for him. It's strange, though, I've always thought magic was so out of reach for people who are not magic bound. But, it seems, it's just as out of touch for those who are gifted with magic as well."

"It is. I've seen many of my fellow soldiers fall because they got overconfident or didn't listen to their instructor. It's the same thing."

"It is." She yawned.

"What are we going to do about Tegan?"

Lanis scrubbed her hands down her face. "I don't know. We should have killed her."

Elson laughed. "Maybe. We know she can't come with us, but she did look pretty occupied with that girl earlier. I wonder if they will allow her to stay here."

Lanis shrugged and stood. "All we can do is ask."

"Yes, and I believe it is probably time for us to get some sleep."

"What? I am not tired." Lanis yawned again.

"Sure."

"Whatever. Where exactly do we do that?" They hadn't been given a full tour when they arrived. She rubbed her arms, but she wasn't cold. The fire pits that were placed everywhere did an amazing job of keeping the place warm. Although, she had an idea that the fires weren't the only thing warming the village. "Excuse me," she said to a woman passing by them. "We were wondering where we could turn in for the night?"

"Oh dear." The woman looked horrified and for a moment, Lanis thought she had said something wrong. "We should have said something earlier. You must be tired. Of course you are. Look at you, barely able to keep your eyes open." She fussed around them. "Follow me." As they passed by Vic and Mitchell, Lanis explained where they were going and Vic gave her a thumb's up. They were walking through parts of the village they hadn't seen when they first arrived. Lanis didn't have a chance to take everything in because the woman leading them was walking so fast. The woman zigzagged around several medium size huts, then proceeded in the direction of a door-sized opening cut into the mountain. Their guide nodded at the two men standing on either side of the door and motioned for Lanis and Elson to follow her in.

Lanis squinted into the darkness and took a moment to allow her eyes to adjust before she attempted to follow the woman. She sucked in a breath and calmed her racing heart as they continued farther into the darkness. The damp tunnel reminded her of being buried alive and it wasn't a welcome feeling. Out of habit, she touched her whip, her feet picked up the pace, and she breathed a sigh of relief when they turned a corner and light started to flood into the tunnel. As the light illuminated the tunnel, hundreds of pictures carved into the walls made themselves known. Lanis ran her hand along the wall, her fingers brushing the exquisite lines of several warriors. Even though the hall was well lit, her unease continued to build, and from the firm set of Elson's jaw, so did his.

"Not much farther," their guide said, and turned yet another corner. Thirty feet ahead of them a large archway stood proud. Two massive warriors were carved into the stone on either side of the opening. It was amazing and quite a feat for the sculptors to accomplish. As soon as they walked through the archway, Lanis stopped short and her breath caught in her throat. She shouldn't be seeing what she was seeing this far inside the mountain. By her estimates, they had walked at least a half a mile inside the heart of the mountain. It was quite obvious to her now that either the people had sorcerers under their employ, or they moved here and found this spot by chance.

They had walked into a huge opening, in the middle of the mountain. A three-foot wide bridge surrounded the perimeter of the opening, a few feet above a large pool of water. Dozens of window size openings were scattered all over the walls of the inside of the cavern. In the center of the ceiling, light poured in. From where, Lanis didn't know, but it was spectacular. She walked to the edge of the bridge and looked down. The water was so clear, she could see the bottom, and it sparkled inside the cavern. She looked up when Elson patted her shoulder.

"It's beautiful, isn't it?" the woman said.

"Yes," Elson said.

Lanis pointed around them. "What keeps it from flooding?"

"The water in here has always stayed this height. As long as we've been here, it has never flooded. All excess water runs into an underground stream. Let's continue." They climbed a long narrow staircase onto another bridge, then walked through a door on their left and into a hallway. The woman stopped beside a closed door and opened it. "This will be your room for the night. Enjoy."

"Wait," Lanis said. "We were wondering if the young lady traveling with us, Tegan, could stay here with you. She only recently crossed our path and she cannot be allowed to come with us."

The woman frowned. "I will ask and see if she would like to, but we will not force anyone to stay. It has to be her choice."

"Of course." The woman nodded and walked out the doorway. Lanis pushed the door open and walked into the room. The room wasn't large but it was comfortable and the floor and walls were stone. It was as warm inside the room as it was in the village. A bed sat in the middle of the room. Only one bed. She walked up to the window and looked out. The water dripping from the ceiling instantly put her at ease. Anya would have loved it.

Elson walked up to her and leaned against the

window. "I'll sleep on the floor."

She had to give him credit; he was always a gentleman. She waved her hand in the air. "Don't be silly." She walked back to the bed. It was big enough for them both, but it would be tight. "But." She turned to him and tried to keep a straight face, but failed.

"Yes," he urged.

"Keep in mind this will be the first and only time you will share a bed with me. So," she grinned, "you better enjoy it and keep your hands to yourself."

He held his hands up, backed away from her, and placed his hands on his chest. "I live to serve." He bowed at the waist.

Lanis laughed. "I just bet you do."

※ ※ ※ ※

Isabel smiled and her footsteps quickened when she spied Abigail waiting for her outside the dining room doors. Considering they had to cancel the first few attempts at having dinner together, she didn't expect it happen, yet, here she was. "Abigail."

Abigail pushed away from the doors and stopped Isabel before she reached them. "Have you found out anything yet?"

Abigail always did get straight to the point. "No. I wish I had some news for you, but I don't. She seems to have vanished. I believe she is still within the town limits, but I don't have any proof of that. Just my gut feeling. I can't pinpoint where she is." The look of defeat on Abigail's face broke her heart. "I am sorry, Abigail, but I will continue to look for her. As long as I am here, I will not stop looking for her."

"Very well." She pointed to the doors. "Shall we?

I believe Sara is already inside waiting."

Isabel nodded, but she knew Sara wouldn't be happy about seeing them arrive together. "We shall." The guards moved from in front of the doors and opened them. Abigail moved aside and allowed Isabel to enter first. The look on Sara's face, if she had been magic inclined, would have incinerated her on the spot. Isabel held her head up and walked with purpose to the table, allowing Abigail to hold her chair out for her when she sat down opposite Sara. "Good evening, Sara."

"Lady Sara."

Not this again. Was she really going to be so trite? "What?"

Sara smiled sweetly and Abigail groaned. "You may address me as Lady Sara, Isabel."

Two could play this game. Isabel unfolded her napkin and laid it across her lap before locking eyes with Sara. "If we are going to stand on such formalities, then I suggest you address me as Queen Isabel, your Highness, your Majesty, or my Queen."

Abigail coughed and motioned to the waiter. "Well then, since that is out of the way, let's see what the cook has prepared for us tonight."

Isabel smiled at Abigail, then turned her attention back on Sara. She knew the tension between Abigail and Sara wasn't entirely because of her presence. They barely looked at each other all evening. Something was going on between the two of them and it was obvious it had started long before she arrived. Her presence only escalated matters. This kind of tension didn't grow overnight.

"I hope everyone enjoyed their dinner?" Abigail said, after their plates had been taken away.

"It was lovely," Isabel said. She had only agreed to dinner because she enjoyed spending time with Abigail. She could have done without all the dirty looks Sara kept throwing her way. Barnet still hadn't found out what Sara was hiding, but he assured her he was still looking. She was a patient woman; she could wait. She was well aware of Sara's alliance with Dimitri and the fact that she was probably behind the attacks on Jalen, she just didn't know why. What would Sara have to gain by taking her daughter out of the picture? It didn't make sense. Her fingers stilled on her wineglass and her gaze strayed to Sara when it dawned on her what Sara had to gain by Jalen's death. Sara was truly one sick woman if her suspicions were confirmed. With shaky fingers, she picked up her wine glass and downed it in one swallow. It was a good thing Jalen was nowhere to be found at the moment.

"You're going heavy on the wine tonight." Sara smirked.

Isabel straightened in her seat. "It would seem you would be too, seeing as how you still don't know where your daughter is," Isabel shot back. "If my daughter was missing, I would do everything within my power to find her."

Sara squeezed her glass so tight it looked like it would shatter. "Don't tell me how to deal with her disappearance."

Isabel knew she had pushed a button, but she was too caught up not to put an end to it. "Tell me something, *Lady* Sara. Do you get to travel much outside the estate? I hear the west is beautiful this time of year." She felt a deep satisfaction as she watched the different emotions cross Sara's face.

Sara turned sharply to Abigail. "Are you going to

allow her to talk to me that way?"

"Sara, it seems to me that you're both doing a good job at insulting and throwing riddles at each other all evening. It's been good entertainment."

Sara patted her hand. "Then I am glad Isabel joined us for dinner. Taken your mind off Jalen, has it?"

Abigail threw her hand off and gripped the table. "Of course it hasn't. I have people all over Hadmore looking for her. I will not stop until I find her and whoever put her in that cell."

Isabel snickered to herself. Sara had always underestimated Abigail's love for her children. They always came first and the crown second to her. Isabel respected that most about her.

"Abigail." Sara rolled her eyes. "We will find her and hopefully, when we find her, we will also find out who threw her in the dungeon."

Sara's words didn't convince Isabel and, by the look on Abigail's face, neither was she. She had conflicting emotions about telling Abigail what she knew about Sara. A smile graced her lips when the staff set a bowl in front of her and she realized what it was. Strawberry ice cream. Her favorite.

Sara eyed her bowl in disgust. "What is this?"

Isabel would enjoy this more than she should. "It's strawberry ice cream, my favorite. Abigail, I can't believe you remembered," she said sweetly.

"Figures," Sara grumbled. "So we're catering to her needs now."

Abigail sighed. "Isn't that what we do when we have guests?"

"No, Abigail, it isn't and you know it. You're the one that always says it's not their comfort, but yours that you care about."

"Look," Abigail said, "I don't know what is causing the tension between you two, but it needs to stop and stop now. I will not put up with this when the Festival starts. Do I make myself clear? If I need to make it an order, I will."

Isabel knew from the tone of her voice that she had pushed it too far. "I agree, Abby. I think we can at least be cordial for a bit. Don't you agree, Lady Sara?" Isabel didn't even realize she had used the nickname until she saw the look on Sara's face.

"Really, Abby," Sara growled. "You have no clue as to what is causing the tension. She," she said, pointing her spoon at Isabel, "should have never been invited and by you no less."

"Sara, I am not getting into this with you again. Sara, wait. Where are you going?"

"I am going upstairs so you two can spend some quality time together. When you get a clue, Abigail, come to bed."

"Well," Isabel said after Sara was gone. "That went well." She pulled Sara's bowl across the table to rest beside hers.

"Isabel, you aren't helping matters."

"That's Queen Isabel to you, remember."

"Isabel," Abigail said as a warning.

Isabel laid her spoon in her bowl. "It isn't my fault that she still thinks there is something between us. Good grief, Abby, it's been twenty-eight years."

It took a moment for Abigail to answer and when she did, Isabel had to strain to hear her. "Thirty-five."

"What?" Had she missed something?

Abigail leaned forward and rested her elbows on the table. Isabel couldn't decipher the look on her face, but her stomach dropped. "You said it's been twenty-eight years, but it's been thirty-five."

Isabel cringed inwardly, but kept her expression neutral. She had said twenty-eight. "It's been a long night and I'm getting old. A little slip of the tongue. It happens to everyone." Abigail frowned and didn't look convinced. Isabel didn't turn away from her gaze and she knew the moment Abigail realized what she meant by twenty-eight. Abigail stood and headed for the door.

Abigail gripped the handle, then turned back to Isabel. "I'm not so sure you're right, Isabel."

Isabel hadn't seen that look on her face since they were teenagers. "About what?" She asked, not sure she wanted the answer.

Abigail licked her lips and smiled softly. "About there not being something between us."

Isabel held her breath until Abigail walked out of the door and she lost sight of her. This was the worst outcome she could have thought of. She would have to think out her words carefully around Abigail from now on. She had grown comfortable when she should have never let her guard down. The fact that Abigail looked amazing tonight, in her black slacks and pale blue blouse, didn't help matters. Sara should be her main focus. No one could find out her secret. She ate the last of her ice cream and stood. The long walk to her room did nothing to quell the uneasiness that had settled within her and when she opened her door and entered, she knew her night was nowhere near to being over with. It seemed anyone thought they could break into her room. She knew who the woman was even before she turned and faced her. The woman standing in front of her was a carbon copy of Abigail, although a much younger version. She looked healthy and didn't seem to possess any signs of distress, but one could never tell. "Princess Jalen, what can I do for you tonight?"

Jalen fidgeted, then straightened, and clasped her hands behind her back. "I need your help and I wasn't sure where else to turn."

"Help with what?" She was pretty sure she knew the answer, but she had to hear it from Jalen's lips.

"I know who had me thrown in the dungeon." She ran her hands through her hair. "Who tried to kill me."

She knew Jalen was a commander in the Queen's Army, but at this very moment, she looked like a lost little girl. "So do I," she said sadly.

❧ ❧ ❧ ❧

Everyone woke before dawn to get an early start on the day. Lanis stretched, trying to motivate and wake herself up. She wasn't looking forward to the long day of travel, but she knew she needed to be at her best for everyone else's sake. It didn't help that every night for the past week, she woke suddenly, drenched in sweat. The dreams were so vivid, they seemed real, and they all ended the same way. With Anya dying in her arms. It was getting to the point that she was afraid to close her eyes at night. Afraid she wouldn't make it in time, again. She, usually, didn't put much stock in dreams, but when they replayed your worst nightmare over and over again, it was hard to ignore them. After the third night of waking up, Elson stood beside her with a glass of water, and every night since then. He never mentioned it the next morning and for that, she was grateful.

Pulling herself from her thoughts, she drank the last of her tea and put the empty cup in her bag. Her eyes landed on Tegan, who stood some ways back from them, warming her hands over an open fire. From the looks of it, someone had given her a large heavy coat and a new pair of boots. Lanis had to give her credit. Even after everything that had happened, she had decided to stay. It was the best outcome for everyone involved. She felt no obligation to Tegan, but she did hope she found what she needed in this place.

Elson touched her arm and she sat down next to him when Mitchell headed their way. Vic shifted on her seat and a smile pulled at her lips. Finley, on the other hand, looked miserable. Vic had mentioned that she had talked to him the night before, but Lanis had a feeling it wouldn't be the end of it. If it weren't, they would deal with it when the time came.

"Morning," Mitchell said, taking a seat beside Elson. He scratched his chin. "I wanted to inform everyone that the route you will take out of here is riddled with many dangers. Bandits lurk just on the other side."

"I can handle her safety," Finley spat.

Mitchell smiled. "I believe you can, friend." He stood and held his hand out to Vic, who readily took it. "May I have a word with you?"

"Of course."

Lanis kept her eyes on them, but couldn't make out anything that was being said. Vic handed him something and he slipped it into his pocket, nodded, and walked away. Vic had a skip to her step as she made her way back to them. After retrieving their horses, a guard led them to the border. "Once on the other side," the guard said, "you're on your own. Good luck."

The guard had led them to a dead end. At least that's what it looked like. But she knew all too well that looks could be deceiving. Tall stone walls surrounded them on three sides. "Vic, I assume all we have to do is walk through the wall."

"I believe so." She trotted up to the wall and stuck her fingers against the stone and they disappeared into it. "Looks like it."

"So," Elson said. "How does everyone want to play this? Anyone want to take a guess as to how many will be waiting on the other side for us?"

"Obviously, we won't know until we get on the other side," Finley said, breaking away from them and walking through the border. Vic pointed to the wall and followed him through.

Lanis shrugged. "I guess we follow them."

"It would seem so." The moment they crossed through the difference was immediate. The air was stifling and Lanis slipped her cloak off, folded it, and reached for her bag when she noticed the terrain behind them. Nothing behind them even indicated that they had just left a bustling village. The illusion was amazing. Lanis slipped her cloak in her bag and turned back around. Vic and Finley were ahead of them, talking. They were on a dirt road that was twenty feet wide, and a hundred foot tall stone walls rose on either side of them. It was at least a half a mile before they would cross into an open space.

Out of instinct, Lanis reached up and grabbed the arrow out of the air that was headed in her direction. Each of them slid from their horses at the same time that a dozen men stepped out of the shadows in front of them. She scanned the area and counted four archers positioned around them. They were well-organized bandits.

"I can take out the archers," Vic said. "You will have to handle everyone else."

Lanis and Elson nodded.

"I am not leaving her side," Finley said.

He was useless. Lanis couldn't wait to put him in his place and it wouldn't bother her if he died right now. The moment Vic threw her hands out, Lanis threw her knife and struck one of the men in the chest. She advanced, flicked her wrist, and pulled when her whip wrapped around another man's leg, sending him falling to the ground and his sword slipped from his grasp. Lanis ran to him, picked up the sword, and drove it into his neck.

Elson ran past her and easily cut two men down with one swing of his sword. Lanis fell to her knees, barely missing a blow by another man, crouched, jabbed the sword up, and into his stomach. She grabbed her knife and slashed out at the man running at her. He screamed and raised his sword to strike her. Without thinking, she grabbed the sword blade, holding back a scream when it cut into her palm. She stuck her knife into his throat and pulled it out quickly. The sword fell from his grasp and slipped from her hand, leaving a trail of blood in its wake.

She was bent over, gasping for breath when Elson walked up to her.

"Lanis?"

"I am fine."

"Here," he said and ripped a piece of his shirt and wrapped it around her hand. "We are going to have to find a healer for you. That's deep."

"I know." She glanced up and Finley was engaged with the last two men. "Finley."

Elson nodded. "I am on it." He easily dispatched one of the men and Finley took out the last one.

Lanis stood and was walking toward them when another man ran out of the shadows toward Elson. "Elson," she screamed. He turned and dropped his sword when the man drove his sword into his stomach. Elson grunted, eye wide, and fell to the ground. "No." Lanis ran to them, picked up Elson's sword, and swung it around, severing the man's head. She dropped the sword and fell to her knees beside him when Vic screamed at Finley to take out another one. Lanis pulled her knife, turned, and threw it at the man racing toward them. She was reaching for her bag when Vic stopped her.

"We have to get out of here." She waved her hand over Elson's wound. "It will bind it until we can get out of here. We will patch him up once we are clear of this area. Here," she said, reaching for Lanis's hand. She waved her hand over it. "It will only last for a short time. We must go."

"Lanis," Elson groaned. "Listen to her." His hand shook in her grasp. "Impressive with that sword."

"I can see the advantage of carrying one." Lanis grasped one side and Vic the other and they were able to haul him to his feet. "Easy does it." He leaned into her and let her lead him to her horse. "You're riding with me."

"Wow. First your bed and now your horse. A guy can get mixed signals you know." Lanis rolled her eyes and looked for Finley. He was already on his horse. "Finley, I could use a little help."

"Finley," Vic said, with a tone to her voice Lanis had never heard before. "Help her get him on her horse."

Lanis grabbed his shirt when he stomped up to them. "You hurt him and I will hurt you."

He threw her hand off. "Elson, can you put your foot in the stirrup?" Elson struggled so Lanis knelt and picked his boot up and placed it in it. "When I grab your waist, you're going to have to lift yourself up and I will help you over."

Elson gritted his teeth. "I'll give it my best shot."

"One, two, three." Finley lifted him up and Elson struggled with getting his leg over. Lanis moved to the other side and helped him. When he was settled, she tied his horse to hers, ran and got her knife, then climbed up behind Elson.

Not bothering to wait for the others, she kicked her horse in motion and easily went from a walk, to a trot, to a run. She slowed when Elson started to slip and they were a good few miles from where they were attacked. "Easy."

"That's easy for you to say." He was much paler than she liked and her hand was killing her. Blood had already seeped through the bandage and coated the reins she held firmly in her grasp. She touched his forehead. He was burning up. The only answer was that the blade of the sword was poisoned.

"Lanis," Vic said, touching Elson's forehead.

"We need to find somewhere to stop." She couldn't lose him, not like this.

"I saw a small shack a few hundred feet back," Finley said. Vic nodded and motioned for Lanis to go behind him. They rode for a few minutes when he took a sharp turn into the trees and entered a dirt pathway. At the end of the path was what looked to be an abandoned building that was grown up with weeds.

"Good. This will have to do. I am going to need

help getting him down."

"I'm on it," Finley said, coming up to them and grabbing Elson by the waist. He easily pulled him down beside him. Lanis dismounted just as an older woman threw open the door to the shack and walked out. When Vic noticed the woman, she stiffened.

"Vic, what is it?" Lanis adjusted her bag.

"I'll go. We will have to ask for permission." Vic walked up to the woman and spoke to her, motioning to them quite a few times. Vic bowed, then motioned for them to come forward. Lanis walked behind Finley, who was half-dragging Elson and half carrying him into the building. He laid Elson in front of the fire, then walked back out the door, saying he would tie the horses off. The woman took one look at Elson, walked to a small hutch in the corner of the room, pulled several small, glass bottles from the shelf, and walked back to them.

"I don't need your help," Lanis said and dropped down next to him.

"Lanis," Vic said quickly. "She is a medicine woman. Let her help you."

"That type of healing always comes with a price and I am not sure I am up to paying it right now." With shaking hands, she reached into her bag and pulled out the vial her grandmother had given her. Lanis opened the vial when Elson grabbed her hand.

"Don't. Not on me. I am not worth it. Use it on your hand."

She slapped his hand away. "Don't be stupid. Of course you are." He laughed and blood started to leak out of his mouth. Lanis pulled his shirt away and sucked in a breath. The wound was already starting to turn black.

  Shannon M. Harris

"Wait," the medicine woman said, kneeling next to them. "Let's use what I have first, then we'll put your ointment on it." Lanis hesitated, but when Vic slid down next to her and put her arm around her waist, she agreed. The woman dabbed the wound and wiped away the black substance and blood that was oozing out. Elson beat his hand against the floor, then passed out. "It's best this way." She opened one of the jars and poured a clear liquid on the wound and it started bubbling and smoking. Elson's body started to jerk from side to side and Lanis grabbed his shoulders and held him firmly to the floor.

"Lanis, move." Vic touched his shoulders and a white, shimmering strap appeared across his chest, securing him to the floor.

"Lanis," the woman said, wiping at the wound. "Put some of your salve on it, then we'll turn him and do the other side." Lanis dipped her fingers into the vile, pulled them out, and wiped the substance all over and inside the wound. "Young lady, loosen the restraints so we can turn him." Vic waved her hand and Lanis helped the woman turn him. She cut his shirt away and held back a sob. The wound looked even worse from this side. They went through the same routine, ending with Lanis putting the last of her salve on his wound. "Now we need to get him on the bed over there." She pointed to the far wall. "While you all accomplish that, I will make up a tea for him to drink to combat the poison and I will get what I need to take care of your hand." She stood and walked away from them and into another room.

Working together, they were able to get him up and onto the bed. The woman hollered from across the room. "Remove his armor and throw his shirt in the fire. We need to burn the poison and someone needs to clean his skin." Finley removed what little armor Elson wore and Lanis cut his shirt off. She bundled it up and threw it into the fire. As she turned to go back, the woman grabbed her hand. "He will be fine. Now, we need to take care of your hand. You're dripping blood all over my floor."

"Lanis," Vic said, wiping his chest off. "I've got this. Let her take care of you."

Lanis followed the woman to the table, sat down, and placed her hand palm up on the tabletop. She winced and bit her lip when the woman started unwrapping the bandage. She turned her head when the depth of the cut was revealed.

"Well, this is something." The medicine woman wiped the blood away and uncorked a vial filled with clear liquid. "The good thing for you was that the blade wasn't covered in poison. The bad thing is the cut is almost to the bone. Hold still, this is going to hurt."

Lanis hissed and steadied herself in the chair when the room started to spin. She lay her head back and concentrated on anything except the intense heat and pain that was exploding in her hand and racing up her arm. The woman continued to pour the liquid and wipe at the wound. Lanis opened her eyes and looked on the table when a coolness enveloped her hand. "I have sterilized the wound, and it is deeper than I originally thought it to be. I will pour medicine and a healing ointment into the cut, then stitch it up. After that, I will scrap what little salve is left in your vile and smear it across the wound. Hopefully that will be enough. It's all I can do."

"Just do it." Lanis turned her head and focused on a shelf against one wall of the shack. Books lined the shelves, but from this distance, she couldn't make out any titles. She sucked in a breath and rounded her neck when the needle pierced her skin. It was a comfort when Vic stepped up behind her and wrapped her arms around her. Lanis rested her head back against her chest and closed her eyes. She prayed to Nia that whatever the woman was doing and what little salve she had left would heal the wound enough for her to be able to function as normally as possible. Her eyes flew open when the pain dulled to a bearable limit.

"There was enough of your salve left to put a light coating over the top. I will wrap it and we'll go from there. No guarantees, I'm afraid."

"Thank you." Lanis stood after her hand was wrapped and walked to where Elson lay. She resigned herself to the fact that they would be spending the rest of the day and probably the night there when the first raindrops hit the tin roof. She stepped aside when the woman walked past her and instructed Finley to lift Elson enough for her to pour some of the liquid down his throat. Vic grabbed a rag and wiped his chest off when the liquid dripped from his mouth.

"Lay him back down." The woman eyed the ceiling when the rain pounded on the rooftop. "Looks like you won't be going anywhere for a while."

Lanis sat down next to the bed and watched him sleep. Another day wasted and she wasn't any closer to finding Anya. At this rate, they wouldn't make it in time. She buried her head in her hands. It was all too much. Elson, Anya, everything. After all this was over, she couldn't see herself ever leaving Anya's side again. She raised her head at the touch on her shoulder. The medicine woman handed her a cup of tea. Lanis arched an eyebrow when the scent reached her nose.

"I thought it would help you relax." The woman walked across the room and settled down at a desk set into the corner of the room. The room was larger on the inside than what the outside showed. Two doors sat across from the main table and a small fire burned in the fireplace that sat adjacent to the main door. Every spare inch of the room had shelves that were jam packed with stuff. A lot of stuff. She smiled at Vic when she sat down on the edge of the bed.

"You do know what she is, don't you?" Vic took a sip of her tea and grimaced.

"No. Am I supposed to?" Lanis savored the first sip of the Maldorna tea. The flavors danced on her tongue and instantly put her at ease.

"She is a wise medicine woman."

"Bit of a mouth full, don't you think?" She shut up when Vic glared at her.

"Nia's chosen and all those that go to her academy must, at some point, train with one. She will teach them invaluable information, associated with all aspects of healing, not just those based in magic. Each student must seek and find one on their own and they are not easily found. It is a miracle we ran into one."

"No, not a miracle. Just someone looking out for us."

Vic shrugged. "If you say so." She poured what was left of her tea into Lanis's cup.

Lanis laughed and held her cup up. "It's an acquired taste." She sat her cup down when Elson moaned and tried to set up. "Lay back down."

"Lanis," he croaked.

"Yes." She placed her hand on his chest and pushed him back down.

He looked from her hand to her face. "If you

wanted to get me naked all you had to do was ask." He laughed, then grabbed his chest. "Man, that hurts. Water."

"Here." She helped him to sit up. "I have something even better." She brought the cup close to his lips.

"Is that what I think it is?" She nodded and held it steady as he took a healthy sip. "Thank you."

She waved off his concern and held back the sob that threatened to take her over. "You would have done the same for me. Besides, I need you and you still have an Oath to fulfill. I am sure Nia has plenty more for you to do." He closed his eyes and fell back asleep. Lanis looked up when a shadow fell over her. "What can I do for you?" The woman wasn't as old as she had first thought. Probably late fifties.

"He will have to stay the night. I only have one spare bedroom and Vic and Finley will be sleeping in there."

"Don't worry. I am going to sleep in here with him."

"Very well." She cocked her head and didn't break eye contact. After a few moments, the woman seemed to have found what she was looking for because she turned and walked away. Lanis leaned back in her chair and raised her legs to the end of the bed.

᪥ ᪥ ᪥ ᪥

Dimitri eased to a slow, then a stop outside one of the Castle libraries when he heard a familiar voice. Queen Abigail. He grinned and was about to enter when he heard her voice: Sara. He didn't see any guards in the hallway or the adjoining rooms so he sidled up to the doorway and listened.

"Abigail, how many times do I have to tell you she doesn't belong here? You're blind if you can't see how she feels for you. She's in love with you," Sara spat.

"Maybe so, but I made a commitment to you long ago and I would never break our vows. Not for her or anyone. Isabel is only here for the Festival. I will not repeat myself again."

Dimitri grimaced when Sara laughed. "You are delusional and in some things, you always have been."

"Is that so?"

"Yes."

"Sara, you're walking a thin line. Do not cross over it."

"And what, my dear, are you going to do if I do?"

"Sara, you may be my wife, but you are not above the law."

Dimitri wished he could have seen Sara's face. She was losing it and hearing her now only proved that.

"Abigail, you can't be serious. You would never put me in the dungeon. Besides, I don't have an outfit to wear down there."

"You can't be serious!" Abigail shouted.

"Abigail, get your hand off me. I am not some common servant that you can touch me this way."

"No, you're not, but you are not above the law. I wouldn't have a problem throwing any law-breaker or traitor to the crown where they belong, especially when it comes to my children."

When Sara laughed, he wished he could have seen Abigail's face, but he stiffened at Sara's next words. "You are so clueless. You don't even realize you have a traitor in your midst."

"No, Sara, you're wrong. I have a lot more than that."

Dimitri didn't wait to hear the rest of the argument. He ran to his office, shut the door, and locked it behind him. His fingers fumbled with the keys and it took him several tries to unlock one of his desk drawers. He pulled out several papers, folded them, and put them inside the inner pocket of his robe. He whipped his head around when the door opened and Queen Abigail walked in, holding a set of keys in her hand, followed by several guards who took up position along two walls.

"Going somewhere?" Abigail smiled.

He didn't detect any malice or hidden meaning behind her words, but her body language spoke volumes. "I was just heading out early today, your Highness. I wanted to spend some extra time with my family."

She nodded and leaned against the doorframe. "Family is important. I would do anything for mine."

He gulped, but there wasn't anywhere to run, and he would be damned if he bowed down to her. "As would I, your Majesty."

"That's one of the reasons I have kept you around so long. You are deeply committed to your family. It is a refreshing change of pace compared to some people I have worked with who only cared about money and power. They spend so much time looking for those things that they lose track of what really matters: family." He knew he was trapped. "I want to know two things."

He took a step back, leaned against the wall, and pushed his hands into his pockets. "Okay."

"Did you have anything to do with Jalen being thrown in the dungeon and do you know where she is?"

He instantly relaxed at the questions. Maybe he would get out of this after all. "No on both accounts. I would have never thrown her or anyone into that foul prison. I would have just killed them. Honestly, my Queen. I don't know where she is."

"I believe you." She walked farther into the room and shut the door behind her. "I have one more question."

"Of course."

"How did Sara become involved with you?" Dimitri opened his mouth to answer when the room started to fill with smoke. All the guards grabbed their chests and started coughing. A few of them fell to the floor and Abigail covered her mouth and nose and turned her head to the side when a figure materialized beside him. Abigail uncovered her mouth when the smoke cleared. "I take it you know her?"

Dimitri was afraid to look and when he did, his heart started to race. Rose. He grabbed her hand when she lifted it toward Abigail. "Do not harm her." Even after all his resources, he still needed to find the remaining spheres and for that, he needed to get out of here alive. Rose didn't need to diminish her power by harming Abigail. He flinched when she grabbed his arm, threw something into the air, and chanted. One minute his feet were on solid ground, the next, it felt like he was flying. Rose whispered in his ear to brace himself, then the next moment the air was knocked from his lungs and he was struggling to breathe. At a touch on his arm, he opened his eyes, steadied his breathing, and realized he was back on solid ground. He accepted her outstretched hand, stood, and pulled her into a hug. "What have you done?" Her magical career was over. He couldn't begin to fathom what she had just given up to save him.

"I saved you like you had someone do for me." She winked. "We're even now."

The surroundings weren't familiar to him. "Where are we?"

"A small valley beyond Manight's borders. We will be safe here for a short time."

He loved her, but what she had given up for him already was far more than he could have ever expected. "You need to get out of here. I am afraid nowhere is safe for you anymore."

She shook her head. "Nowhere is safe for you either. I'm sticking with you." She held up her hand. "For now, you need me. Queen Abigail did get one thing right. Family first."

When did his little girl grow up? He didn't know whether he would see the rest of his family again, so he was grateful she was by his side. If it was the last thing he did, and it very well might be, he would make sure Sara paid dearly for her betrayal, but unlike Lanis, he didn't care how she died or who killed her. Sara was a dead woman and she probably didn't even know it.

Lanis's eyes flew open and she grabbed the chair arms as she became aware of her surroundings. Elson was still sound asleep and she lifted the bandage away from his chest to check the wound. The skin was pink and it had closed completely. Good. She unwrapped the bandage from around her hand, not sure what to expect. Her skin was a bit red, and the wound hadn't completely closed. She would have to keep an eye on it to make sure infection didn't set in. After rewrapping it, she turned and took in the rest of the room. A fire was burning in the fireplace and the medicine woman sat at the table, mixing what looked to be several different types of herbs together. Vic and Finley must still be asleep.

"Come have tea with me," the woman said.

Lanis settled into a chair at the table across from the woman. Most of the herbs scattered around the table she recognized, but several she had never seen before. Some, she knew, were very hard to come by. A few she wouldn't even risk collecting. For this woman to have collected them told her more than words ever could. It was a bit unnerving that she still didn't know the woman's name. The woman picked up and dropped a bunch of different herbs into two mugs, then poured hot water over them from the kettle that set on the corner of the table. Lanis hesitated, but accepted the cup the woman offered her. She raised the mug, blew on the tea, and took a small sip. She eyed the woman over the rim when the woman continued staring at her.

As soon as she set the cup on the table, she grabbed her chest and fell from the chair onto her knees. She gulped in deep breaths and clutched her throat, trying and failing to slow her racing heart. Blood pounded in her head. She fell sideways onto the floor, her vision unfocused, and took one last breath.

Her eyes shot open, she took a deep breath, and took stock of her body. Everything seemed to be in working order, but she couldn't make out where she was. With deliberate purpose, she rose onto her knees, then stood up. She grabbed her chest when sharp pains raced throughout her body. When her eyes finally adjusted, panic started to set in. Was she dead? Did a cup of tea really take her out? She wouldn't have written that as the ending to her story, but everybody's had to end sometime.

She spun in circles, but everything remained a wide-open space. As far as she could see there was nothing but white. She assumed she was standing on the ground, but nothing gave her that indication. There was no floor, ceiling, or walls. Nor were there any doors of any kind or any living beings. If this was Nia's idea of an afterlife, there wasn't much to it. Elson would tell her everything had an explanation, but the more she walked, the more everything stayed the same. In the future, she would learn to watch what she drank. She stopped walking. If she were dead, there wouldn't be a future.

She clutched at her chest again, then frowned. Surely, if this were the afterlife, you wouldn't be able to feel any type of pain. At least that's what Nia's teachings foretold. This had to be something else. But what? Meeting the Holy Ones was just a dream, yet they still gave her something to take with her. Maybe this was just a dream too. Her heart started racing, when off in the distance, a shadow appeared. She squinted, trying to make out what was coming at her and when the shadow took shape, she started running toward it. But the closer she got to Anya, the farther away she became. Were they both dead? Would this be their ending? To be so close, but not be able to touch each other. It would be a cruel twist of fate.

She stopped running, bent over and gasping for breath when more figures started to materialize on either side of Anya: Elson, Vic, and Finley. Were they all dead? Nothing made any sense. Did the medicine woman kill them all?

That thought completely vanished as other

figures took shape: Rose, Jalen, Mattea, and Merek. How could they be here? Lanis closed her eyes, then reopened them, but everyone was still there. They stood in a straight line and were far enough away that she couldn't reach them, but close enough that she could make out their features.

Without warning, she fell to her knees and grabbed her head when a loud, buzzing sound filled her mind. She screamed and pounded her fists in the air when the sound stopped. Panicking wouldn't help her. She had to stay calm and figure out whatever this was. If the woman had put something in her tea, she must have done it for a reason. She took several calming breaths. She could do this. She had to do this. When she stood up, all the figures were gone. She remained still when a sound reached her ears and continued to stand still even when the footsteps stopped behind her. She knew who it was even before she turned around.

The medicine woman stood with her hands behind her back. "All actions have consequences, not just yours."

Lanis groaned. She hated riddles. "What did you do to me? Why did you do it?"

"You will have tough decisions to make." She pointed behind Lanis. "Turn around."

Lanis was afraid to. Afraid to see whatever it was she wanted her to see, but she turned around anyway. Again, several figures were standing off in the distance: the Jester, Queen Abigail, Queen Isabel, Sara, and a woman she didn't recognize. The medicine woman walked past her toward the group, spoke to the stranger, then took her spot. The closer the strange woman got to her, the clearer her features became. It was Pash, the woman who traveled with the missionaries of Acker, and she was clearly pregnant. But what did that mean? Pash stood a few yards from her, got down on her hands and knees, and put her face to the floor.

Lanis stepped back when her body jerked, blurred, then started to morph. She watched in awe as a blank panther completely replaced the young woman's body. The cat stretched, sniffed the air, stood up, then walked toward her. Lanis was trying not to react, but the closer the panther got, the more her fear started to show itself. She stumbled back when the panther leaped at her and landed hard on the ground. She closed her eyes as the panther walked around her. When nothing happened, she opened her eyes and the cat's face was only a few inches from hers. The inky pools of black didn't scare her as much as she thought they would and when the panther licked her face, her tension vanished. The cat stretched a few times, then laid down beside her. Lanis looked up, but everyone was gone. She lay down beside the cat, wiped her cheek off, and closed her eyes. She flinched when something touched her hand and tried to open her eyes, but they felt like they were glued shut.

She grabbed her throat and sucked in several deep breaths, but they didn't want to come. The prayer of Nia lay on her lips, but the words died on her tongue. She shot up and her eyes flew open when someone squeezed her hand.

"Lanis," Vic said. "Look at me."

Lanis pushed her away and shook her head, but everything was still fuzzy.

"Lanis, look at me," Vic insisted. She pulled Lanis's face around and searched her eyes. "Are you okay? When I woke up, you were on the floor."

"I don't know." She shook her head. "Give me

a minute." She closed her eyes, savoring the fact that when each breath came, she felt a little more grounded to the here and now. "Help me up." She grabbed Vic's hand and stood up on shaky legs. She grasped the edge of the table and steadied herself.

"Are you really okay?" Elson asked. "We were worried." He licked his lips and ran his hands through his hair. "I was worried."

"I'm fine. How are you?"

"Better than you, I suppose."

"Yes." She nodded. Even though it was a dream, it felt so real. She wouldn't soon forget this nightmare. She rounded her shoulders and searched the room. Finley held the medicine woman's arm in a firm grip. She didn't look the least bit sorry about what had happened, but she didn't look boastful either. "What was the meaning of that?"

"Only you know the meaning. Dream visions don't always make sense at first, but in time, everything will be explained."

"Why me?" Why did it always have to be her?

"I sensed you needed guidance in dealing with future events. It never hurts to have knowledge to go along with a skill. Now, does it?"

Lanis couldn't argue her logic, but she didn't like being tricked either. It would have been a completely different story if she had been allowed to make the decision to enter into the dream vision herself. However, at this point, the damage had already been done. "Finley, you can let her go." Vic nodded and he released her and walked toward them. "I think we should leave."

"Sounds good to me," Elson said, guiding her toward the bed where they started gathering their belongings. "You sure you're okay? I got to tell you, you scared the life out of me."

"I am." She felt his forehead and it was cool to the touch. His coloring had also returned to normal. By unspoken agreement, they headed outside to wait for the others.

Elson slipped his hands in his pockets. "I'm kind of glad all of this weird stuff happens to you and not me. A stab wound I can deal with, but I don't know how I would handle things waging war on my mind."

"Trust me when I say, you would be able to handle it and to be fair, you almost couldn't handle the stabbing."

"I know, but to be fair." Elson grinned. "It was laced with poison."

"Are you still hurting a lot?"

"Not hurting really. But there is some pressure."

"When I was stabbed, Kaylynn told me it would take time even though most of my injuries were healed."

"How's your hand?"

"It's sore, but nothing I can do about that right now. In time, it will heal too."

"Fair enough." He pulled a tightly wrapped bundle out of his pocket. "The medicine woman gave me these herbs. She told me to add a few to my cup and add hot water. She told me if I drink it a couple of times a day it will help me to get my strength back." They both eyed the herbs, then each other. Lanis bit her lip, but kept her mouth shut. Elson slipped the bundle back into his pocket. "Let's hope she didn't give me the same thing she gave you."

"Well, if she did, let's hope you can understand what everything means."

He bumped her shoulder. "Want to talk about

it?"

She explained everything about her vision in detail, ending with the panther. "So, do you know what it means?"

They were quiet for several seconds when he shook his head. "No, I've got nothing. I'm sure it's important in some way, though."

"Hasn't everything been?" She slapped him on the shoulder, grateful he was all right. She knew she wouldn't be able to make the rest of the trip without him, especially with her hand the way it was.

They both swung their heads around when the door opened and Vic and Finley walked out, followed by the medicine woman. She held out a bundle, like the one she gave Elson, to Lanis. "I don't have to drink it, do I?" Without getting an answer, Lanis accepted the bundle and slipped it into her bag. She mounted her horse and took up the rear.

⁂

They traveled all day, only stopping when Elson needed a short rest. Even with all the stops they made, they were making good time. For once, it was an easy ride. Besides what had happened that morning, all had been quiet. Lanis knew it wouldn't last, but when it happened, it was a welcome change. By the time they stopped for camp later that night, everyone was ready for a good night's sleep.

After making camp, they sat around the fire, Lanis and Elson on one side and Vic on the other side. Finley, surprisingly, had taken first watch. Lanis frowned, but kept her mouth shut, when Elson lifted his cup to his lips and took a tentative sip of his tea. When nothing happened, she relaxed and tossed another stick onto the fire. "I propose before we reach Laramore's border we sell the horses."

"I agree." Elson pulled the map from his bag and Vic rounded the fire to sit next to them. He pointed out the village of Tanmore close to the border. "This is our best bet. It makes sense to sell them and go on foot to the border. The Jester said the cave we sought was just over the Laramore line."

"And we made pretty good time on foot last trip," Lanis said.

He rolled the map up and put it back in his bag. "We did."

Vic retook her seat and ran her hands through her hair. "I don't know if I should ask, but I was wondering if you both could tell me about Anya?"

"I have no problem telling you about my High Priestess; however," Elson said, "I wouldn't feel comfortable listening to Lanis talk about the woman she knows."

"Of course," Vic nodded and turned to Lanis.

Lanis couldn't believe it had taken her this long to ask about her and she had hoped she wouldn't have. The one thing that kept her going was focusing on anything besides Anya. "I don't mind. Elson, you can start."

He leaned back against the tree and kicked his legs out in front of him. "I can only tell you my impression of her. She is my High Priestess above everything else. I would gladly lay my life down for hers. Even if she hadn't earned it, which she has, she still deserves my respect. If for no other reason than because of who she is. I believe with my entire being in everything Nia stands for and I know High Priestess

Anya feels the same way. Love and compassion always fill her monthly sermons. When she speaks of Nia, you can't help but believe every word she says. Before I was chosen for my Oath, I had met her once before. I had just completed my initial training and she, personally, welcomed each new member. There were hundreds of us, but for those few minutes she spent with me, I knew her full attention was on me. It made all the difference in the world. She doesn't act better than any one person. She treats everyone with dignity, respect, and her position notwithstanding, she treats everyone as an equal. She is a true follower of Nia's ways and what we all strive to be."

"It doesn't bother you, now, to know that she wasn't born in Malora?" Vic asked.

Elson scratched his beard. "I think," he said, standing, "that Nia works in mysterious ways and that her ways are not our ways. She knows our lives and what our journey is even before we do and I trust her impeccably."

"Elson," Lanis said. "Trust me when I say you are definitely on the right track."

He squeezed her shoulder. "With that, ladies, I will leave you both to talk."

"He's a good man," Vic said when he walked away. She then stood up and joined Lanis.

"I was lucky to be paired with him. His faith has carried us quite a long way."

"So your views are different from his?"

"No. Everything he said is true about Nia; it just has taken us walking quite a road to figure it out."

"How do you see Anya? Do you see her the same way he does?"

"Yes and no. I get to see all that, but I also get to

see the side of her no one else does. I will not get into her role as High Priestess, but I will tell you about the woman I know."

"Sounds good."

Lanis took a sip of her tea before speaking. "I love her for who she is, including her being High Priestess. It can be tricky at times."

"Have you ever wanted to walk away?"

Lanis shook her head. "No. I could never walk away from her. She is the air I breathe and without her, I know I couldn't make it. She has a wicked sense of humor, loves music, dancing, and when she has time, cooking. Although, to be fair, cooking is a new skill for her. She loves easily, laughs without reservations, and fights for what she believes in. She would never do or say anything to harm the people of Malora. She weighs every decision she makes without bias and always gives it her full attention. I've seen her stay up all night contemplating how to handle certain situations. She was chosen as High Priestess and she accepts that with everything that she is."

"It doesn't bother you that you will always come second to her?"

Lanis rubbed her neck. "We've been together for three years and I wouldn't change a thing."

"Before Mom asked me to meet you, she explained the situation regarding Anya. I won't repeat it, because it is her story to tell, but I will say that it was hard for both of my parents to give her up. Mom said that it wasn't until I was born that she realized how hard it had been for my father to give up Anya. The person you just described fits my dad. He loved music." She swiped at her cheek.

"How long has he been gone?"

"A few years." She grew quiet. "His death hit us both hard. It was unexpected and unwelcome. We moped around until we both realized that he wouldn't want us living that way."

"If Anya is like him, we would have gotten along great. She's genuine."

"That's a hard trait to find in a person."

"Yes, it is."

The fire was starting to die down when Lanis threw a few more sticks on it and Vic spoke again. "You trust Elson?"

Lanis welcomed the change in subject. "I do. He earned my trust."

"Do you trust me?"

"Not fully, no, but I like you and in time, the trust will come." Lanis drank the last of her tea. "I don't trust Finley."

Vic laughed. "Fair enough." She set her cup down. "Thank you. You and Elson have painted a well-rounded, two-sided picture of her to me."

"You're welcome."

Vic stood up and dusted her black leggings off. "I am going to find the guys."

"Wait."

Vic sat back down. "Yes?"

"There has been something bothering me and it probably has a really simple explanation, but it still bugs me."

"Why do you look so nervous? Must be some question." Vic snickered.

Lanis bit her lip. "Jalen and her siblings. I know Jalen is Abigail's daughter, but the other two, are they also? I mean." Lanis laughed and turned away from Vic. "Abigail and Sara both can't be their biological mothers." She grinned and looked back at Vic, but her smile vanished at the frown on Vic's face. "Vic?" Vic held her hand up.

Vic took a deep breath. "There is only speculation." She ran her hands through her hair. "What I am about to tell you, you cannot tell anyone. Not even Anya."

She hated keeping things from Anya, but from the look on Vic's face, she would keep her mouth shut. "Okay."

"Okay." Vic sighed. "Yes, Abigail gave birth to Jalen and Sara gave birth to Maya and George, but they are both their biological mothers." Vic held her hand up when Lanis opened her mouth to speak. "Let me finish. The sorceress that created the desert and survived the green orbs also created something else. I, personally, think it was the reason why she was shunned, feared, and why, ultimately, the complete magic world and all of Adearian eventually turned on her. Some things, Lanis, should never be messed with. No matter how badly someone wants something. You see. The woman fell in love. Madly, deeply, in love with another woman. Which is fine. Nobody cares if two people of the same sex are in a relationship, but with everything, there are limits to such a relationship and certain things just can't be done."

"I know."

"Yes, well. The sorceress didn't know. They wanted a child, which is fine also, but the sorceress wanted a biological child of their own." Vic stopped talking when Lanis raised her hand.

"But, isn't anything possible with magic?"

Vic grinned. "The dead can be raised with magic, but that doesn't mean they should be."

"I understand."

"So, the sorceress did what she had always done. And let me stop here and say that she was the most powerful sorceress ever to walk Adearian. I don't know why, but she seemed to be blessed with all the Gods' powers and I think that also scared everyone in charge. But, back to the story. She found a way around the restrictions. When people found out that her girlfriend was pregnant, they were, of course happy and excited. That is until they found out how it had happened." Vic stood and paced, then sat back down. "With magic comes responsibility. There are limits to what we can accomplish, now, because of this sorceress. We sign a binding contract that we will never practice magic that could alter the human body, or, for two women, to create a new life. The people of the time were scared and rightly so. Here was a young sorceress who had attempted and succeeded with DNA splicing and created a new life. A life made between two women. Just imagine how that could have been seen back then. It, really, wasn't that long ago. Only a hundred and fifty years." She shook her head and grew quiet. "But can you also imagine their happiness shattering because of everyone else's fears."

Lanis had never heard about it before and for good reason. No one should be able to manipulate human DNA. But a part of her wanted it to be possible. She would love to be able to have a biological child with Anya. "So Anya and I could have a baby together?"

Vic smiled sadly at her. "No. Maybe then, but not now. And that brings me to Abigail and Sara. The only way they could have children together is if the sorceress passed her knowledge to someone who continued to use it and pass it along. Which is forbidden, but

Hadmore has a way of getting whatever they want. It has never been written that they are both the children's biological mothers, but to be fair, considering who they are, no one would have the nerve to ask. And before you ask, yes, I do believe that to be the case. The royal family has some sort of plan in place to make sure the heir is acceptable to the throne. I don't know how, but they do. And before Abigail, there has never been a ruler that was married to someone of the same sex. So, in this instance, they were able to make sure that all three kids have the same bloodline. I, personally, don't have an issue with being able to help two women have a baby, but I signed an Oath and I would never break it. But, Lanis, I am not saying that there isn't someone out there who would be willing to help you and Anya. It just can't be me."

"I understand."

"There are limits to what we can do, or at least there should be. We are not Gods and, to be fair, if it got out that this could be accomplished." She shrugged. "Not many people would be able to do it. Could you imagine the strain that would be put on the few people who could? Thousands of couples would want a child. Not just two women in a relationship, but couples of the opposite sex, who have attempted to have a baby, but it hasn't happened for them. The sorcerers wouldn't be able to keep up with demand and in turn, it would destroy their life. Magic takes a toll on the human body and it takes time to recover. It's simply not feasible."

"I completely understand. Couples would come from all corners of Adearian if such a thing were possible." Lanis and Vic sat in a comfortable silence until Lanis spoke. "Is Abigail really that powerful?"

Vic stood up. "Yes, she really is." She patted

Lanis on the shoulder and walked off.

This whole thing was unsettling. It would be a dream come true if she and Anya could have a baby together, but no one should be able to yield that kind of power. She shook her head. You learn something new every day.

She saw quite a lot of Anya in Vic. It was refreshing to have a reminder of her around. She hugged her knees to her chest. Deep down, she knew, she would find her, but she also knew that she couldn't allow her fear of what she might find when she got there cloud her emotions. She opened the flap of her bag and pulled out the Book of Damrek. She fingered the binding and flipped it over in her hands. The book couldn't have been more than fifty pages, maybe not even that many, she hadn't bothered to look. It was amazing how such a small book could wreak havoc on so many different lives. She turned to a random page and read.

Life's injustices are vast. Life's different turns are hard. Decisions rule the core of who we are. Make the right ones for your life. Draw upon yourself to guide your steps. Follow not those that request servitude from you. True Gods should never take all that you are and twist it for their own amusement and pleasure. Draw from the power within yourself. It lays dormant, waiting, and hoping to come alive within you. Listen and heed my words. I ask that you not give yourself up to false Gods, but live life as a testament to yourself. In the end, the only person you will have to answer to is you.

Lanis shut the book and slipped it back into her bag. The words rang true and she couldn't disagree with them, but it didn't set right with her agreeing with them either. The more she read, the more apparent it became how easily his words could sway someone. It wasn't a comforting thought. The book held so many mysteries and she still didn't know why it was given to her. It didn't make any sense. A lot didn't make sense.

She unwrapped the bandage on her hand and was satisfied to see that the skin was a healthy pink and the wound was finally starting to close. She made a fist, wincing, when pain shot up her arm. The only thing she could rely on now was time to heal it. After getting a new bandage, she rewrapped it, stood up, and glanced down at her bag. Elson was right, though: the book had to mean something to her. All she had to do was figure it out.

It was late afternoon and the roads were considerably more congested the closer they got to Laramore. Thankfully, most of the people on the road hadn't paid any attention to them and those that did quickly dismissed them and finished their own business. Conversation had been light between everyone, except Finley, who had been quiet all morning. Vic, on the other hand, continued to surprise Lanis. From her magic, to the concern that she felt for Anya. Lanis did a double take and came to a stop when Finley rode past the city sign.

Finley stopped and turned around. "Why did we stop?"

"We agreed to stop and sell the horses at the first available village," Elson said, and took the lead into the city. Lanis followed behind him. His stomach had healed nicely, but her hand was still causing her a bit of trouble. She was grateful that they happened upon a medicine woman, because if they hadn't, she feared, Elson wouldn't be riding in front of her now. She wouldn't have been able to save him. Then there was her dream vision. She still didn't know what that was about, but considering everything she had been through, it would probably come to pass.

The village was a lot bigger than she expected. The large buildings that lined the main road looked to be well kept and the road they were currently on was paved with stone. Elson stopped and asked a woman directions, then preceded to head toward the stable.

Once there, Lanis dismounted and was adjusting her bag when a tall and solidly built woman walked out of the building. Her short scabbard rested on her hip, against her black leather pants. Lanis couldn't read her and that bothered her.

"Excuse me," Vic said and walked up to her. "We wanted to inquire about selling our horses." The woman eyed Vic, then the horses.

She crossed her arms across her chest. "Most people that come to me want to buy horses and I have to be honest. No one ever wants to sell horses this nice." She walked up to Lanis's horse and ran her hand along his mane.

Finley pushed past Vic and walked up to the woman. "All we need to know is whether or not you want to buy them. If not, we can take them elsewhere."

Vic grabbed his arm and spun him around. "Do not talk to her that way."

"It's all right," the woman said, stepping away from the horses.

"No, it's not. Finley, you will not speak to anyone the way you just did to her." He was angry, but nodded, turned, and walked away. "I am sorry," Vic said to the woman.

"That's quite all right. I've heard worse." She shrugged.

Lanis held her hand out to the woman, who accepted it. "Would you be interested in buying them?"

The woman examined each horse before answering her. "I would."

After settling on a price, the woman directed them to the closest Inn. After being seated, everyone kept quiet while they ate.

"We may have a problem," Elson said. "I don't know if anyone's noticed, but as soon as we sat down a small group gathered outside."

"I noticed." Lanis picked up her cup and took a drink. Three men and four women had been standing across the street since they sat down, watching them.

"I noticed too," Finley said.

Vic gestured with her hand. "I can take care of them, but it would be a problem if the entire town decided to attack us."

Lanis understood that. Your gifts could only get you so far. After that, it was all luck. She sat back when the waitress cleared the table. "So," Lanis said. "Let's take a page out of Vic's book. What are we waiting for?" As soon as they walked out, Elson in the lead, the group took notice. It didn't take long for them to step forward. One of the men broke away from the group, walked up to them, and held a piece of paper in the air. Elson and Lanis exchanged glances. This was about the bounty.

"We will be taking you both in. Do not fight us. You will not win," the leader said. Vic laughed, swung her hand through the air, and all seven of them flew backward and landed on the ground. A couple of them looked frightened, but the others looked pissed. The leader stood up. "Do you really think magic will stop us?"

"No. I don't think so, I know so." Vic lifted her staff and pounded it on the ground. The group tried to move, but they couldn't. "Don't force my hand. You won't like the outcome." The leader nodded and Vic waved her hand. They jumped up, turned, and headed into the woods. Vic buffed her fingers on her shirt. "Piece of cake." Lanis grinned and noticed the stable master headed their way.

She looked both ways before speaking. "I'm not one to interfere, but you gave me a fair price on your horses," she said. "You should have killed them. They're nothing but trouble." She nodded and walked off. Lanis agreed with her and if it had been up to her and Elson, they never would have allowed them to walk away, but Vic had her moments.

"Let's get going," Elson said. They headed out of the village and entered onto a well-worn dirt path. Lanis would have much rather kept the horses, but the practical thing was to sell them. She reached into her bag for an apple, when her fingers brushed the bundle the wise medicine woman gave her. She pulled it out, unbundled it, and frowned. Nestled within the fabric was a combination of herbs, spices, and what looked like twigs.

"Let me see," Vic said and moved the contents around with her finger. "You don't know what it is?"

"No. Should I?"

"It's a protection spell."

"I don't understand." Why would the woman give it to her? "What's it supposed to do?" She rewrapped it and dropped it in her bag.

"Well," Vic said. "From the ancient text a…" Vic threw her hands up and Lanis crouched and uncurled her whip. Arrows rained down on top of the shield Vic had created around them. "Come out and fight us! Cowards." When more arrows continued to hit the shield, Lanis saw a change come over Vic's face. "I will not warn you again. I can and I will kill all of you." As dozens of arrows continued to fly at them, Vic took a deep breath and pushed her hands out. The arrows leaped from the ground and floated in the air. Vic waved her hand and they all flew back into the trees. There were dozens of screams, then bodies started falling out of the trees and landed on the ground. It was over in a matter of minutes.

Vic dropped one hand and lifted her staff with the other one. She mumbled a few words, then swept the staff in a circle. Lanis felt a warm sensation engulf her. Vic dropped her hands and turned toward them. "Let's go. I put a temporary shield around us, but it won't last long. I think it would be best if we stuck to the roadway." As Lanis eyed Vic, she couldn't help but feel like something had changed. Vic was the same, but her compassion only ran so deep and Lanis knew it had run out.

"Agreed," Elson said, taking up the rear. They headed out of the woods and stepped onto the dirt road. After only a few minutes, five people stepped onto the road in front of them. It was the people from the town.

"We told you we would get you," the leader spat.

Vic touched Lanis's arm. "I can see why you kill everyone."

"It does make things less complicated." Lanis eyed the people and knew they would put up a good fight. Her hand still hadn't healed and Elson wasn't a hundred percent either and she knew Finley would be useless. As she crouched and pulled her knife, a woman walked through the crowd and Vic tensed. The woman threw her hand out and a blue orb of fire raced toward Vic. Lanis rolled out of the way when Vic brushed it aside and it crashed into the closest tree, shattering it. She stood, uncurled her whip, and threw her knife. It embedded itself into one man's chest and she advanced. She jumped back, barely missing the blade of a sword as it swung at her stomach. She grabbed her whip in both hands, looped it over the woman's head, and kicked her in the stomach. Lanis dropped to her knees, pulled the woman's legs out from under her, grabbed her neck, and twisted.

Lanis rolled over, grabbed her knife, and stood up. Vic and the woman were still engaged and she ducked when something pink flew at her. She stood her ground when one of the women swung at her. She blocked her punch, grabbed her arm, and twisted it. She drew her elbow back and slammed it into the women's face. Lanis screamed when something sharp pierced her hand. She ripped the dagger out of her hand and drove it into the women's neck. Vic was still engaged, but by the looks of it, Elson had taken care of the others. Finley stood back from them and his clothes didn't have a speck of dirt or blood on them.

"Here," Elson said. He lifted her hand and wrapped several pieces of cloth around it.

"Thanks." The Rogue Vic was fighting winked, jumped in the air, and disappeared.

Vic wiped her hands on her pants. "For the record, I could have done that too. It takes more than that to impress me." Her smile quickly turned into a frown when she spotted Lanis's hand. "What happened?"

"Battle wound." Lanis grimaced and held her hand to her chest. "Someone will have to stitch it for me."

"Lanis, we can stitch it, but," she turned her hand over, "it went clean through and the last wound hasn't healed yet. It doesn't look good." Vic said, then she noticed Finley. "Did you even help them?"

"I stood by you. That's my job and I won't apologize for that."

"Here." Elson slipped her bag over her head, took the knife from her hand, and slipped it into her boot.

"Thanks. I should be fine for a while. Let's get farther down the road before we make camp, then someone can patch me up." Her hand was on fire, but they needed to get away from this area.

"If you're sure?" Vic slipped her hand through her arm and walked along beside her. "You sure you can wait?"

"No, but it will have to. I'm afraid the damage can't be undone."

"You'll be fine. I took a class that taught the basics of surviving in the wild. I am confident I can pick the right herbs to put on the wound. We'll make it."

Lanis hoped that was the case, but if her hand didn't heal, she knew she wouldn't be able to defend herself when she went for Anya. "Our luck sucks."

Elson handed her and Vic a piece of jerky. "I know, right? You think you're doing pretty well, then a Rogue steps out into the road."

"That's happened to us twice. Let's hope that's the only thing we have repeats of."

"I hear you."

Vic patted her arm and fell back to join Finley.

"Elson, what if we're too late?"

"Not possible."

He sounded so sure of himself, Lanis couldn't help but believe him. "You're amazing."

He laughed and pulled her to his side. "I know." She punched his side, but laughed along with him. At this point, it was better to laugh than cry. No use in dwelling on what was to come, until the time came. Every time the pain shot from her hand into her arm, she would take several slow, shallow breaths. First, she had to fix her hand up and make sure she stayed alive, then she could worry about Anya.

❧ ❧ ❧ ❧

Dimitri ran his hand through his hair and kicked the feed bucket out of the path as he made his way across the barn, to the small table Rose had set up for them to eat at, and sat down. It wasn't his ideal choice for a hideout, but Rose had been adamant that no one would look for them here. He couldn't fault her reasoning. The barn had already collapsed in several places and looked to have been deserted for several years. He couldn't wait for the day when all this was over and he was able to be who he was meant to be.

Out of everything, Rose was his rock. Since they left the Castle, she had been nothing but a support for him to lean on, but he knew that would change. He could see it in her eyes every time they talked. She was his daughter, after all, and he knew her far better than she knew herself. Magic was the one constant in her life, and now, for what she had done, if she was ever caught, she would be stripped of her bands and her abilities would be permanently disabled. They were both on the run and wanted by Queen Abigail. He would have loved to have been a fly on the wall when Abigail realized he had slipped through her fingers. He picked up his glass and took a sip of the clear liquid. The water wasn't his usual drink of choice, but for the remainder of their time away, he would need to keep a clear head. He rolled his neck and replayed everything that had happened thus far. So much had happened, but he couldn't let anything sway the end result.

Treg was supposed to stop by tomorrow evening with an update on Anya. He still wasn't sure what the Jester was up to, but he continued to keep a close eye on him. It would put a smile on his face to wipe the Jester's off for good. Treg had told him it would be possible to take the Jester out, but it would take more resources than what he had at the moment. At least he would have the satisfaction of getting rid of Lanis, Merek, and Anya. The only hiccup in his plans were the last two spheres. Everyone had their ideas about where they were, but nothing was concrete.

Thoughts of his family constantly bombarded his mind. At one time, he had loved them above everything else in his life, but when the opportunity came along with the spheres, it fueled something long buried deep inside him. Surely the Prophecy would reveal something of the spheres. Otherwise, what was the point of it all? He would have to disguise himself for the reading. Rose had tried to discourage him from going to the reading, but he wouldn't miss it for anything. He shut his notebook and looked up when Rose walked up to him. She looked so much like her mother, it took his breath away. He knew deep down, no matter what happened, he would never see his wife or his other two daughters again. "Rose." His smile vanished when she turned to him. It was time. "What's on your mind?"

Rose laid her bow, along with a dead squirrel, down on the table, then walked to a basin in the corner of the room, and splashed some water on her face. After drying her face and hands, she turned to him. "I have a lot of questions, but I will start with one." He nodded. "Who are you?" When he began to speak, she held her hand up to quiet him. "Do not lie to me. I want to know the truth about everything. After what I've done for you, I deserve at least that much. I don't want to hear that crap Treg told me back at the Ruins of Treko when I was traveling with Lanis and Elson. I want the truth."

Dimitri shifted in his seat and took a long, deep breath. He watched in awe as she flexed her fingers and tempered her magic. "It all started fifteen years ago when a man came to see me at the Castle. He gave me a sphere and a small black book." He paused when Rose sucked in a breath. "Before you ask, I don't know why he chose me. What I can tell you is when I held them in my hands, it felt right, like a missing part of the puzzle had been put back it its rightful place. The man informed me it would be my job to collect the remaining six spheres and bring them together inside Damrek's Cave. In the past fifteen years, I have found four of the remaining spheres. I have an idea where one is, but I don't have a clue where the last one is. In fact, I don't even know where the original Book of Damrek is." He couldn't decipher the look on her face; anger, hurt, sadness, or maybe it was disappointment.

Rose sat down opposite him. "You seem rather calm about all of this. Do you have any idea what you're messing with? Damrek's magic isn't something to be toyed with. There is a reason it's forbidden to practice it. You're not magic inclined." She shook her head. "What exactly do you think will happen when the spheres are brought together?"

He shrugged. "I honestly don't know what will happen, and for the record, Damrek wasn't magic inclined either and look what he accomplished."

She rolled her eyes and leaned back in her seat. "Yes, let's look at what he accomplished. He wiped out entire villages and killed tens of thousands of people. And we can't forget he created his own race of people. There is no telling what he destroyed in the process. Even today, no one truly knows the true extent of what occurred on that fateful day. There are still so many unanswered questions and here you are, stirring the pot."

Dimitri ran his hands through his hair. "I know all of that, but I am confident I will be able to handle whatever happens. First, though, we have to find the cave and Damrek's original book." He needed her help for this, but he would never ask her for it; he would wait for her to volunteer it.

"So, even though Damrek couldn't handle his magic, you think you can." She lay her head back and looked at the ceiling beams. After a few minutes passed, she raised up in her seat and looked at him. "You betrayed Queen Abigail and the crown for this. That's not even taking into account our family."

"As did you," he said quietly. She had to have realized by now that she was wanted to.

Rose stood. "I know. Mom will be worried. By now, the Queen's Army would have already paid her a visit."

It broke his heart knowing what his family was

likely going through, but it wasn't enough to stop him from continuing with his plan. He stood and drew Rose back against him. A weight lifted off his shoulders when she didn't resist, but leaned farther back into his embrace. "I know, but right now there isn't anything we can do about that. When the time comes, we will both go home to her and to your sisters." Maybe, if she believed the lie, so would he. "You have always been the strongest of all of them. I love all of you the same, but you've done more than your mother or I ever dreamed of. You are the only magic inclined in both of our families."

Rose broke away from him and leaned back against the wall. "Isn't that odd?"

"Not really. It happens when Shara wishes it to. What?" He asked when a puzzled look crossed her face.

"You speak of Shara as if you still believe in her."

"That's because I do, but I also know that magic is what the future holds and not just those born with it. I believe Shara would understand and maybe even accept that. Shouldn't everyone who is interested in magic be allowed to practice it?"

Rose shook her head. "No, they shouldn't. That would be far too dangerous and you've gone way off track. I know I'm not as powerful as Treg, but if I am to help you and if you want that help, I have to know more. I love you, but I won't risk my life for a lost cause. I know you have five spheres. Is there anything else I should know?"

"I don't know how much you know about the situation involving Lanis."

"Not much. She was pretty tight lipped. She only discussed matters that pertained to the journey."

He nodded. "It was rumored that deep inside

Malora, inside the Central Temple, a sphere was buried. I needed a way to get in. Lanis was my opportunity. I hired a Rogue and he took over Priestess Tion's body. She was the woman escorting Lanis to Malora. I needed Lanis to get in, but that plan went horribly wrong. Suffice to say, I had to come up with a new plan."

"How did you know Lanis would be traveling to Malora?"

He debated how much to tell her, but she was his daughter. She may not go along with him, or even believe in his cause, but he knew she would never betray him. "I have an ally inside Malora. He wasn't hard to turn to my side. He wanted something, and in exchange for his help, I agreed to help him get it."

Rose snapped her fingers. "That simple?"

"Yes. I have people everywhere." He brushed his fingers down his beard. "That brings me to one last thing. I don't know what you know about High Priestess Anya or that she's missing, but that was also my doing. It wasn't my intention to kidnap her, but in order to get to her Protector, I had to. I have her trapped in an enchanted cell in Laramore." He walked back to the table. "It has recently come to my attention that Lanis is also her Protector and I know for a fact that she is headed to Laramore." It brought him a bit of comfort when shock spread across Rose's face. "A couple of things are going to happen when she arrives in Laramore. Knowing what type of person she is, I know she will kill my ally from Malora for betraying Anya. After she does, Treg will capture her. Only then will I be able to question her about being a Protector."

"Do you really think it's going to be that easy to capture her?"

"Love makes people do foolish things."

Rose sat down across from him and leaned forward on the table. "It's a lot to take in."

"I can appreciate that." He clasped his hands together on top of the table. "Something has been bothering me about Lanis."

"What?"

The look on her face gave him pause, but he needed to know. "Lanis withstood a green orb and I can't figure out how she did it. It is said that only one other person has ever withstood one. Do you know who that was?" She was quiet so long, he thought he had gone too far, then she told him what he wanted to hear.

"All accounts of her have been erased from the history books. She withstood not one, but three green orbs some hundred and fifty years ago. She accomplished magic beyond what anyone, even Damrek, could comprehend. Those in positions of power considered her actions a betrayal and they punished her for it. Her name was Asher and she has accomplished what some of us can only dream about."

Asher. He would send someone to gather all the information they could on her. The name didn't ring any bells with him. And to withstand three orbs was simply unheard of. "How did she withstand the orbs?" When Rose grinned, his pulse quickened.

Rose grasped his hands in hers. "It is rumored the reason she withstood the orbs is because she held a sphere somewhere on her body."

Dimitri squeezed her hands and matched her grin. Lanis had one of the last two spheres. It was the only reasonable explanation to how she withstood the orb and she was on her way to Anya. If he let things play out as they should, within the next couple of weeks, he would be holding the sphere in his hand. Circumstances were certainly looking up. "It's a good thing she is traveling to Laramore then, isn't it? However, the Jester did seem concerned that Victoria was traveling with her. Do you know anything about her?"

Rose slipped her hands from his and stood. "Princess Victoria of Candor?" He nodded. "Oh boy. You do realize that she is a very focused sorceress for her age, don't you? Victoria is a One Sorceress. They train different in Candor then we do here. I am not sure any Rogue would be able to defeat her if she is zeroed in on her objective. If she is traveling with Lanis, then Lanis has a powerful ally with her. Your men better be prepared." She held her hand up to ward off his question. "Do not underestimate Victoria. I am sure she would not hesitate to kill, if that's what it came down to. If she is traveling with Lanis, she has a good reason for doing so."

He waved off her concerns. At this point, nothing could damper his enthusiasm. "My men are prepared. Don't worry about that."

"What now?"

"Now, nothing. We wait. The time will come when we need to act and I know you don't agree, but I must be in Malora when the Prophecy is read."

"I understand now. I will make sure you get there safely."

"Thank you." It was a comfort having her here with him. He just couldn't let her distract him from his task. He loved her, but what was happening was far bigger than either one of them. Her life meant so much to him, but he wouldn't risk his to save hers and he was sure she knew that.

"Queen Isabel," Harrison said and sat at a vacant seat in front of the fireplace. "You wouldn't believe what some of these people would divulge to a total stranger. Most information wasn't pertinent to our case, but there was one servant who had a lot to say." He grinned.

Harrison had always been loyal to her and she trusted him almost completely. "What did this person have to say?"

"It seems this woman has taken a liking to one of Lady Sara's personal guards. After a night of drinking, the guard revealed to her that he had accompanied Sara on many different outings outside of the estate." He leaned forward in his chair. "It seems that they would disappear inside of a tree, only to reappear in a different part of Adearian altogether."

"Is that so?"

He laughed. "My Queen, it is."

Isabel knew exactly what he was talking about. It wasn't well known, but hundreds of years ago, a group of magic bound individuals thought it would be fun to create passageways between different parts of Adearian. The governing magic body didn't take well to the idea and, supposedly, all the passageways were destroyed. Isabel never believed that to be true. They did have their advantages. She had created several in Candor to make it easier to travel. It beat travelling by carriage for weeks when all you had to do was walk through a channel.

"My Queen, the Castle is also awash with rumors about Councilman Ramus's disappearance."

"It is quite perplexing how so much magic can be going on inside the Castle, isn't it?" They both turned at the knock on the door. Harrison held his hand up, stood, and answered the door. He bowed when Queen Abigail walked in. Isabel nodded at him and he left. "Abigail, what can I do for you at this hour?" By the look on her face, what she had to say wasn't good news.

"Do you mind if I sit?"

"Of course not." She would wait for Abigail to start this conversation. It didn't take long.

"How long have you known Sara was involved in everything that has been going on?"

Isabel leaned forward on her desk and contemplated her words. The last thing she wanted to do was alienate Abigail. "I've known for about a week and before you ask, I didn't feel it was my place to tell you. We may have a past, but that was a long time ago, and I didn't know if you would believe me."

Abigail scooted to the edge of her chair. "Not your place. I trusted you enough to give you access to my Mages and the shields that protect my country. Of course I would have believed you."

"She's your wife and the mother of your children."

Abigail stood and leaned against the wall beside the fireplace. "She had Jalen thrown in the dungeon. She almost died."

"I know." Isabel's heart was breaking to see Abigail look so defeated.

"Did you lie to me? Did you know where Jalen was the whole time?"

"No, I didn't know where she was. I did, however, know who rescued her. I didn't feel that information would be prevalent considering I didn't know where she was."

"I should tell you that a short time ago Sara along with Norris and Sadie were arrested."

Isabel stood. "Abigail, I am so sorry. I can't imagine what you're going through."

"I still can't wrap my head around the fact that she did it. Jalen is our daughter. How could a mother do that?"

"I know I couldn't."

They were both quiet until Abigail started to chuckle. "If you know any reliable and loyal Mages, I am down two." Abigail sat back down and crossed her legs.

"Can I ask about Councilman Ramus?"

"Yes, Dimitri. His daughter, Rose, helped him escape."

"I wouldn't think she would be capable of that type of magic."

Abigail shrugged. "Defeat can be a powerful motivator." Abigail bit her lip. "Do you know what he is after?"

"I know what and who he's after. He is confirmed to be a member of the Holders of the Spheres and is looking for all seven spheres."

"Are you serious? I knew there was something off about him, but I would have never believed he would forgo his faith. Even if he did the impossible and found the seven spheres, he would have to find Damrek's Cave."

"He has five spheres."

"Five?"

"Yes. Your Councilman has been very determined."

Abigail waved off her statement. "I am sure he won't find the other two. What are the odds of that happening?" Isabel wouldn't push the issue, but

Abigail was holding something back. She remained seated when Abigail walked to the door. When Abigail wanted something, she was always quick and to the point. She grabbed the handle, then turned back to Isabel. "Do you ever wonder what could have been?"

This was a slippery slope and one that wouldn't end well, but she had to be honest with herself and Abigail. "All the time, Abby. All the time," she said quietly. Abigail turned and walked out. Isabel rested her head back against the chair and closed her eyes. In a few days, the Prophecy would be read. Surely, Vic wasn't messing up as badly as she was.

⁂

Dimitri nodded at Rose as she kicked her mount, sending him into a trot. Morning had come all too soon after his meeting with Treg and his guards. Treg had assured him everything was in order. He hoped that to be the case. His guards, on the other hand, didn't have anything new to tell him. After this mess was dealt with, he would find new guards, more capable of what he asked of them. That morning, he had shaved his beard after Rose insisted that he needed to change his appearance. When he mentioned the same to her, she only shrugged and said he was more recognizable than she was. She wore her hood pulled up and compared to the clothes she usually had on, the ones she wore now were quite dull. She would be forgettable as long as no one saw her hair. He kicked his steed and slowed when he was beside her.

"Do you have a place in mind?" Rose asked.

He bit his lip. "Yes, since we are early, I have set up a meeting with the Jester. I believe our best bet would be to enter into the town limits and from there, you can lead the way."

"Very well."

They rode in silence until they reached an outpost into the city. Without missing a beat, Dimitri rode up to them and past them. Rose followed behind him. It wasn't until they were a good distance into the city that he let out the breath he was holding. "See, I told you it wouldn't be an issue getting in."

She cocked her head. "Maybe because the guy at the outpost is working for you."

She had always been observant. He laughed. "He does."

"Figures."

"Let's stop and tie our horses up here. Someone will come and fetch them. We should walk the rest of the way."

"Okay." She dismounted and tied her horse off. "By now, the city should be packed with people."

"That is my hope. It will make it much easier to get around." She had grown into a fine young woman and he hoped she didn't resent him for this later on. Once they were free, he would make sure she had the life she deserved. He followed close behind her as she weaved in and out of numerous alleyways. He didn't anticipate the Jester doing anything he asked. He would have to find someone else that could complete the job. It seemed some things were even out of reach of a Rogue. When she stopped, he knocked on the door twice, and it was immediately opened. The Jester stood back and waved them both in. Dimitri stiffened when his eyes landed on High Priest Lantor, who sat in the corner of the room.

Dimitri turned to the Jester. "What's he doing

here? This was supposed to be between us." He hated surprises.

The Jester cocked his head and glared at Rose. "It seems to me that we are even. She shouldn't be here either." He smiled. "Why don't you both sit so we can get started?" He gestured to the two empty chairs in the room.

Rose dropped her hood and reached for Dimitri's arm. "We'll stand."

The Jester clapped his hands. "Magic isn't allowed here."

"I just bet it isn't," she said. "We'll stand."

He nodded in her direction. "Very well."

Lantor stood. "Dimitri, your daughter is lovely."

"Lantor, I am warning you. Do not go near my family." He would be glad to wipe that smirk off of his face.

Lantor held his hands up. "Now, now. We have an agreement. I stand by my word."

Dimitri shook his head. How were these two men involved? It didn't make any sense. Sure, Lantor could have hired him, but he knew it was something else. Lantor wanted the spheres and the Jester had plenty of opportunities to steal them, but he hadn't. The Jester, of course, had his own agenda, but something was off about them. It didn't seem likely that the only thing Lantor was after were the spheres. Time would tell. That he had plenty of. "Have you had any success with anything I've asked of you?"

The Jester sat in the seat Lantor had vacated. "I told you it wouldn't be easy to take Princess Victoria out and, what can I say, Lanis is Lanis." He sighed. "Besides, they should be nearing Anya by now. Surely, Treg is capable of handling them. Otherwise, he wouldn't be in your employment. Now, would he?"

"I think," Rose said, "that you need to watch the way you talk to him. If it wasn't for people like him, you wouldn't have a job." She sneered.

The Jester cocked his head from side to side. "I will concede that point." He smiled. "Dimitri, I do believe I have information that will come in handy for you."

"What will it cost me?"

"For you, nothing. I just thought you would want to know that two of Queen Abigail's Mages, Sadie and Norris, were arrested. Seems our Queen is cleaning house."

Dimitri couldn't believe his luck when Norris came to him with a proposition. He was a capable sorcerer, but very egotistical. All in all, the arrangement worked out quite well. Sadie, on the other hand, was a complete surprise. She didn't work for him. "It is a shame. They are both quite accomplished."

Lantor nodded. "Shame indeed. If you can't trust your own people, who can you trust?"

"I also find it my obligation to tell you Lady Sara was also arrested," the Jester said.

Dimitri knew it was only a matter of time before she done herself in and Abigail had to take action. Abigail really was cleaning house. "That's a shame."

"And I must say," the Jester said, tapping his finger on his chin. "That your disappearance is also causing quite the stir. Tell me, Rose. How did you do it?"

"I don't owe you any explanation," she said.

"No, I guess you don't," the Jester said. He turned to Dimitri, "Do you know how she did it?"

Dimitri wasn't sure what the Jester was getting at,

but he knew Rose was capable of what she did. "If that's all, then we will be going. Anything else, gentlemen?"

Lantor grasped his arm. "Be careful. I wouldn't want anything to happen to you or your spheres. Or your family," he added as an afterthought.

Dimitri flung his arm off and followed Rose out the door.

"You're not worried," she said.

He shrugged. "What's there to be worried about? I am confident we won't be found inside city limits and I am confident that Lantor is all talk. Besides, I do have you." He pulled her close to his side.

"Yes, you do. I only wish we could see Mom. At least one last time."

"Rose," he said, touching her arm. "We will see them again. I promise you."

"I will hold you to that."

"You can count on it." It didn't take them long to reach the edge of the marketplace. They heard the shouts of the people long before they actually saw them. Dimitri saw where Rose's gaze was and offered to buy her an apple turnover.

"No." She frowned. "I'm not really hungry."

"Very well. Let's head that way." He pointed to a small building off to their right, but before he could take a step forward, he was grabbed from behind and pulled backward. He struggled to free himself, but the man behind him was a lot stronger than he was. The last thing he saw before a bag was thrown over his head was Rose being thrown to the ground and cuffed.

❧❧❧❧❧

It had been an easy morning of travel and they

easily made it to Laramore's border and crossed over it without a problem. Their borders, unlike Hadmore's, weren't guarded. They continued to stay adjacent to the tree line, but they followed along the water's edge. Lanis had never been to this part of the country and she wasn't sure how long it would take them to reach their destination. The landscape was both beautiful and dangerous. It had been two days since her hand injury, and even though Vic had patched it up nicely, it still throbbed all the time and she still couldn't make a fist. The element of surprise would be the only thing on their side or at least, she hoped it was.

Elson had climbed up a tree that morning and had spied the cave system. It was a cluster of caves set back from the hillside. From where they had started that morning, it looked like an impossible task to reach it, but the terrain was flat and an easy walk. They were almost there. They had passed several people already and would have to be vigilant. No one paid them any attention, but she was sure that wouldn't always be the case. They were dealing with a completely different world now. There was a reason no one ever traveled to Laramore for leisure.

"Lanis," Elson said. "I think we should climb up this small embankment here. That way we can scope out the area and get an idea how we can reach the caves."

She accepted the water he offered and nodded. It was a good plan, but Elson would be disappointed. She would be the only one going to rescue Anya. She wouldn't risk anyone else's life. "I agree. I'll go first." She hated climbing, but it wasn't that far, and she'd handled worse. As soon as her head popped up over the embankment, she slid on her belly and lay atop the small hill. Elson crawled up beside her, followed by Vic and Finley.

"I wasn't expecting that. I couldn't see them when I climbed up earlier," Elson said, glancing at her.

"Who are they?" Vic asked.

"The Black Brigade." Now Lanis really felt defeated. How in the world would she get past them? Vic couldn't come with her. The front entrance of the caves and the surrounding area were littered with members of the Black Brigade and dozens of tents. "Let's climb back down and come up with a plan." Once everyone was back on the ground, Vic spoke.

"I think it would be best if Finley and I made our way as close to the caves as possible and wait for you. When you get back, I will need all my power to get us back to Manight. My power is best used for when you get her out."

"You are better off here," Elson said. "Lanis and I will be fine. Once we…Lanis, what is it?"

"I'm going in by myself."

He shook his head. "No, you're not. We've been through too much."

"I need you outside of the cave, for when I bring her out. It's going to be hard enough for me to find a way in and I have my blending to depend on. You don't have that to fall back on."

"As long as I draw breath…"

Lanis stiffened and gripped her whip. Elson, Vic, and Finley were all frozen in place. The last time that happened, it was the Jester's doing. She stepped back when he stepped out of the tree line in front of her.

"Lanis, Lanis, Lanis, what have you gotten yourself into?" he said, walking up to her.

"No games this time?" she asked. He looked tired.

"Not this time, no. I do have something for you, though."

"Can you help me get in?"

"Not in the way you're thinking." He pulled his shirt up, slipped the dagger out of its scabbard, and handed it to her hilt first.

Lanis accepted it and turned it over in her hands. It was made of the finest woods and had gem stones embedded within its handle. "What's this for?"

"That, my dear, is your ticket in. I don't know how long the ruse will work, but it will get you in the main door. From there, it will be up to you. You are holding in your hand a very rare dagger that one only acquires by becoming a guard in the Holders of the Spheres. Every guard that has one would rather die than give up theirs. They are not easily attained and they are never given to anyone that hasn't earned them."

She pointed behind her. "The Black Brigade has seen my face."

He shrugged. "That's your problem. Keep your hood up and keep your mouth shut. Keep your eyes only on the door. Do not let your gaze wander."

This was too easy. He was up to something. "What will I owe you?"

He looked pained. "I want you to rescue High Priestess Anya." He turned to walk away, but Lanis stopped him.

"I have to do this by myself. Can you keep them frozen until I get away?"

"I can."

"Thank you."

He laughed. "Don't thank me. Take the main road and take my horse."

Lanis took one last look at Elson, hoping, praying,

he would forgive her. She mounted the horse and turned it toward her destination.

With every step that drew her closer to Anya, her anxiety rose. As soon as she hit the main road, the guards took notice of her, but they didn't stop her progress. She took the Jester's advice and kept her eyes on the door to the cave. She wouldn't lie to herself; she was terrified and she had to force her hands not to shake on the reins. The only thing keeping her going was knowing that after this was said and done she would have Anya back. She gulped but kept her calm when a guard stepped away from a larger group and stopped her a quarter of a mile away from the caves. She stilled her features and glanced down at him.

"You have to turn around," he said.

"Dimitri sent me."

"I can't take your word for that," he spat. She pulled her cloak back and showed him her dagger. He took a step back and seemed to consider his options. He nodded and let her pass. With each hoofbeat, her heart pounded. She kept her eyes straight ahead, but could feel every guard's eyes on her. The road to the caves wasn't long, but it was the longest ride of her life. She pulled up to the entrance and dismounted.

The guard at the door held his hand out and she showed him her dagger. "Dimitri sent me to keep an extra eye on his prisoner, High Priestess Anya." He nodded at the guard on the other side.

"This way. I will escort you in," he said, and motioned her in. "It's down this hallway." It still felt like a trap. They walked down a long hallway and turned right. He stopped at a shut door, knocked three times, then opened it to allow her in. She stopped dead in her tracks, but masked her features when she realized who was in the room. Merek stood up and walked up to them.

"Who are you?" he spat.

He obviously didn't recognize her from her time in Malora. She would enjoy killing him. "Dimitri sent me to keep an extra eye on Anya."

"Is that right?" He leaned against the desk and crossed his arms over his chest. He looked her up and down and shook his head. "Follow me." Instead of going back the way they had come, they continued straight. The farther they walked, the stronger the stench became. "It won't be long now. She's fading fast." He laughed. Lanis clinched her fists and resisted the urge to kill him. At a crossroads in the hall, they turned left and she noticed a man at the end of the hall. When they walked up to him, he turned around, and she sucked in a breath when she realized whom it was. The Rogue that held Rose captive. That's why he didn't hurt them. He was working for Dimitri the entire time. When he looked at them, Lanis dropped her hood.

"Welcome, Protector," Treg said.

❧❧❧❧

Isabel nodded at the guard and thanked him when he directed her to the cell Sara was in. She shouldn't be here, but she couldn't resist the urge to confront her. Her feet felt heavy, but she pushed on, and stopped in front of Sara's cell. She was standing in the corner of the cell and sneered when she spotted Isabel.

"What do you want? Come to gloat, did you? I will get out of this, of that I am sure."

"Really, because Abigail is not happy. I don't see you getting away with anything. However, that's not why I am here. Tell me, Sara, everything that you did, was it worth it? Throwing your life away and trying to have your oldest daughter killed."

Sara laughed and gripped the bars of her cell. "Isabel, we both know that Jalen isn't my daughter. Give me a break. Maya deserves to be Queen, not Jalen."

"It's funny, because Abigail told me that Jalen had mentioned to her before she left for the Brown Pass that she felt Maya would be better suited to be Queen than her. Over the years, that never dawned on you. Obviously, Abigail was teaching Maya for a reason."

Sara's smile vanished. "You're lying."

"No, I'm not. Jalen doesn't want to be Queen and Abigail was respecting her wishes. If you had only waited, you would have had everything you wanted, without scarifying Jalen's life in the process."

She moved away from the bars and leaned against the back wall. "Whatever. You're probably thrilled, aren't you? With me out of the picture, now's your chance to swoop in and claim Abigail for yourself."

"Actually, that's not why I am came to see you. I am afraid after I leave here, I will be forfeiting any future I might have had with Abigail." Sara walked back to the bars and frowned. She was broken and Isabel could clearly see the regret of what she'd done written on her face, but she had come here for a reason.

"What are you talking about? You're talking nonsense." Isabel grabbed Sarra's hand that rested on the bar and pricked it with a safety pin she had concealed in her hand. "What did you stick me with? What have you done? Guard!" She screamed. Two guards skidded to a stop in front of the cell. "Arrest her. She just pricked my hand with something. Look."

She held her hand up. The guards eyed her hand, then looked at each other.

"I don't see anything," Isabel said.

"What?" Sara looked at her hand, but there wasn't any pinprick. "How?"

"I don't know what you're talking about." She turned to the guards. "Would one of you gentlemen be willing to walk me back to my room?"

"Of course, Queen Isabel." She slipped her hand through his arm and allowed him to lead her back down the hallway. She ignored Sara screaming her name.

❧ ❧ ❧ ❧

"What?" Merek said. He eyed Lanis up and down then recognition dawned in his eyes. "Treg?"

"He's not going to save you." Lanis smiled, and before Merek could react, she pulled the dagger free and plunged it into his chest. She felt satisfied when he slumped against the wall. "That's for Anya." She twisted the dagger and pulled it out. "And that's for me." As his body slid to the floor, she took a step in Treg's direction.

Treg started clapping. "Very good, but very predictable. We knew you would kill him."

"Did you now?" He was standing in front of what had to be Anya's cell.

"Yes." He raised his hands and two green orbs appeared in his palms.

She slipped the dagger back through her whip and said a silent prayer. No one was going to come to her rescue. She put her hand in her pocket and grasped the stone the old women had given her. She didn't know how, but she knew this was the time to use it.

"You do realize you won't get out of here alive. Don't you?" He flicked his wrists and the orbs flew at her. She braced herself and only felt a slight discomfort when they connected with her chest.

"How?" he stuttered.

Lanis thanked Nia, then took off running toward him. Right before she reached him, she tightened her hold on the relic, turned left, and jumped into the wall of Anya's cell. Her body hit the ground with such force that it knocked the wind out of her. She rolled onto her stomach, then raised up on her knees. The smell hit her first, and she gagged into her hand. The second her eyes landed on Anya laying in the bed, she jumped up and slowly approached her. Her body was curled up into a ball and she was facing the wall. The sores on her feet were puss filled and bleeding. The baskets that sat in the corner of the room were empty. She only allowed herself to breathe when Anya took a breath.

She sat down next to her on the bed and ran her hand down Anya's side. Her fingers stilled when Anya's next breath never came. "Anya." Lanis turned her body around and Anya's face fell to the side. "Anya." She picked her up and hugged her to her chest. "Anya, I am so sorry."

"Lanis, too tight."

Lanis wasn't sure she heard what she thought she had. She eased Anya's body away from her and Anya was awake. "I'm sorry. I thought." She wiped frantically at her tears. "Never mind."

"You came for me?"

"Of course I did. Nothing, nor anyone could have stopped me. I didn't think I would make it in time."

"Love, I'm not doing well. With each breath it's harder to breathe."

Lanis laid her back down and jumped up off the bed. She had to get them out and fast. The room hummed from the enchantment the Jester put on it. The Rogue stood just outside the door, looking in at them. She could hear guards running down the hallway. How was she going to get them both out safely? Think. Think. She turned when Anya spoke her name.

"I love you." Lanis stiffened at the way she said it. Like it was goodbye.

Lanis shook her head. "Not now. Not today. Anya, you have to hang in there for just a little bit longer. I am going to get us out of here." How would she get them both out of the room and get them home alive? Having magic abilities or being immortal would have come in handy right about now. She stopped walking and stared at the wall. *Or being immortal.* She didn't know if it would work, but she had to try. "I am High Priestess Anya's Protector and I demand that my mask come to me." When nothing happened, her heart sank, then the air changed and the room vibrated with energy. One minute there was nothing in her hand and the next, the mask lay nestled in her palm. "Anya, hold on for a bit longer."

"I won't make it home alive."

"Yes, you will. Besides, I've had that part covered before I even came in here." Lanis slipped the mask on and felt an instant connection to it, but this time it felt different, she felt different. She was more herself, more aware of what needed to be done. "I will be back in a few minutes." Lanis pulled the sword that manifested when she slipped the mask on, walked to the door, and kicked it open. It flew off the hinges and into the waiting guards. She walked through the enchantment and easily killed the five waiting guards. She ran down the hallway to make sure she had gotten them all. When she was walking back, Treg was staring into the room. He laughed at her and walked to the door, but the instant his body touched the shield, it threw him back against the opposite wall. Lanis lifted her sword and plunged it into his body. She pulled it out, raised it up, and cut his head off. Satisfied he was dead, she walked back into the room. She pulled the mask off and knelt next to Anya. "Ready?"

"Yes. I've had better days."

"You're beautiful." Lanis ran her hand down her cheek. "This is going to be unpleasant, but when I put the mask back on, I will have to put you over my shoulder. It will make it easier to get out of here and still allow me to use my sword."

"Okay."

Lanis lifted the mask to her face, then easily lifted Anya and placed her as gently as she could over her shoulder. She held her legs securely to her chest, and picked up her sword with her free hand. When she walked out of the room, no guards were waiting for her. She stepped over the bodies on the floor and walked back the way she had come. It wouldn't be as easy getting out as it was getting in. Right before she turned the corner to walk out, she said a silent prayer to Nia. She turned and walked out the door and came to a complete stop. There wasn't anyone waiting at the entrance to the cave because every one of the guards were lined up in front of it, four deep. She knew she could kill every one of them, but she couldn't allow anything to happen to Anya. Out of the corner of her eye, she spotted Elson, Vic, and Finley off in the distance. They weren't close enough to be of any help. She would have to make her way to them.

When a noise caught her attention, she turned to her right and thanked Nia for answered prayers. The horse she had rode in on walked up to her and nudged her shoulder. The Jester's horse. She laid Anya's body over the beast's back and climbed behind her. As soon as her hands touched the reins, the horse started trotting back and forth. She would have to make her move. When she saw Vic lift her staff, she knew now would be the only chance they got. When the staff hit the ground, spikes flew out of it, and embedded themselves into at least a quarter of the Black Brigade. She kicked her mount and jumped into the crowd. She swung her sword and when they were halfway across and were clear of the guards, she jumped off and allowed the horse to reach Elson. When she knew Anya was safe, she turned around and started cutting down the Brigade, one by one. She felt a deep satisfaction when the remaining guards took off running away from them. She sheathed her sword and started running. When she reached them, she took her mask off, and relaxed when she saw Anya in Elson's arms.

Vic grabbed Lanis's arm. "Everyone get in a circle." Vic took a vial out of her bag. "Everyone needs to be touching. Quickly!" She murmured a few words, threw the contents of the vial onto the ground, then slammed her staff into the ground. Lanis's knees buckled, but she kept a hold of Elson's arm. The air shifted around them, and Lanis closed her eyes. She fell to her knees and her eyes shot open. Isabel jumped up from her chair and screamed at the guards outside her door. They had made it.

It took a second for Lanis to register where they were. "Elson, put her on the bed." Lanis gripped the bed and pulled herself up. Anya's breaths were shallow and her skin was a sickly gray color, and she was burning up. Without looking away from Anya, she screamed. "Someone get Kaylynn in here. Now!" She jerked her arm away when someone grabbed it. Isabel walked to the other side of the bed and sat down beside Anya. "She's in bad shape. I don't know if I got her back in enough time." Isabel nodded, stood up, and walked away. Voices floated her way, but she ignored them. She grabbed Anya's hand, slid to her knees, and prayed. She prayed for Anya, for their life together, and she prayed for favor. Anya meant too much to too many people for it to end like this. If she didn't make it, Lanis would make it her life's mission to hunt down everyone who had a hand in her death. She swiped at the tears running down her cheeks. She felt, rather than saw, Elson kneel beside her.

"She's going to be okay. We did not come all this way for this to be the outcome."

She accepted his hand and stood up. She settled down beside Anya. "I wish I had your faith."

He wrapped his arm around her shoulders. "You already do; you just haven't realized it yet." He patted her on the back and walked around the bed. He knelt on one knee and bowed his head.

Lanis ran her hand along Anya's arm. It was warm and clammy. She sucked in a breath when Anya opened her eyes and leaned forward.

"I guess we made it," Anya said quietly.

"I told you we would. Haven't you learned by now that I would do absolutely anything for you? I would destroy all of Adearian if it meant you would be safe."

Anya took a deep breath and started coughing. "I…it's getting harder to breathe."

Lanis jumped up from the bed and turned sharply toward the others in the room. "Someone better get the healers in here now. You don't want me upset."

"Young lady," Queen Abigail said. "They are on their way."

Lanis gritted her teeth. "They're not coming quickly enough. She's dying and so help me, if she does, I will destroy this Castle and everyone in it."

Abigail bit her lip. "Do not threaten me. I don't care how upset you are. I will cut you down and make sure the healers do not come."

Lanis stepped forward when Isabel grabbed Abigail's arm. "Abigail," Isabel said. "Please don't. Not now. You don't know everything that is going on. Please believe me. If something happens to Anya because you stopped the healers from coming in here, I will help Lanis bring this Castle and you to your knees."

"Mom?" Vic asked.

Abigail threw her hand off. "What is it to you? I will not be threatened in my home. Who in the hell do you think you are?"

"Have you looked at her?" Isabel pointed to the bed "She is my daughter."

"What? You can't be serious." Abigail walked to the bed and looked at Anya, then Isabel.

Lanis jerked her head around when the door opened and the healers ran in. Two people she didn't recognize followed Kaylynn.

"Everyone needs to leave!" Kaylynn raced toward the bed and leaned over Anya. "I need everybody out! Including you, Lanis."

"I will stand back, but I am not leaving." Lanis crossed her arms and stepped back from the bed. She watched as the other two people surrounded the bed.

"Lanis," Elson said. "We need to go. Let them do their work."

"No."

"Lanis," Queen Abigail said. "We need to leave and that includes you. If you don't leave on your own, I will have someone remove you. I am your Queen."

Lanis turned to her and sneered. "You're not my Queen." She stood her ground when Abigail's guard walked up to her.

"Mom," Jalen said from behind Abigail.

"Not now, Jalen."

"Mom, cut her some slack. She's been through a lot."

"How would you know what she's been through?"

"I've been through the paces too. Trust me, I know. Besides, I trust her." She turned to Lanis. "You need to do what you're told. I understand what you must have been through, but I will not allow anyone to disrespect my mother or my Queen."

Lanis knew the way she was feeling she wouldn't be able to defend herself. After one last glance at Anya, she stalked past everyone and out the door. Elson pulled her to his side and she buried her face in his neck and let the tears fall. He squeezed her even tighter when she screamed and beat into his chest. After her sobs quieted, she pulled away from him and accepted the cloth Vic handed her. She wiped her face and nose, then put the cloth in her pocket. She learned long ago never to be ashamed of your actions or your reactions. Elson returned her smile.

"I think," Vic said. "It would be best if we went

to my room to wait. It's big enough for all of us." She slipped her hand through Lanis's arm and tugged her away from Anya's room.

"No," Lanis said.

Vic squeezed her arm. "Are you a healer? Because the last time I checked, you weren't. Has that changed?"

Lanis knew when she had been outwitted. "No."

"We are all worried about her. We got her this far, and I am not sure how we did, but we did and now we must let the healers do their job."

Lanis nodded and let her lead her down the hallway. Once inside the room, she slumped into the chair that Vic directed her to and blindly accepted the glass someone handed her and downed the water in one swallow.

"I hope you killed all of them inside of the cave," Elson said.

"I killed Merek and the Rogue that captured Rose."

"Good."

Vic sat down on the arm of the chair and slid her arm along the back. "You killed a Rogue?"

"Yes." Lanis caught Abigail's eye. "I hope you know where Dimitri is, because I am going to kill him too." Abigail pulled a chair away from the desk and sat down. Lanis hated to admit it, but she looked every bit of a Queen and just her presence demanded respect. Jalen stood directly behind her mom's chair and there was a guard on either side of her. Isabel took a seat at the desk, along with Finley.

"I am sad to say, Dimitri got away," Abigail said.

"Figures. If you want something done right, you have to do it yourself." Lanis debated on what to tell Abigail about Sara, but the way she felt, she could care less about Abigail's feelings. "Sara is involved in this mess."

Abigail leaned forward in her chair. "You won't have to worry about her. She's dead."

That was news and she had a feeling it wasn't by Abigail's hand. Jalen was gripping her mom's chair and her jaw was clenched, but she looked far better than the last time she saw her. She hoped whoever healed her was working on Anya. "You look better than the last time I saw you."

Jalen nodded and didn't break eye contact with her. "You have no idea."

Abigail looked between them. "You two know each other?"

"Mom, Lanis is the one that got me out of the dungeon. If it hadn't been for her, I would be dead right now."

Abigail leaned back in her seat. "I see. Thank you, Lanis. I will do everything I can to see that nothing happens to High Priestess Anya."

"I would hope you would, but not for me. If she was to die in your care, it wouldn't sit well with the people of Malora." Abigail didn't say anything, but she smiled.

"What I want to know is how you got Anya out," Isabel asked.

Elson nodded. "We still haven't forgiven you for leaving us on that hillside. One minute you were there and the next we saw you, on a horse, off in the distance. How did that happen?"

She didn't want to talk about this, not right now, but it would keep her mind occupied for the moment. "The Jester wanted to speak to me so he froze all of you." She stood up, took her cloak off, and laid it on the bed. She slid the Holders dagger from within her whip and laid it on the table. "He gave me that dagger and told me it would get me into the caves. It used to belong to a guard of the Holders." She shrugged. "I knew I couldn't trust him, but I didn't have a choice, and he was right, it did get me in. Once I was inside, a guard led me to an office and Merek was inside. He took me to Anya's cell and a Rogue stood outside of it. Elson, we saw the same Rogue before the Ruins of Treko. I killed Merek and the Rogue produced two green orbs and he threw them at me, but they didn't do anything. I held onto this." Lanis dug the stone out of her pocket and laid it on the table as well. "And I ran for Anya's cell. I ran through the wall and entered her cell."

Vic picked up the stone, then dropped it back on the table. "Where did you get this? You never mentioned before that you had this."

Lanis licked her lips. "Three old women gave it to me. Elson, do you remember in the Ruins when I wouldn't wake up? Well, I felt like I was dreaming and three old women gave me that stone and told me when the time came, I would know when to use it."

Isabel slowly stood up. "Three old women? Good grief, Lanis. You saw the Holy Ones." The awe in her voice put Lanis on edge.

"I take it that doesn't happen that often." Lanis looked between Isabel and Vic.

"That often?" Isabel said. "How about never. I haven't heard of a sighting in hundreds of years. It just doesn't happen. They can never be found."

"When I was there, they told me those that seek them, would never find them. Maybe that's why no one does. Whatever the reason, I am glad they did give it to me. Without that, I would never have gotten into Anya's cell."

"Amazing," Vic said, and closed her notebook.

"Is that how you survived the green orbs?" Abigail asked.

Lanis rubbed her neck. "Well, no. It wasn't the first time I had survived one."

"Really?" Abigail asked.

"Vic told me that she knew of another woman who had survived one."

"That's interesting," Isabel said.

Vic rolled her eyes. "I didn't tell Lanis her name, but I did explain that she was a very powerful sorceress. I told her it was rumored that she had a sphere somewhere on her body."

"Before we get to that," Abigail said. "I would like to know how you got yourself and Anya out of her cell. Did you use the stone for that too?"

Lanis shook her head. "No." She dug in her bag and lifted the mask out. "I used this." Every guard in the room took a step back. "I summoned it to me and it allowed me the opportunity to get us out. Once outside, Vic did what she does so well."

Vic winked. "Why, thank you."

"Queen Isabel, your daughter is amazing," Lanis said.

"I second that," Elson chimed in. "The way she slammed that staff into the ground and all those spikes flew out was pretty cool."

"Vic cast the spell and here we are." What was taking them so long with Anya?

Abigail stood up. "Do you have a sphere?"

"What? No," Lanis said. "Of course not. I don't even know what they look like."

Jalen frowned. "If you don't know what they look like, how do you know you don't have one?"

"I have an idea," Isabel said and walked up to her. "Close your eyes. I am going to scan your essence. It won't hurt." Lanis closed her eyes, felt a warmth flood her body, and sucked in a breath when the warmth pooled at her waist. "Open your eyes. What part of your body did the warmth pool at?" Lanis looked down at her whip. "Take your whip off."

"My Papa gave it to me. You won't damage it?"

"No." Lanis uncurled her whip and laid it on the bed. "Vic, come here. I know you're tired, but I will need a secondary to help me."

"Whatever you need." Isabel whispered in her ear and they both held their hands over the top of the whip. The whip started bouncing on the bed and Lanis took a step closer when the handle began to shake uncontrollably. She watched in awe as the handle worked itself loose from the rest of the whip. Isabel picked the handle up and turned it over. A small white sphere landed in the palm of her hand.

"No way," Lanis said. "Can I touch it?"

"I don't see why not; you've had it this long." Isabel dropped it in her hand. She was a bit disappointed when nothing happened. Jalen walked up to the bed, looked at her hand, then walked out of the room.

"Can I see?" Elson asked. She handed it to him and it looked so small in the palm of his hand. "Something so small has caused so much death and destruction." Lanis accepted it back and looked up when the door opened and Jalen walked back in. She held her hand next to Lanis's and opened her closed fist. In the palm of her hand was an exact replica of Lanis's, except for the color. Where Lanis's was white, Jalen's was black.

Abigail grabbed Jalen's shoulder. "Where did you get that?"

"It was in the trinket box that Grandfather gave me. I didn't realize what it was until I saw hers."

"Let me see." Isabel held their hands side by side and looked from one to the other. "You both have one of the remaining spheres Dimitri is looking for."

"Yes," Jalen said in awe.

Lanis shrugged. "I guess." She jerked her head up when the door opened and the woman that was helping Anya walked in.

"Casten?" Queen Abigail said.

"We've done all that we could. Between the three of us, we were able to heal most of her injuries. She's stable, but we all believe that after a long rest and plenty of sleep, she will be fine. Lanis, Elson, she asked for both of you."

"Good." Lanis picked her whip up, reattached the handle, and tied it around her waist.

"Lanis," Elson said. "Your bracelet is gone."

It made sense. She saved Jalen, but Anya was the Princess she was sent to save. She picked up the sphere and, without missing a beat, laid it Jalen's outstretched hand. "Now you have two." She didn't look back when Jalen called her name. She followed behind Casten and didn't have to look to know Elson was behind her. She walked into the room, not sure what to expect, but when Kaylynn smiled at her, she knew, at least for the moment, that Anya was okay. Kaylynn patted her on the shoulder and walked out with Casten.

"I'll stay by the door," Elson said.

Lanis nodded and walked up to the bed and sat down beside Anya. She picked up her hand and stroked her palm.

Anya smiled and opened her eyes. "Aren't you a sight for sore eyes?"

Lanis kissed her on the cheek and let the tears fall. "I am never leaving you again."

"Never say never, Lanis."

⁂

Isabel walked swiftly down the hallway with Barnet a few feet in front of her, holding a lantern. Morning was still a few hours off. At the end of the hall, she stopped, pulled her hood up, and motioned for Lanis to do the same. It wasn't until they were outside of the estate and halfway to Isabel's ship that Lanis spoke.

"Queen Isabel, I mean no disrespect, but this better be important to drag me out of bed and away from Anya."

"It is and no matter what you see or hear, keep your mouth shut. Understand?"

"Yes."

"Good. As soon as we enter the room, blend with the wall and stay blended."

"Okay."

Isabel accepted the Captain's hand and climbed aboard the ship, followed by Lanis, and Barnet.

"My Queen," the Captain said. "They are below deck."

"Have they said anything?"

"No. Very tight-lipped, those two."

"Thank you." She patted him on the arm and directed Lanis to follow her. At the bottom of the rugged, wooden staircase, she winked at Lanis, opened the door to her right, and walked in. Her two captives sat back to back in chairs in the middle of the semi-large room. Lanterns littered the enter space, masking it in an eerie glow. She nodded and two guards ripped the sacks from her captives' heads. The woman kept her head down.

The man spat in her direction. "You."

"Dimitri, it would seem everyone is looking for you and by chance I was the one to find you. And as a bonus, I have your daughter as well. She must be quite the sorceress to get you out of the Castle single-handedly." She laughed. "Quite a feat, if I do say so myself."

His eyes narrowed and he struggled against the ropes that bound him to the chair. "What do you want?"

She grabbed a chair by the wall and sat down a few feet in front of him. "I want a lot of things; however, it's what I know that is the interesting part." She lifted a finger. "I know you have five of the seven spheres and I also know you're the one who kidnapped High Priestess Anya. Tell me something, Dimitri. What in the world did you expect to gain by kidnapping her?"

"You have no idea who you're dealing with."

She sighed. "It seems to me I am doing quite well for myself and I am pretty confident in knowing my opponent's weaknesses. Have you seen your wife or other two daughters recently?"

He snickered. "Only a true coward goes after someone's family. You are a Queen. What do you think would happen if your people in Candor knew what you were doing? Don't you people have morals?"

She stood and smoothed the slight wrinkles out of her shirt. "I think you have me mistaken for Queen Abigail. Abigail will do whatever is necessary to protect her family, but she draws the line at going after someone else's. I, on the other hand, don't care whom I have to take out in order to reach my endgame. Your family included."

Dimitri's features softened, then he whistled. "She looks just like you, you know. Same hair, same eyes, same everything. Of course, she didn't look so good the last time I saw her. Fading fast, that one was. She might be a High Priestess, but as a human, she is pretty weak. She should be dead by now."

Isabel shrugged. "She and Lanis both looked pretty good when I saw them yesterday. I should probably tell you that Treg is dead and half of the men that were guarding your cave are also."

The blood drained from his face. "What do you want?"

"I am curious to know where the five spheres are."

"You and everyone else, it seems. The last thing I would ever do is tell you where the spheres are."

"Well, at least you admit to having them."

He smiled. "Why lie? It would seem you have me at a disadvantage."

"It would seem I do." She pointed at Rose. "Untie her."

"She didn't have anything to do with this." He stiffened when a guard brought Rose to stand in front of him. Isabel accepted the guard's knife. "You wouldn't stoop to such levels as to hurt her. What could you possibly gain by that?" He caught Rose's eyes. "I am sorry."

"I'm not," Rose said.

"What?" Dimitri looked between the two. "Rose?"

Isabel slipped her arm around Rose's waist. "I would never hurt her. Why would I when she is the one that brought you to me?"

"Rose? Why? Why would you betray me?"

"Why? Maybe we should start with what you've done to our family. All because of some stupid spheres. That doesn't take into account that you kidnapped a High Priestess and at every turn you tried to kill Lanis. She saved my life when she didn't have to. She paid a price for me and did so freely, because it's who she is. Why would I betray her? She was loyal to me and fought beside me. I can't say the same about you. I would never betray that kind of loyalty to help you worship a false god. You only had five. Tell me, Dad, where are the other two? You can't do much if you don't have all the pieces."

"Don't talk to me about our family. What do you think your mother and two sisters are going to say when they find out that you turned on me? I am so disappointed in you."

Rose took a deep breath. "They would stand behind me."

He shook his head. "No, they wouldn't."

Rose's smile was bittersweet. "I talked to Mom a few days ago and told her everything. I wanted one last chance to see her and tell her I loved her." Isabel couldn't help but feel a bit of elation that he deflated before her eyes. A so-called man of power brought down by his nineteen-year-old daughter.

He spit on the ground. "She was in on this, wasn't she?"

Rose scrunched her nose. "Who?"

"Queen Abigail. I knew she didn't fight that hard when you rescued me."

"Actually," Isabel said. "You're wrong. Abigail didn't know anything about that. I was the one that helped Rose get you out."

"I see. You have been deceiving me this whole time. You are no longer my daughter and Isabel, if it's the last thing I do, I will make sure you and your kids pay dearly for this and I will find the remaining spheres."

"I am fairing pretty well so far. It blows my mind how you think you are going to get out of this alive. Besides, I happen to know where the last two spheres are. It seems I would be at the advantage, not you."

He stiffened in his seat. "Lanis has one."

"Well, she did. That Lanis is quite the giver."

"Did Jalen have the other one?"

Isabel slapped her hands together. "My, my, Dimitri. You knew more than you gave yourself credit for. Now, actually, Jalen has two. How does it feel to know where the last two spheres are and not be able to do anything about it?"

He started laughing. "You have no idea what you've just done. I am a vessel for Damrek's work."

"If you're talking about the mark on your back, there is no need to worry. This part of the ship is shielded. The information I just spoke of will die with you."

He jumped in his chair. "You have no clue who you're dealing with. There are others who will take my place."

"Yes, I am sure there are. Rose has already told me about the Jester and Lantor. I will deal with them when the time comes."

"You will pay for this." He turned hate-filled eyes to Rose. "And so will you."

"Rose, no need to be worried. That's what they all say." She took a step to the right and drove her knife through Dmitri's hand, pinning it to the chair. She ignored his screams and grabbed his face in her hand. "I don't take too kindly to people hurting my family. My kids have always comes first to me. I may not know Anya that well, but she still has my royal blood running through her veins." She reached toward the guard and accepted the knife he handed her. She fingered the blade and rolled it over in her palm. A rose was etched into the black wooden handle and continued onto the blade itself. "I have to say, Dimitri, your knife is exquisite." She clutched the handle and drove it into his other hand. She turned to Rose. "Are you sure you want to be here for this? Rose, there is no shame in wanting to leave."

"I'll stay."

"All right." Isabel accepted the piece of cloth Barnet handed her, pushed it into Dimitri's mouth and tied it around his head. She picked the sack up off the floor and pulled it over his head. She whispered for Rose to keep quiet, turned to where Lanis was blended into the wall, and motioned for her to join them. Rose's eyes widened when Lanis stepped away from the wall and walked up to them. Lanis squeezed Rose's shoulder when she stood beside her. "Do you want to do the honors?" She was talking to Lanis, but Dimitri didn't know that.

Lanis nodded, leaned down, and pulled her knife from her boot. As she rose up, she kicked him in the chest, and his body lurched backward, and landed on the floor with a thud. She walked up to him, put her boot on his stomach, gripped her knife handle, inhaled, and flicked her wrist downward where the knife embedded itself in his chest. She looked at Isabel, then at Rose, squatted, and ripped the sack from his head.

His shocked eyes bore into hers when she placed her hand over the handle of the knife and started pushing it into his chest. A smile graced her lips when the life dulled from his eyes. She stood, pulled the knife out, grabbed the sack that had covered his head, and wiped the blood off the blade. She sheathed it and turned to Rose. "I felt it only fitting that my face was the last one he saw, and not yours."

"Thank you," Rose said.

"Lanis, Rose," Isabel said. "No one is to know what has occurred here this morning. No one. You cannot tell Anya or Elson and I will not tell Abigail or Vic. This will be our secret. If Abigail knew what's happened, it wouldn't bode well for any of us."

Lanis nodded. "All right. I don't like keeping secrets from Anya, but I will forget this ever happened."

Rose stepped around Isabel and stared down at her dad. After a few minutes, she wiped her eyes and turned to Isabel. "What's going to happen to me?"

"You, my dear, are in for a new life. You must stay on this ship. If Abigail knew you were here, she would put you to death. She has been on a killing spree as of late. You are not safe here. In a few days, we will leave for Candor and you will be coming with us. I would never leave you to Abigail's fate since I got you into this mess. You will be welcome in my home."

Rose sniffled. "How do you know I am not just like him? That I won't turn on you like he did me and our family?"

Isabel shrugged. "I don't know that you won't, but if I didn't trust you, even a tiny bit, you wouldn't even be on this ship to begin with. I don't think you're a bad person. You stood up for what you believed in and you stood up for Lanis. I respect that. Besides, if you betray me, or my country, I will kill you." She had a feeling that wouldn't be the case, though. In Candor, Rose would have a chance to let her magic flow freely.

"Rose," Lanis said. "Thank you. I don't know if I would have been able to do what you did."

"Don't be silly. Of course you would have." She smiled.

"And," Lanis said. "I have a feeling you'll be right at home in Candor." She ran her hands through her hair and pointed to Dimitri's body. "What's going to happen to him?"

"The Captain is going to take the ship out and Dimitri's body will be put on a small skiff, pushed out to sea, and set on fire. His body needs to be completely destroyed. Rose, it's the way it has to be."

"I know. He wasn't the man I remembered. It had to be done."

Lanis squeezed her shoulder. "I have to leave. Anya will be expecting me."

"Yes," Isabel nodded. "Rose, you must not leave the ship."

"I won't, and thank you for my second chance."

"No, thank you." Isabel followed Lanis off the ship and settled into the carriage that awaited them both. She wasn't at all sure she had made the right decision with Rose. Only time would tell. The closer they got to the Castle, the more her excitement grew. After everything that happened, she was looking forward to the reading of the Prophecy.

❦ ❦ ❦ ❦

Lanis leaned against the window and looked down at the crowded courtyard and marketplace. It made her nauseous thinking about all the people crammed into such a small space. Yesterday, her life was in shambles, not knowing whether Anya would live or die; today was an entirely different story. She was still weak, but moving around at a good pace. Kaylynn had told them both it would take months for her to get back to her old self. Lanis could handle months and she knew Anya could too. She smiled and relaxed when two arms embraced her from behind. "How are you feeling?" She breathed a sigh of relief when Anya kissed her neck. She would never again take for granted these small moments.

"I am breathing and you're in my arms. What more could I ask for?"

The night before, Anya had insisted on talking about everything that had happened. She held her as they relived every moment leading up to her capture and the time she spent in her cell. Lanis knew how hard it was for Anya to give up control and talk about what she had gone through. They cried, laughed, and spoke about the future. When Anya finally fell asleep, Lanis laid awake and thought about their future and before she fell asleep, she realized what had to be done.

"You still with me?" Anya asked. Lanis turned, pulled her into her arms, and brushed the hair back from her face. "Lanis, I am fine. Thanks to you and everybody that accompanied you."

Lanis shook her head and choked back the tears that threatened to fall. "Elson never doubted. I did. I thought we were too late."

"You weren't. I knew you would come for me. Nia knows what she's doing."

It was time. "Yes, she does." Lanis pulled away from her and tried to shake the tension from her hands, but failed. She picked up her bag and carried it to the bed. "I didn't mention this last night because I didn't know how you would react, but I don't want you to find out later that I had this." She rummaged through her bag and stopped when her fingers brushed the all too familiar leather. Without thinking about what she was doing, she pulled the Book of Damrek out of her bag and handed it to Anya.

"Where did you get this?" Anya ran her finger along the title.

"The simplest explanation is a water Seer gave it to me. It made me angry and I disregarded it at first, but Elson said it might be Nia's way of lending us a helping hand." She shrugged and bit her lip. "I don't know."

Anya whistled and turned the book over in her hand. "This is an original. I have never seen an original before. It is rumored that the original version holds several different passages that aren't in the revised editions. Have you read it?"

If the original held different passages that could be why no one's ever found Damrek's Cave. She would have to get her hands on a revised edition and compare the two. "I have read some of it. Enough to get the gist." She sat down on the bed. Anya settled down beside her.

"Did you learn anything?"

"Have you read it?" Lanis asked, stalling for time.

"I have read the revised edition."

When Anya didn't offer anything else, Lanis knew she would have to answer her original question. Yes, this was her lover, but this was also Nia's High Priestess. She would be cautious. "It's not what I expected." She squirmed on the bed when Anya didn't say anything. How could she tell Anya that she didn't disagree with everything that she had read?

Anya patted Lanis's bouncing leg. "It is all right. It's not what I expected either." She tapped the book. "I can understand why people would follow it. Don't get me wrong. I know it's fake, but everything has a grain of truth."

Lanis relaxed when the reprimand she expected never came. Anya kept surprising her. "I don't believe what's written, but I don't disagree with everything either. You know how I feel about magic. I can see, though, how that can draw followers to him. Having something that was once out of reach within your hands is very tempting. From what I read, it wasn't hard to determine that Damrek was troubled. What I don't understand is why no one tried to help him. He clearly needed it."

"I think that by the time anyone realized what state he was in, it was too late. I would hate to know his problems were ignored on purpose." Anya squeezed Lanis's hand. "You don't have to feel bad, or feel like you're turning away from Nia, because of your views. Nia doesn't love you any less because of this book."

"Elson never strayed from his faith. He's a good man. My faith, on the other hand, was tested at every turn. Nia never left us, though."

"Lanis, some people's faith comes easy to them; others have to try a little harder. It doesn't mean one person's journey is easier than the other's. It only means that two different people can come to the same conclusion by walking separate paths. Here." She handed her back the book, "Keep it. Nia obviously wanted you to have it."

Lanis slipped it back in her bag then lay back on the bed, pulling Anya with her. She closed her eyes and relished the feeling of Anya's body tucked up against hers. She sucked in a breath and her skin popped out in goosebumps when Anya ran a finger down her cheek. She would die for this woman. The woman she wanted to spend the rest of her life with. "I want more," she blurted out. Lanis raised up on her elbow.

Anya smirked and ran her hand down Lanis's chest. "Right now?"

Lanis smacked her hand away and lay back down beside her. "No, not that. At least not now and not until you regain your strength. And besides, we don't have time for that."

"Okay."

Lanis grabbed her hand and held it between hers on top of her chest. "I want kids. I want everything. I think we deserve that." If anybody did, they did.

"I want those things too."

"When we…" Lanis groaned and swung her head around at the knock on the door. Her mask still lay inside her bag and that's where she intended for it to stay. She raised up and saw surprise in Anya's eyes when she didn't put it on, but only shrugged. "That would be your guests." Lanis stood and held her hand out for Anya, who readily grabbed onto it.

"We'll discuss all this later."

"You can count on it. Nervous?"

"Yes. It's strange. I don't even know them. I know Queen Isabel gave birth to me, but I don't know her or Victoria."

Lanis raised their joined hands and kissed the back of Anya's. "They are good people and I trust them with my life." Lanis winked, dropped her hand, and walked to the door. She took a deep breath, nodded at Anya, then pulled the door open. Vic stood on the other side, her hand raised to knock again. She looked pissed.

"Took you long enough." Vic huffed, then a smile split her face and she grabbed Lanis in a tight hug. "We did it," she whispered in her ear. She grabbed Lanis's hand and turned it over. "I see you're all healed."

"You bet we did it and yes, Jessop patched my hand up yesterday. You're incredible. I owe you a debt that I know I will never be able to repay."

Vic pushed her to arm's length and clasped her hands. "Don't be silly. You don't owe me anything."

Lanis looked her up and down, then winked. "You look good."

Vic pulled her hand back and curtsied. "Of course I do. What did you expect?" Lanis grinned and stepped aside to let the others in the room. She did a double take when a man and a young boy followed Queen Isabel in. Mitchell and Steven. She patted Steven's shoulder as he walked past her, but seeing Mitchell almost knocked the breath from her chest. Gone was his long hair and in its place, he wore a short, layered look, and he was clean-shaven. Vic had to have noticed the resemblance. He looked happier, and younger than the last time she had seen him, but he also looked exactly like the water spirit they encountered at the onset of their journey. Exactly like him. She smiled and accepted his hand, trying to curb her unease.

"You okay?" he asked.

She rubbed her neck. "You look good."

"Ah, I see. Rendered speechless by my good looks." He flashed a smile then pointed to her feet. "Boots still doing okay?"

"Didn't even have to break them in."

"Good. Good."

Lanis shut the door, then quickly joined Anya, who looked nervous with Vic standing directly in front of her, staring. Lanis rolled her eyes and pushed Vic back a couple of feet. "Queen Isabel, good morning."

"Good morning, Lanis."

Isabel also looked nervous and now that she and Anya were standing in the same room, no one would be able to deny that they were mother and daughter. Lanis slipped her arm around Anya's waist. However, when Vic took a step forward, Anya took a step away from her.

"I am sorry," Anya said when Vic reached for her again. "I don't know you. I cannot allow you to touch me." Lanis groaned. She understood Anya's reasoning, but she trusted them and Vic looked both horrified and ticked off.

Vic planted her hands on her hips. "I would never do anything to harm you, but rest assured I am quite capable of doing my fair share of damage."

"I am sure you wouldn't, and I am sure you could. Just the same," Anya said.

Vic seemed to weigh her words and Lanis knew Anya was about to get a lecture. "High Priestess or not we carry the same blood. We will have some sort of relationship whether you want to or not. And whether you agree, or not, I intend to stay in touch with Lanis, so you will also have to deal with that." She motioned Steven and Mitchell to her side. "This is my husband, Mitchell, and our son, Steven."

Lanis snickered when both boys' eyes lit up. "Husband?"

Vic grinned, showing off her dimples. "When you know, you know."

Lanis understood that. She felt the same way the

first time she met Anya, but Vic had to have noticed the resemblance between the water spirit and Mitchell. But, in the end, it was her choice. "Good for you."

"I know, right?" Vic laughed.

During the entire exchange, Queen Isabel stood in the background, taking everything in. Lanis couldn't imagine what was going through her mind. She stepped up to her side and slightly bowed her head. "Queen Isabel."

Isabel smiled. "Lanis."

"I told you I would bring both of your girls back to you."

"I never doubted you for a second."

"Don't worry, I doubted myself enough for the both of us."

"Lanis," Anya said. "I have never seen you bow to anyone. Not even Nia."

Lanis paused only briefly at the surprise on Anya's face and in her words. "Queen Isabel has earned my trust and my respect. I will forever be in her debt."

Isabel grabbed Lanis's hand. "Any debt you think you owe me has already been paid." She let go of her hand and turned to Anya. "I didn't think I would ever see you again."

It was the first time Lanis had seen Anya fidget. "Honestly, I don't know what to say. All this is new to me and to be fair, I am not sure I like it. I am used to being in control of everything around me." The room grew so quiet, Lanis didn't know what to expect next.

"Lanis," Vic said, breaking the silence. "Why don't we leave these two alone?"

Leave it to Vic. "Good idea." Lanis kissed Anya on the cheek and whispered in her ear. "I love you."

Anya smiled. "I love you, too."

Lanis knew Anya was safe with Isabel and felt comfortable leaving them alone together. She grabbed her bag, slipped it over her neck, stepped out into the hall, and joined Vic. Mitchell and Steven were gone. Maybe Vic would be the first one to bring Mitchell up.

"That went fairly well," Vic said. "She looks just like Mom." She bit her lip.

"She does." Lanis waited for Vic to say something, but she kept quiet, staring down the hallway. "The resemblance is uncanny."

Vic nodded. "I know. She looks like Mom and I look like my dad."

Lanis crossed her arms and sighed. "I'm not talking about Anya."

Vic glanced at her, then turned her face away. "Oh, who then?"

"Vic, don't do this. You know whom. Mitchell looks exactly like the water spirit we saw, right down to his boots." Lanis took a step back at the look in Vic's eyes.

"You have no idea what you are talking about."

After all they'd been through, Lanis wouldn't allow it to play out like this. "Don't I? Vic, you're only kidding yourself if you are telling me you haven't noticed." Vic's shoulders slumped forward and she walked to the far wall and sat down on one of the chairs that lined the wall. Lanis sat down beside her. "Want to talk about it?"

"What's there to talk about? My husband looks exactly like a water spirit. A dead man. Whom, I might add, attacked and tried to kill us. The only difference between the two is Mitchell doesn't carry an axe." She buried her head in her hands. "The moment I saw him cleaned up my heart skipped a beat. Until my head registered what my heart felt." She turned her face to Lanis. "It's probably a coincidence, right?"

She was looking for reassurance, but that wasn't something Lanis could give her. "Vic, I don't believe in coincidences. It also threw me when I saw him. I don't know what to think, but I do know what I see. You look happy, he looks happy, and so does Steven. Believe in that. Trust in that. Everything else will play out, with or without our permission or participation. Enjoy the life you've been given. I plan to."

Vic jumped up and pulled Lanis with her. "You're right. I needed that. Live life and steer clear of obstacles. I can do that."

"No." Lanis pulled her around to face her. "You can't avoid the obstacles. You have to meet them head on and bust through them. It's not about avoiding them. It's about having a plan for when you finally do meet up with them." She winked. "Or having quick reflexes."

Vic kissed her on the cheek and pointed down the hall. "I am going to meet my boys. Mitchell's nervous about standing up with me."

"He may be nervous, but trust me when I say nothing will stop him from being by your side."

"I am a lucky woman and so is Anya." Lanis watched her until she was out of sight, then turned and headed the opposite way. She had unfinished business to attend to. She stopped and knocked twice on the door and it was opened almost immediately. "Can I come in?"

"Of course." Elson grabbed her arm and dragged her through the doorway. "Shouldn't you be with High Priestess Anya?"

"She and Queen Isabel are talking." Lanis fiddled

with the hem of her shirt.

"Good. I hope they are able to find some middle ground." He leaned back against the table.

"I do too." She rubbed her neck then started pacing. She stopped when he glared at her and touched her arm. She grasped his wrist. His Oath bracelet was gone. That was the final push she needed to know she was doing the right thing.

"Lanis, what is it? What's wrong? You can talk to me."

She swallowed, patted her bag, then ran her hands through her hair. "I have a proposition for you." His answer would determine her future.

⁂

Lanis had agreed to meet with Jalen this morning and discuss how she was able to save her, but she hated leaving Anya. She had to admit, Jalen wasn't at all what she was expecting, but after their conversation, Jalen had assured her all of her questions had been answered. At the end of their talk, Jalen had surprised her when she handed her a revised copy of the Book of Damrek to go along with the original one she had, so she would be able to compare the two. But now she was glad to be back at their room. She knocked once, then opened the door and walked in. Anya stood by the mirror, wearing a long gold dress with a white bodice and red stitching. Her hair was put up, and around her neck, she wore a simple purple stone. She was breathtaking, but she still looked tired. They had all been through a lot.

"My, my," Anya said. "Don't you look fetching?" Lanis looked down at her clothes. She took the opportunity while she was with Jalen to ask her for a change of clothes. Jalen had readily agreed and outfitted her with a pair of brown wool trousers and a long, sleeveless, blue tunic. She wore the boots Mitchell had given her, kept her hair down, and her whip was wrapped around her waist.

"I think I clean up pretty nicely." Lanis turned in circles.

"That you do," Anya said, and fingered Lanis's rabbit necklace. "But I really don't see the point when it's going to be camouflaged by your Protector getup." She frowned when Lanis bit her lip.

"Things are going to be different from now on," Lanis said. "It's time for us."

"I don't understand."

"You will." Lanis kissed her on the cheek, walked to the door, and opened it. Elson walked in and bowed before Anya.

"High Priestess Anya."

"Elson." She looked to Lanis. "I still don't understand." She sucked in a breath when he stood and raised the Protector's mask to his face. The transformation was instant. "Lanis?"

"It was time and he is dedicated to you. I trust him and he would lay his life down for either one of us." She held her hand up. "I know I promised to never leave your side, but I trust him with your life, and it will give us a chance to have somewhat of a normal life. Elson and I understand each other. He knows I would do anything for you and he knows he can trust me alone with you. We have an understanding. We get our time together and he does what he loves: protecting you."

Anya smiled and pulled Lanis into her arms. "I don't know what to say."

"Then don't say anything." Lanis leaned forward

and took her lips in a tender kiss. "I hear you have something big to do today."

Anya laughed and rubbed Lanis's arms. "Indeed, I do." Lanis led the way out of the room, followed by Anya and her Protector. It felt weird, like a dream come true to be able to walk beside her, instead of behind her, covered up. Lanis smiled when Anya grasped her hand. They walked down a long hallway and stopped when they reached the wide, double doors. Anya nodded at the guards.

"I guess it's time," Anya said and raised Lanis's hand to her lips. "Wish me luck."

Lanis laughed. "Oh, Anya. Trust me. You don't need luck." Lanis stepped to the side when the doors where opened and Anya walked out, followed by her Protector. The crowd went crazy when they caught sight of Anya. Anya winked at her, then stepped up beside Queen Abigail.

"Ladies and gentlemen," Queen Abigail said. "I welcome you to the reading of the Prophecy. High Priestess Anya has traveled a long way to make this happen. I bid you to respect her, as you would me." Queen Abigail turned to Anya and smiled.

Anya stepped up to the railing and looked out at the crowd. Lanis couldn't even imagine what she was thinking or feeling. The entire courtyard and beyond was packed with people. Tens of thousands had come for the reading. Jalen had told her that it was the biggest crowd they had ever had and that the majority had come only to hear the Prophecy. Lanis took her place beside the Protector.

"I have been blessed by Goddess Nia to come and read the last Prophecy ever written. Danath was the receiver. Let us say a silent prayer of thanks." When everyone bowed their heads, Anya reached back and Lanis placed a sealed parchment into her hand. "Let it be said that every word read will become law. No one can abolish the words once they have been read." Anya tore open the seal and unfolded the page. Lanis was sure no one else would have noticed but she did. Something was wrong. She was stepping toward her when she felt a hand on her arm. Anya's Protector held her back. She moved back to the wall and held her breath when Anya began to read.

Dawn will break on the third moon day. The Second Daughter and the Fourth Kin will be Bonded by Light.

Two will become one.

A Linex will rise and one will fight under the Gilded Star.

Near and far, high and low, many shall walk the path.

Red will stain the way.

Night will strike without warning and the Feline will be powerless in the fight.

The Mountain will tremble and Sectors of the Sun will flee.

Time will be won and the Fourth rotation will begin again.

A hush fell over the crowd when she finished reading. Lanis noticed Queen Abigail grip her chair handles and looked shocked, as did Queen Isabel. Lanis wasn't sure what any of it meant and from the way the crowd was reacting, neither did they. Anya folded the parchment up, nodded at the crowd, and headed toward Lanis. The guards opened the door and Lanis followed Anya and her Protector through. It wasn't until they were in their room did Lanis ask what was bothering her.

Anya turned to her and frowned. She handed Lanis the parchment and told her to unfold it. It was blank. "I don't understand. You read the prophecy."

"That's because I memorized it. That parchment being blank didn't have any bearing on what I had to do."

"So what does it mean for you? For us?"

Anya stood. "As far as I'm concerned it doesn't. I will admit it threw me for a second, but I don't see what someone would have wanted with it or what they could want with it now."

"It doesn't bother you that someone stole it."

"To tell you the truth, I don't know when the original was stolen and what point would it make to look for the thief." She let her hair down and embraced Lanis. "I am not going to let what someone did have any interference on our lives."

"Do you know what the Prophecy means?" Lanis asked.

"No."

"Did you see Queen Abigail and Queen Isabel's faces?"

"I can't worry about what might happen to others. My work here is done and all I want is to go home. With you. As soon as possible."

Lanis wasn't so sure that was the best course of action considering everything that had happened so far. Anya hadn't actually experienced what took place. This only added to the whole picture. But Anya was right; she couldn't let her worries interfere with their happiness. Though, she wasn't a hundred percent sure her involvement was over with. She ran her hands down Anya's back. "I think that is the best plan I've heard in a long while. We have the dinner tonight, then tomorrow morning we will head home."

Anya smiled and pulled her close. "Even though the future holds many unknowns, I wouldn't trade spending them with you for anything."

Lanis grinned. "I couldn't agree more."

ᴥᴥᴥᴥ

Lanis blew out a breath and fidgeted. They'd arrived at the dinner, in the banquet hall, less than an hour ago and she was already ready to go back to their room. She kept her eyes on Anya, who stood on the main platform, talking with Queen Abigail, when an arm wrapped around her waist.

"She's fine, you know," Vic said.

Lanis nodded. "I know. It's just strange. It's as if the last few months never happened. Gone so fast."

"Well, maybe to you. I, for one, will never forget being trapped underground. Or the countless other things we experienced. We have everything we've ever wanted. Life is good."

"Vic," Lanis said, tugging on her arm.

"What?" Vic said, looking where Lanis pointed.

"What is she doing here?" Great. That's all they needed. Another troublemaker in the bunch. Tegan stood near the wall, talking with a woman Lanis didn't recognize.

Vic sighed and frowned. "Mitchell told me she begged him to bring her and he couldn't tell her no. And Queen Abigail invited her to dinner." She held her hands up. "I don't know why either." She looked around the hall. "Where's Elson?"

Lanis knew she couldn't tell her the truth, but

she would probably see right through her. "He got a new assignment." She shrugged. "Couldn't be helped."

"That's a solider for you. Heads up, Princess Jalen and Casten are headed in our direction. Jalen's not at all what I expected."

Lanis had to agree. Jalen wore her military dress uniform and Casten wore a simple black dress that contrasted nicely with her long, curly auburn hair. They were both stunning. She nodded when they reached them.

"Lanis, Princess Victoria," Jalen said.

"Some dinner," Lanis said, noticing Jalen wore one of the spheres around her neck and Casten wore the other one.

Jalen laughed. "I want to leave as well, but it wouldn't sit too well with my mother." She pulled Casten to her side and for the first time, Lanis noticed a black mark through the bands on Casten's wrist. "Although, it would be nice if they would serve dinner."

"I hear that," Vic said, quickly quieting when her mother walked up to them.

"If you all don't mind," Isabel said. "I would like a word with Lanis."

"What can I do for you, Queen Isabel?" Lanis said when the others walked off.

"After everything we've been through, I felt it would be only prudent to tell you that High Priest Lantor is the only person who could have the five spheres. Rose told me Dimitri met with him and I believe he is the only one that could have them."

"I've never met him." She jerked her head around when there was a commotion at the front of the hall. "No. Not now."

"What?" Isabel asked.

"Be prepared." Lanis walked up to Vic, who already had her staff drawn, and her gaze was locked onto the Jester's, who jumped up and landed on top of the main table. A handful of guards surrounded Queen Abigail and Anya's Protector stood firmly in front of her. "Vic?"

"I'm ready."

The Jester looked around the room, a grin plastered on his face, then stopped when he spotted Anya. He bowed in her direction. "You look better than the last time I saw you and I have to say, Lanis did a very good job." He sighed and pulled three cards from within his pocket. "Well, what do we have here? Two queens and an ace. Tell me!" he screamed. "Princess Jalen, how does it feel to be the heir to two different thrones? My, my, Isabel. You have been busy." He laughed and turned back to Anya. "Anya, I am sorry. I hope you have no hard feelings." He stretched his fingers and threw two green orbs into the crowd. One hit Jalen in the chest, but it didn't affect her. Vic waved her hand in front of Lanis and the one headed in her direction disappeared. The Jester jumped up and down and laughed. "My, what secrets everyone holds." He nodded at Tegan. "Lanis, you do have a way of adding people to your inner circle. Don't you?" He flipped off the table top, landed on his feet, and his eyes landed on Steven.

"Vic," Lanis said. "Be careful." But she could tell by the look on her face that that wouldn't be the case. At the same time Mitchell grabbed an axe off the wall and ran toward the Jester, the Jester threw a green orb at Steven and Vic waved her hand, averting the orb before it connected with Steven's chest. Lanis screamed, uncurled her whip, and ran toward Mitchell when the Jester winked at her and threw a green orb at him. It connected with Mitchell's chest and he was thrown off his feet and through the open window.

Lanis stopped cold, with her heart in her throat, and caught Vic's eye. Vic licked her lips, then raised her staff, and walked forward toward the Jester. With each of Vic's steps, Lanis's heart pounded faster and faster. The Jester smiled and raised his hand, but Vic stood her ground, and continued walking. When he raised his hand again, and nothing happened, for the first time Lanis saw what looked like fear in his eyes. Vic swung her staff in his direction and he fell back onto the floor, clutching at his chest. He scrambled to get up, but Vic was quicker, and hit him in the chest with her staff. He grabbed his chest, and rose onto his knees, disbelief etched into every line of his face. He reached for her, but she stayed out of his grasp.

"Lanis!" she screamed. "Help me."

Without thinking, Lanis ran toward Jalen, pulled her sword out, and ran in Vic's direction. Her feet skidded to a stop and she raised the sword. She could hear people shouting at her, but she ignored them. She swung down and felt a deep satisfaction when his head hit the floor. "Vic. I am so sorry." Vic dropped her staff and buried her face in her hands. Lanis pulled her into her chest and held her as she cried.

"What just happened?" Abigail asked. "Who was that?"

"Lanis," Anya cried. "What have you done?" She looked at his body, then at her. "Why?"

"Why? Why? He was evil and he earned his fate justly. He deserved worse." Lanis swiped at the sweat on her forehead.

"Lanis," Isabel said. "I've got her."

"Mom," Vic cried. "Mitchell."

"Sweetheart, I am so sorry." Steven ran up to them and buried his head in Vic's stomach.

For the first time since she and Anya had gotten together, Lanis felt like Anya was disappointed with her. It was easy for Anya to ask why; she hadn't gone through what they had. She didn't have to deal with the Jester at every turn. He deserved his fate and she wouldn't hesitate to do it again. Lanis frowned when Tegan pushed away from the wall and headed in their direction. Lanis held the sword out and Jalen accepted it back, and without wiping the blood off, she slid it back in her scabbard.

Tegan stopped a few feet from them and Lanis rested her hands on Vic's shoulders. "It's started," Tegan said. Lanis stepped forward and Vic raised her head up and caught Lanis's eye. Tegan's eyes glazed over and her blank stare looked right through them. "You are all a part of everything that's happened. Your lives are intertwined. Death is inevitable. Your lives will never be the same." Her body fell forward, but a guard caught her before she hit the floor.

"She's a Seer," Anya said.

"What's started?" Jalen asked.

Lanis cursed under her breath and Vic squeezed her hand. Why her? Why them? Why now? "The Prophecy," Lanis said. "The Prophecy's started."

About the Author

Born near Chicago, but raised in Southern Illinois, where she still lives, Shannon spends her free time writing. When she isn't writing, she enjoys binge watching fantasy, science fiction, or true crime shows.

You can contact Shannon at -

Website: smhfiction.com
Email: smh1981@live.com
Facebook: facebook.com/smharrisauthor
Twitter: @smhfiction

www.ingramcontent.com/pod-product-compliance
Lightning Source LLC
Chambersburg PA
CBHW051648180726
48284CB00006B/1908